Dedication

I would like to dedicate Perils of Passion to my children, Adrian Elzy, Andrea Elzy, and Cameron Hekmatnia, for their love, patience, and understanding throughout this journey. It was a long one! My children have given me the resolve, and the inspiration to shoot for the stars. To my parents Frank and Maria Marquez for encouraging me to push boundaries and giving me the confidence to do anything I set my mind to! To my sisters: Liza, Olga, Norma and brothers Frankie and Ronnie for your support. Special thanks to my sister Cookie for being a thought partner, giving me the support to push on and stay the course. To my family friend Elaine Emmanuel for her enthusiasm and support. Last but certainly not least, I would like to thank my husband, Behrouz, for his support and love over the years.

May this book be an inspiration and legacy that lasts a lifetime, and an example to my grandchildren Jack and Luna that anything can be achieved with passion, perseverance, and hard work.

Love.

I0662316

Book Cover by: Cam Hekmatnia & Jenn Haro

Preface

Delirium finally came, as she lay huddled in an alley in New Orleans. No one would have ever thought she was once from one of the richest and proudest families in Atlanta, Georgia. Reduced to rags and degradation, Brana Prescott, only twenty years of age, had traveled an unknown journey like so many other southern families, who had met their demise with the War Between the States. However, Brana was worse off than most since she had no recollection of her family, friends, or her home.

Touched, was what was whispered about her amongst the crowd of vagabonds that considered her to be crazed and would clear their paths as she walked down the surrendering roads of Atlanta, along side them. Fearing for their children when she was near, no one tried to comfort her, a mere child herself, who had lost everything the Southern culture was known for, leaving her to survive on meager scraps not nearly fit for the starving animals along the road side.

Greedily, the union soldiers took everything. They had robbed her of the life before the war, her carefree youth, stripped her of the love of her family, friends and ultimately even taken away her identity. Now, the only link she had to her past was a gold locket that she treasured and managed to hide throughout her long journey, praying every night for some recollection of the past, trying desperately to remember who she was. She had no choice but to drift with the other tortured souls from city to city, looking for a place that welcomed the reminder of defeat.

No one cared as she fell to the ground because they knew that it might be that she carried a far worse death sentence than being shot between the eyes by a blue-bellied Yankee.

It was the fever!

CHAPTER 1

The bleached white plantation stood proudly on a hill surrounded by a valley filled with luscious green foliage and mature groves of brilliant oak. The younger saplings stood at attention swaying gently with the mild summer breeze. The smell of lavender sweetened the air and clung to the tender young branches that weren't yet strong enough to spread their leaves and whisper in the wind like their almighty ancestors while their mighty elders dominated the Prescott landscape as they had for hundreds of years. In the fields, miles of white fluff was being picked with skilled ebony colored hands, as gently as if the cotton were the lilac flowers that were picked every morning for the mistress of Prescott Plantation. Gorgeous wild flowers and bushes of fragrant rosemary made the gardens almost as famous as the plantation itself along with the magnolias and azaleas that, in season, adorned the manor.

"Cameron, I really wish you would talk to your sister. She's totally uncontrollable," Olivia Prescott said, shaking her head in disapproval. "Young girls her age should be learning the pianoforte or embroidery, but no, Brana has to be different. She would rather spend her time at the stables with that beast you bought her. Really, couldn't you have bought her a new ball gown, trinkets or something far more suitable?"

"Don't blame Cameron for your daughters wild nature, luv," her husband teased her. "She reminds me of the spitfire I married years ago."

"Mother, mark my words, this is just a passing fancy," Cameron replied uncertainly. "Next week she'll forget all about Beauty and start amusing herself with new gowns or other things girls of her age do."

Right now Brana Prescott's fancy was riding Beauty as fast as she could. She loved the feel of the wind in her face and always pretended the devil was at her heels. Moreover, she loved the freedom of sitting astride her beautiful stallion, her waist-length blue black hair flying wildly in the wind, while her heart and eyes danced with excitement. She could never thank Cam enough for buying Beauty for her, even though she was used to getting what she wanted from the men in her life, all she had to do was tell her secret wishes to Lynnie.

Lynnie, being Brana's confidant, was Cam's informant, sharing secrets ever so cleverly. As a result, he spoiled his younger sibling quite rotten, catering to her every heart's desire. Despite the fact they were six years apart, they were very attached to each other. The way he indulged her whims and extravagant fancies made her the passionate envy of all her friends.

Just so, Cameron Prescott was the envy of all Southern men. Exceptionally handsome and born with riches befitting a king, he had inherited not only wealth and beauty, but incredible charm as well. Even when he was a mere teen, he had females of all ages in Atlanta begging for his affections. Furthermore, with an intuition beyond his years, his behavior in public at an early age was that of a true Southern gentleman. However, in the private chambers of the most notorious harlots in the city, he was quite a rogue. He had become quite skilled in the art of love- making before he learned to calculate figures. His affluent standing in the community had every mother in the city keeping a very close eye on him when he was around their daughters. They watch, waited, schemed with cohorts and prayed to the heavens above, for him to make an inappropriate advance that would seal his fate of bachelorhood forever.

Meanwhile, Cameron was enjoying bachelorhood, not quite ready to claim a wife yet, even though his parents were plotting with Southern beauties at every turn, although he had promised his beloved mother that he would consider a serious relationship in his nineteenth year or so, by that time he might just be ready to claim a wife and settle down. After all, so much could happen before he hit the milestone of twenty, as he had once informed her.

"Miz Brana, your mammy sho' was fussin' at Master Cameron when she knew you done went a' ridin by your lonesome again." Scrubbing her mistress' back, Lynnie began to tell Brana about the conversation she had overheard in the parlor that morning.

Brana smiled to herself, remembering her morning ride. "Oh Lynnie, I just couldn't bear it if I had to give up riding Beauty. He's the only friend I can tell my secrets to, and he really does understand me." Feeling a gentle tug of her hair, she quickly added, "and of course, I can always count on you, to keep my true feelings secret." Brana lied blatantly, attempting to soothe her nursemaid by accentuating her already deep Southern drawl, knowing that whatever she confided in her, all the slaves on the plantation would know within the hour.

Lynnie started washing Brana's hair more gently now, taking special care to rub in the leaves of fresh dried lavender before rinsing the perfectly shaped ringlets at the base of her neck. "Now you effin know Miz Brana, we done do this ebery time you take a bath. You need to get' on outta this here hot water. Your body cant' take much moe' of this! You almost red as Miz Olivia's prized roses. Effen your mammy sees you this here color she'd whip me good!"

"I declare, Lynnie!" Brana exclaimed, ignoring her maid's pleas and letting herself sink even further into the foamy water, "you have never been touched a day in your life! I'm not ready to leave my bath just yet!"

"You get 'on out now girl!" Lynnie exclaimed. "I'm fixin to go and tell Miz Olivia. I will, Miz Brana. You just wait an see effen I don't!"

"Lynnie, don't threaten me with the same threat over and over again! I declare, you think I'm touched!"

Brana fell back against the tub laughing as she skimmed her hand over the water while Lynnie screeched as the water soaked the front of her body and trickled down her face.

"Well, I declare!" her tormentor cried. "I'm ready to be dried now. All the bubbles are gone!"

"Look what you done did to me, Miz Brana!"

Stepping out of the porcelain tub, Brana looked at her reflection in the bureau mirror. It was difficult to believe that it was really her body she was looking at. She should still look like a young girl but, in fact; she was already blossoming into womanhood. Her exquisite black hair streamed down past her waist, and her eyes were the color of violets. Her long black lashes, the same color as her hair looked as though they had been painted. She would have had Southern gentlemen already swooning at her feet; if it weren't for the fear they felt when her name was mentioned in the presence of Cameron. Cameron was always so protective. Because of him, her small round breasts, and slim waist were hidden under a corset and her shapely legs were always kept well hidden under several layers of ruffled petticoats.

A couple of weeks had passed since Brana had ridden Beauty, and she couldn't understand why Cam and her father had been so adamant about her not riding Beauty. Furthermore, she was not to leave the grounds. And yet no one would tell her why. Could the rumors of war Lynnie had told her about possibly be true? Today she was going to demand an explanation as to why her family was behaving so strangely.

Dressing for breakfast, Brana saw that they had early morning visitors, their friends from the neighboring plantation. Finishing her toilet in a hurry, Brana ran down the stairs and heard sobbing coming from the direction of the library. Realizing that it was her mother, she opened the library door and slipped inside, undetected. The morning visitors were in what was obviously a serious discussion with Cameron and her father. Her mother was crumpled on the sofa. When Brana started toward her, she caught the attention of everyone in the room.

Cameron was the first person to speak to her.

"Brana, what are you doing here?" he spoke with such sternness that Brana was taken aback. "Go have your breakfast and we'll talk later."

"I'm not leaving Cam, until I find out what the hell is going on here!!"

"I suggest you moderate your tone, daughter. You will not use such language in front of your mother and our guests!" Franklin Prescott said angrily. It was a rare occasion when he would raise his voice to Brana.

"I apologize," Brana said, flushing, trying to keep her voice even. "But as I said, I'm not leaving until I find out what has made mother so upset! Do not mind me, I'll wait until you are finished."

Franklin Prescott looked at his daughter, her defiance reminded him of her mother at that age. His heart melted. He knew they would be facing difficult times ahead.

"Cameron, Mr. Prescott, Mam, Brana. Thank you for your hospitality, but it would be disrespectful at the ladies if we continue talking about war," the eldest Alden announced. "We'll be back for you later Cameron."

Olivia Prescott, sobbing hysterically, ran out if the room leaving bewildered Brana behind.

"Thank you boys for coming and God be with you. " Franklin said, shaking their hands, and in that instance, he could not hide the fact that his eyes had filled with tears.

CHAPTER 2

"No Cam! You can't, I won't let you!" Brana screamed. "Papa, you can't let him go, you can't! Tell him you need him here! Please Papa, Tell him!"

"I'm afraid I can't stop him, honey." Franklin Prescott said, as he took her in his arms and hugged her.

"Father, let me talk to Brana alone please," Cameron said, seeing this was going to be more difficult than he had imagined.

Franklin nodded, giving Brana a kiss on the cheek before leaving the room.

"Luv," Cameron said softly, "you know I have to go. But I promise to write, and who knows? The war might be over before I see any blood shed. Everybody knows the North is no match for the South!"

Until this moment, he supposed, he had lived with the illusion that the differences between the States could be settled with civility and without the need of bloodshed. Now, the reality terrified him. Pulling a gold chain, with an ornate golden locket dangling from it out of his pocket, he handed it to Brana. "I was going to wait for your fourteenth birthday," he said, "but this is a good as time as any. I hope you like it, go on open it."

The inscription read, "Brana, I love you, Cam." Brana was trembling and could not speak. Realizing that she was powerless to stop Cam, Brana threw her arms around him and held him tight.

"Please, Cam, I need you, don't leave me! I declare, I'll die without you here. I love you! Please don't leave me!" Brana's body was now shaking uncontrollably, as her heart wrenching sobs filled the room.

Cameron was holding her tightly, unaware that the salt he tasted were the tears that were streaming down his face as well. "I'll be alright, luv. Just remember, whatever happens, I'll always love you!"

Brana, unable to control herself any longer, pulled herself out of Cam's grasp and like an animal fleeing for its life, ran past him and out the door. When she reached the stables she ordered the boy to saddle Beauty. Then, pulling her petticoats high, she swung herself up to straddle the back of her prized stallion.

The wind tangled Brana's hair as she rode Beauty faster until finally, blinded by the tears that were streaming down her face, she slowed to a trot as the black stallion arched its neck and tossed its handsome head.

Trying to control her sobs, she reminded herself that Cam had told her not to worry, that everything would be all right. Once Cam talked to the general and told him who he was, they'd send him back home.

They'd realized that Papa needed him here. And then how Cam would tease her for being such a whiny little goose.

Turning to ride back to the plantation, she stopped and realized that, although she knew that she was surrounded by vast green valley and cotton fields, everything seemed dark and empty. Unhappiness tugged painfully at her heart and she was aware that the wind was turning cold. Shivering, she saw that a storm was fast approaching. The trees started to sway violently. Dark clouds suddenly appeared overhead and the sun that had been shining just a few minutes before tried in vain to protest the forthcoming downpour. In a few days when everything was normal again, she would remember this as one of the worst days in her life. But she had to be strong for Cam. Papa would never let anything happen to him. As for her, she would pray that the good Lord would give her the strength to endure.

Beauty snorted as though he knew what she was thinking. Brana forced herself to sit straight upright in a show of proud defiance as she forced the horse into a trot, knowing that, at this distance, no one could see the tears streaming down her face.

CHAPTER 3

The carriage Lacy was riding in had once been elegant but now, scarred and tattered, it seemed to have all it could do to wobble slowly down the cobbled streets on her way to the dressmaker's shop, which she had told Simmons she must reach before it closed. She was relieved to leave the dirt trails of Vicksburg, Mississippi behind her, at least for a few hours anyway. Reaching the confines of the big city she tried to remember how New Orleans had looked before the war, but it wasn't easy. In the two years since, New Orleans had seen more than its share of sickness and death. The epidemics that the city fathers had assumed was finally under control, had once again found new ways to claim more victims. Many diseases were widespread and made their way to almost every surrounding city. Lacy could still remember holding her last loving relative in her arms.

She remembered, watching helplessly when her father had drawn his last breath. Pox, the doctor said it was, and since Lacy had nursed him until his death, she had thought it would claim her life as well. However, Lacy had been one of the lucky ones who cheated death. But in its wake, the disease had left her with a scarred and pitted face which she could never hide, no matter how clever her use of cosmetics.

The pox had gone for now, but Lacy knew it would be back in the summer months when, the heat combined with mosquitoes, it would strike down even more unsuspecting victims, some of whom actually welcomed the death, no matter how painful. Poverty stricken with nowhere to go, many wanted nothing more than to be relieved of their misery. Sadly, children were among the first to pass into darkness and the unknown.

In the years that had followed her father's death, Lacy had succeeded in continuing the successful operation of her father's gambling establishment, La Petite Salone, a brothel and gaming house overlooking the docks in Vicksburg, Mississippi. Having become a skillful gambler as a young girl, under her father's tutelage, she was skilled at emptying the full purses of her richer patrons, many of whom sought to make her their youthful prey and thus becoming a legend of the sort that made her father proud. Child or not, she had a gift that some called luck and others found more malevolent.

La Petite Salone's reputation was well known throughout the state as an establishment that catered to all sorts of indulgences, providing Lacy with quite a sizeable income and a reputation as well. Its customers were all sorts with one thing in common; every one of them had serious expectations that a roll of the dice could change their life forever.

The once white two story framed building with its wrought iron fences and balconies overlooked the hustle and bustle of one of the more demanding ports on the Mississippi river. The color of the outside walls had changed through the years now more grayish and dull, just like the color of smoke, smoldering from a burning cheroot. The overgrown gardens that surround the building and the moss that slowly made its way up the second level, still gave La Petite Salone the hint of elegance it had before the war had ravished some of its beauty. Ten acres of green pastures and several formal gardens had been used during the war to tend to the sick and dying. Imported fountains of marble and stone courtyards had been a prelude to the mansion and a Union cannon ball was still lodged in its walls in the grand parlor.

Lacy was known for running a fair business. Even if the house lost heavily, Lacy always honored the winner with an expensive bottle of port, and the services of one of her ladies for the evening, thus giving her frequent returning customers. Most of the heavy losers were rogues from the elite Garden district of New Orleans, men who had all seemed to have survived the war with enough riches to maintain the lifestyles they had formerly been accustomed to.

In the summer business was less brisk because of the pox epidemic that usually raged through the city which was fortunate since importing such items of champagne and even regular port and claret was extremely costly during those months, thanks to the reluctance of ship captains to dock there.

The tasty dishes that came from the kitchen had been served to the customers of La Petite Salone since Lacy was a child. The cook jealously kept guarded her recipes, even from Lacy, providing delicacies no matter what the season. Most customers never even noticed a lack of variety on the menu, preoccupied as they were with the smoldering heat of the sun. However, one item to be kept in good supply was spirits. Lacy's customers mostly drank and gambled, with only a handful bedding the women in her employ. Granted that they were willing to pay a tidy sum for their pleasures but more was spent at the gambling tables where the sprits provided false courage.

A sudden jerk of the carriage jolted Lacy out of her musings and, looking out of the window, she shook her head as she saw more beggars and homeless than the last time she was in the city. She could never get used to the sight of poor Southerners trying to rebuild their lives on nothing but hopes and dreams. The honor and glory they enjoyed before losing the war had turned into poverty and defeat, leaving them with nothing but gray rags which many of them simply refused to remove as a sign of defiance and loyalty for their Southern brothers and fathers who had lost their lives.

So many soldiers, homeless, often with missing limbs, were drinking themselves into oblivion. But, Lacy felt most, heartbroken for the children who could not remember what it was like before the war. She feared that the only life they would ever know would be one of hunger and despair. Even the gay music that the city was once known for now carries a different tune, as the city mourned not only family and friends but itself since it might never be restored to the life and beauty it once had. Lacy was tired of so many reminders of death, and defeat. She wanted to put the war in the past, and concentrate on the future.

When she finally reached Estelle's dress shop, she gave a sigh of relief. The place was lit, which meant Estelle was still there, finishing a large order for one of her customers. Simmons, Lacy's driver and groom for many years, pulled the carriage directly in front of the white brick shop and came to a screeching halt, carriage wheels flinging wet clay mud on pieces of broken cobble stones. As Simmons helped Lacy out of the carriage, the black men across the street began to edge closer to them and they could hear their rumbling punctuated by drunken laughter.

Relieved that Lacy was already in the shop, Simmons knew there was going to be a confrontation.

"Old man don't you nos you is free?" one of the men demanded, slurring his words.

"That be none of yer business friend." Simmons replied shaking his head as he always did when he was rattled.

"Well now, looks like we done got er'selvs an uppity white lover, you probably bedding the whore, huh old man?"

"Why don't you share with me an me partners some of that tasty white flesh," a second man demanded, spitting at the carriage at which all three partners doubled up in laughter. "That pox-marked bitch must not know what it be like to have a real man!"

"You fools betta get outa here, or old Simmons gonna hafta put holes in yer heads since you ain't got no brains," Simmons said drawing out a pistol and aiming it directly at them with one shaky hand.

"One of these here days," he reflected, "I'm gonna hafta remind myself to get this here gun loaded. Yes,siree!" Tucking the pistol back into his trousers, he prayed that Mis Lacy would finish her business soon. This was not the part of town to linger in for long. Not since the war, at least.

Inside the shop, Estelle looked up from the counter and saw Lacy, one of her most valued customers hurrying toward her, accompanied by the crisp rustle of petticoats and the crackling of satin.

"I'm so glad to find you still here Estelle," she said, "Antoinette promised me my orders for the satin gowns would be ready today."

"Mondieu! Antoinette has already left for the day!" Estelle exclaimed in her heavy French accent. "That irresponsible child told me nothing about your orders being ready! But not to worry madam. Here they are, already boxed and ready to be carried out to your carriage. Did you bring your driver? Madam, did you not hear me? I've found your orders. Do you have help to carry them to your carriage?"

"I'm sorry Estelle," Lacy said. "It's just that my mind is on tonight's entertainment. My newest girl is supposed to sing, and I'm just wondering how the customers will react."

"You have nothing to fear, madam. Even if this new girl can't sing, your gentlemen will only notice how breathtaking she looks in her gown. I do believe this is my best creation yet!"

"And I believe you're right, Estelle. With the help of your wonderful designs, I should have nothing to fear. I'll get Simmons to carry the boxes, and you can just put these purchases on my account."

On her way out the door, Lacy paused by a counter piled with spools of lace.

"A shipment from Paris just yesterday," Estelle told her. "Simply sinful, is it not?"

"Sinful and deliciously wicked," Lacy replied with a smile. "Only a virginal bride would wear this on her wedding night."

And then suddenly, as if the lace had burned her fingers, Lacy threw it aside, remembering her wedding night, which she tried for so many desperate years to forget.

"I'll send Simmons in for my gowns," she said stiffly. "Thank you for having my order ready so soon. I'll see you again in a few months' time."

"I'm just happy to serve you madam," Estelle assured her. "Your girls really know how to display my work." Seeing the unhappiness in Lacy's eyes, she couldn't help but wonder if the gossip about Lacy's husband was true. That certainly would explain her strange behavior when she had mentioned brides.

When all the boxes were piled in the carriage, there was barely enough room for Lacy.

"Take the back alley," she told Simmons. "I can't bear the way the town looks now. So much poverty and the homeless are at every street corner. This town was once so elegant."

Why had she had to think of Jeb? She wondered. Certainly, she did not want to bring up the horrible memory of the first night that she and Jeb slept together as man and wife. The business agreement she had been forced to make with him had her nerves constantly on edge. Even now, it sickened her that she had, had no choice but to succumb to his treachery. Lacy would run La Petite Salone, and Jeb would stay on as a card dealer, and to keep disgruntled customers from breaking up the place. As for Lacy, she tried to avoid him entirely, only speaking to him when it was absolutely necessary for business reasons.

The first night Lacy had slept with Jeb was on their wedding night, a night she would never forget, not as long as she had the constant reminder of his presence. The pain and humiliation she had suffered was burned forever in her memory. How could she have let her beloved father, who had given his only daughter so willingly away to the only man he had ever trusted, know that this very man had taken her with such brutality, that she had had to be given laudanum to ease the pain? Fear forced her to keep Jeb working at La Petite Salone after her father passed.

The sinister look in his eyes, a look that Lacy remembered all too well, had convinced her to ignore his despicability, if only to protect her father when he was alive. And now, as long as he didn't seek her out to share his bed, the situation was bearable, at least for the time being.

Lacy's girls at La Petite Salone knew that she and Jeb were married. They also knew they didn't share the same bed. They wondered if Lacy knew that Jeb was seeking out their favors.

Taking the back alley to La Petite Salone meant that it would take them longer to get back. The thunder that had started rumbling in the east a few minutes ago was pounding her brain. Finding the fresh smell of rain welcome, Lacy poked her head out of the carriage window and breathed deeply. It seemed so long ago since they had had their last rainfall. The only smell in the air lately had been that of the filth of the river that seemed to cling to everything.

The explosion of lightning was more frequent now, and she realized that the tattered carriage might not even reach its destination before being drenched by a downpour. A flash of lightening illuminated the rows of dilapidated buildings that lined the alley as well as the body of someone lying in the dirt.

Lacy's eyes widened.

"Simmons pull over!" she cried. "You must stop the carriage this instant."

Simmons reined the carriage to a halt.

Not waiting for him to help her out of the carriage, Lacy flung the carriage door open and stepped out, ignoring the rain, as well as the mud. A rat scurried over what looked like a young girl's body and Lacy nearly retched at the foul smell as she tried, trying to hold her as she thrashed about and clutched at the rags that covered her. Lacy let out a gasp when she saw a pale breast, a woman's breast.

"Simmons, come help me hold this woman down!" Lacy called, appalled. This was no ordinary street urchin; it was a woman.

"I ain't gonna get near that there thing with it smelling the way it do. It's diseased for sho. No, not me Miz Lacy!" Simmons replied, already climbing up the carriage to regain his station.

Lacy stood up, put her hands on her hips and spoke with such fierceness, that even the horses became restless.

"Simmons," she announced, "you will help with this, child-woman now! We are going to carry her to the carriage, put her in and take her back to La Petite Salone. If you don't help me, I'll find somebody that will!"

Lacy had never seen Simmons move so fast. Jumping from his seat, he looked in the direction of the woman's body, and then looked at Lacy, clearly knowing what had to be done.

"That's better," she said, when the girl had been lifted onto the seat beside her. "And for heaven sakes, stop that infernal muttering!"

Lacy wiped the girl's brow with a lace handkerchief and realized that she was burning up with fever. Her hair was matted with mud and her bare feet and hands caked with blood. Since she was unable to sit upright, Lacy laid her gently on the cushioned seat, rearranging the boxes of gowns.

"You sure you want to be seen sittin' here with old Simmons Miz Lacy?" Simmons asked her as she settled herself beside him, head held high.

"Don't worry about me," Lacy answered, amazed that Simmons could think riding up there with him could possibly tarnish her already soiled reputation. "Besides, it will give them something new to talk about over afternoon tea."

"Simmons," she said, "you were right about her. She has the fever."

"Lawdy Miz Lacy, we done touched her, an you're takin' her back with us. Masta Jeb shore ain't gonna like this. No sir."

"That's why no one must know we have her. Drive to the back entrance and we'll go up the back stairs. I intend to keep her alive. The poor girl has been through enough. Even if death claims her, she won't be alone."

The raging storm was now upon them. The only noise that accompanied the thunder was the sound of a rickety carriage, and the muttering of a faithful friend.

But all that Lacy could think of was the girl whose fevered brow she wiped. Would she be able to save her or would she fail, once again, to stand in the way of fate?

CHAPTER 4

Santelle, Josephine, Mimi and Ruby, Lacy's girls, were waiting in the upstairs parlor for her to return from the shop so that they could dress for the night's entertainment. Ruby, the newest of the girls was remembering the way the cool satin felt against her bare skin when she had her last fitting for her new gown. The color suited her dark hair, which would be pinned up in curls tonight. The rich gold satin gown, embroidered with tiny light brown rosebuds along the bodice, was enhanced by a daring, low cut. Any sudden move might just prove disastrous, unless of course, it involved Weston.

"I just can't wait for Weston to see me in my new gown!" exclaimed Ruby as if she were a child.

"I'd rather let Weston see me without my gown on," laughed the saucy Creole, Santelle, ignoring the murderous look Ruby threw her.

No, no one else would have Weston, Ruby vowed silently. The first time she had seen him had been at the gaming table where he had towered over the other men, his wavy, light brown hair brushed back from the bluest eyes she had ever seen. And the first time he had taken her, she had given him something she had given no other man, her love.

Having lost heavily at the gaming table, he had decided to quit while he had coin enough to buy a beautiful woman to console him and a good bottle of whiskey. After downing the contents of his shot glass, he headed up the stairs just as he had so many times before, this time coming to her. And she knew why. She overheard Lacy tell him that she was skilled in the art of lovemaking, that she knew exactly how to pleasure men. There had been eagerness in his eyes when she had greeted him clad only in a transparent chemise that revealed the soft curves of her body.

Now, just the thought of what happened that night filled Ruby with desire.

"Let me see if you can make me forget the price I just paid for you!" Weston slurred as the whiskey began to take effect.

"Don't you worry yourself, handsome," she told him seductively, drawing him to the high postured bed. "Ruby never gets any complaints."

As Ruby undressed him slowly, she noticed every scar along his chest. His muscles looked like they wanted to burst out of his skin. She had never seen a man built quite like him before. Finally, as Weston stood nude before her, she gasped at the size of his swollen member, and he, in turn, had chuckled at the look of disbelief on her face. As he pulled her close to him, she saw a scar running down the side of his face from his cheek to his jaw. One that was barely noticeable from a distance. This was, she realized, a man who had fought many battles.

Soon, however, she forgot all that as she looked into his eyes and was lost in a whirlpool of desire. He kissed her hungrily, his tongue forcing her lips to part. He pulled her onto the bed, falling on top of her, as she moved seductively beneath him. She knew he felt pleasure, as his tongue flicked at her now hardened nipples. His hands were leaving a burning trail, as they roamed all over her soft body, finally resting at the curly mound between her thighs.

Expertly shifting herself to lie on top of him, she started kissing his hardened muscles from his arms to his chest, while his fingers were probing her juicy tunnel of ecstasy. When she knew he could no longer control his passion, her hot, wet kisses went lower, lingering at the bulging muscle between his thighs as his fingers probed deeper and deeper.

Finally Ruby touched his hard, throbbing member, replacing her hands with her hot, swollen lips to catch his flowing juices. Turning over, Weston threw her underneath him and together they flew to the heights of wild, unabandoned passion.

As Ruby began to feel a stir in her loins, she quickly returned her attentions to Simmons who was bringing in boxes of silks and satins, silently praying for Weston to return tonight.

CHAPTER 5

Lacy could not believe her good fortune that Jeb was not about La Salone. Probably, instead, he was indulging himself at Under the Hill, Natchez. If he had been waiting for her, she knew that he would never have allowed her to bring the disease stricken waif into the house.

Simmons carried the girl through the back entrance with Lacy following closely behind him.

"Put her in the room next to mine and close the door," she told him. "Make sure you bolt it, I always have the keys with me, so I won't have any trouble getting in. Oh, and Simmons, remember not a word to anyone just yet. I don't want to have a panic on my hands."

"You can trust me Miz Lacy," Simmons replied, while trying to hold his breath, praying he wouldn't catch the fever. "I won't say nothin' to nobody."

"I know you won't, Simmons, and I can't thank you enough for all your help today," Lacy said with a smile, knowing how hard this was for him. When his beloved Eliza had caught the fever, Simmons had never left her bedside, even as Lacy had made preparations for her burial. She had been there for him, just as he was there for her when her father's death dealt her a cruel blow. She and Simmons had always had a special relationship.

"You bess get out of them wet clothes a' fore you run into someone you don't want too!" he said just before starting up the stairs.

Simmons was right, Lacy thought. If someone were to see her in this condition they would ask all sorts of questions, and she wasn't a good liar. The wet fabric of her ruined gown was so heavy, that she hoped she could manage to remove it by herself. But that would come later when the girl had been cared for.

They made their way up the stairs, unnoticed. The room next to Lacy's was clean and inviting. The smell of pine filled the air. A colorful patchwork, a mosaic of reds and blues and velvety greens, covered the four poster bed. Smoothing out the crisp white linen sheets beneath it, Lacy fluffed the pillow just before Simmons laid the girl on the bed.

"Simmons, I need you to bring up buckets of water," Lacy whispered as she looked at the girl. "And be careful not to be seen."

"Now, er what do you suggest I do, effen I do get seen?" his voice was a harsh whisper.

"Shhh! Be quiet! Do you want to help me or not?" Lacy scolded.

"Don't make no sense, Miz Lacy. What are you gonna do effen this here girl dies?" Simmons asked in a lower tone than before. "I ain't carr'in out no dead body. I done had enough deaths in my life, yes sir ree."

"I'll think about that when the time comes. Now go on, get! You need to be quick about it. We don't really have much time to spare," Lacy said knowing in her heart this girl would not survive the night. "Last time I looked, I was in charge here. Now go on. Everything will be fine, Simmons."

The girl had fine cheekbones and tiny feet. What was left of her clothes looked like the fine fabrics that could have easily come from Estelle's. The solid gold chain around her neck was adorned with a locket which read, "Brana, I love you, Cam." Neither of those names sounded familiar to her.

"Simmons, have you ever heard of these names?" Lacy asked and repeated the inscribed names.

Simmons shook his head. "She ain't from around these here parts, she from New Orleans. If she wer from Vicksburg, I wood had seen her a'fore now."

''She could be from just about anywhere. Well,'' Lacy said, "whoever she is, it looks like she had some kind of wealth. That locket is made from real gold, and her clothes, or what's left of them are made out of fine silk.''

Lacy tried to picture the girl as a gentle bred southern belle, but quickly dismissed the thought as absurd and totally ridiculous, her clothes must have been borrowed or stolen.

Lacy started undressing the girl. How long, she wondered, had she been in such a state? Certainly, she was mostly skin and bones. As for her ebony black hair, Lacy thought, she just might have to cut it.

Lacy heard a little tap on the door and then saw it open slowly. She stood still and held her breath, until she saw Simmons enter carrying buckets of water. Then she exhaled.

"I'll need you to help me put her in the tub," Lacy told Simmons, knowing that he was going to refuse, but that eventually, he would give in to her, complaining the whole time.

"I can't do that, Miz Lacy, she don't have no clothes on!" Simmons responded, squirming uncomfortably.

"Don't you play the innocent with me, Simmons," Lacy told him. "I know you're not afraid to look at a woman's body. At least, not from what I've heard in the kitchen."

Simmons wasn't shocked when she revealed his secret. He knew Cook has never been one to keep her passionate nature to herself.

"Thank you, Simmons," Lacy said as he lowered the girl gently into the tub. "You can fetch some extra water now. And don't stay longer in the kitchen than you have to."

Lacy bathed her as though she were a child and washed her long dark hair as gently as she could. When she was finished, and with Simmons help, they dressed the girl in one of her white, cotton nightgowns. Lacy couldn't believe her eyes. This couldn't be the same person she had found in a back alley. Her skin, the color of porcelain, contrasted vividly with her blue-black hair. From time to time, her eyes fluttered open and Lacy saw they were a strange violet color. What on earth, she asked herself, could have happened for such a beauty to have been left alone with no one to care whether she lived or died?

As Lacy finished the task she set out to do, she left for her chamber to dress for tonight, reminding herself to check with Cook for some broth to feed her little sleeping beauty. With some nourishment and tender care, she just might pull through this terrible ordeal. Until then, Lacy would just have to wait to get the answers to the questions that had been racing through her mind since finding her.

CHAPTER 6

Lacy applied the finishing touches and left her chamber to go to the already noisy salon below. Reaching the last steps of the staircase, Lacy looked in the direction of the gaming rooms. Smoke and laughter from her regular customers filled the room. Tonight was going to prove to be very profitable, she thought, because it was early and there were still patrons coming in.

Stepping into the room, Lacy saw her girls already in action, lounging about and drinking, with her clients and most importantly showing off their bodily assets. Estelle was right, those gowns looked simply marvelous on her girls. But her smile soon faded as she looked at the corner table near the bar, the noisiest section in La Salone. Jeb, back from gambling and drinking with his cronies as usual. Why Jeb fancied himself a gambler, Lacy would never know. The whole town must have I.O.U's from him. Sooner or later he'll have pay up. That was probably the only way she'll ever get rid of him. But Lacy had never admitted her feelings about Jeb to anyone. He had ways of getting information out of people and if he knew she confided in somebody about what happened their wedding night, he would make her suffer a much worse fate than what she did then, if that was even possible.

Seeing one of her favorite customers in the foyer, Lacy went to greet him, "Weston, you devil," she said, standing on tiptoe to kiss his weather-beaten cheek, "where have you been hiding?"

"Lacy, luv, good to see you too. I see you can manage to keep the place running when I'm away," Weston replied with a wide grin. He was chuckling as he walked in with his friend Rawlings. He towered over Lacy and bent over to give her his cheek freely. His grin was impish and his dimples looked like dark caves beneath the turbulent sea. The sun had gently kissed his skin, blessing him with a golden hue. His brilliant blue eyes sparkled with mischief.

"Oh stuff," Lacy protested, "you know damn well I can run this place without you losing at cards, Weston Yates. But wherever have you been hiding lately and with whom? That's what I want to know!"

"Now, now Lacy," Weston said dryly, "you know I don't kiss and tell. Besides you're the only woman for me. You already know my evil ways so I wouldn't have to change," he laughed, flicking a piece of imaginary lint from his frockcoat. His broad shoulders filled every inch of the dark blue velvet trimmed coat, the exterior pockets at the waistline adding a stylish effect. The crisp white muslin shirt, unbuttoned, showed the glistening of his golden skin.

"So, she found out you are a black hearted rogue, and made demands on your life, and you probably thought what better way to forget her than to drink heavily and bed another," she told him. "You men are all alike, wanting us women to do all the changing while you continue with your evil ways. One of these days Weston, you are going to fall in love and want a family and no decent woman in her right mind will have you, and it will serve you right!"

Lacy scolded Weston as if he were her child, daring to take liberties that no other would.

Both Weston and Rawlings were laughing heavily at the thought of Weston married.

No, Lacy thought, Weston was definitely not the sort you could picture with a loving wife and family. The reputation he had made for himself sure took care of that. Rumors of the ruthless way he used women just for sport and pleasure had been spread through the city. But even with that reputation, he managed to attract women from the society district, smitten with his impertinent behavior. His extreme good looks were irresistible and many women forgive his deplorable nature, simply because of his devilish charm, not to mention his wealth and the mystery of his background. However, as Lacy knew well, he was not about to let anyone enter his heart. He was a black hearted rogue with a barrier of thick ice surrounding his heart.

"No thank you Lacy," Weston said now. "Love is for fools, I intend to stay as I am. Emotional entanglements are definitely not a part of my life. Of course, as you may have heard, I have other certain insatiable needs which I depend on this establishment to help satisfy."

Weston knew nothing he could do or say could shock Lacy. In fact, he always enjoyed the look of astonishment on her face by the casual way he spoke of his conquests.

"I have a good mind to throw your sassy mouth out of here, Weston," Lacy told him. "Now you two get to your table before I call Jeb."

Lacy realized her mistake instantly as she saw the twitching of Weston's jaw muscle at the mere mention of Jeb's name.

"Oh stuff, Wes," she pouted as she led them over to the table that had been reserved for them, only belatedly realizing that it was right beside the table Jeb was playing at. Futhermore, Jeb was staring at her as if she had planned it that way.

"Let me see if there's another table available," she said, knowing how the two men felt about one another. "This one's much too close to the noise."

"That won't be necessary Lacy," Weston said, looking directly at Jeb, "I like this table. I like the thought of seeing how vermin play cards."

If Jeb heard the menacing remark, he didn't show it, as he continued to play out his hand unperturbed.

"Well, I have to go see Cook," Lacy said, relieved to leave the tension between Weston and Jeb behind her. "You two enjoy yourselves."

"Wes, how come every time we play cards here we always end up next to Jeb's table?" Rawlings said, smirking.

"That scum," Weston said loud enough for Jeb to hear. "I'd just like to intimidate him into a card game, the winner take the loser's life."

Unable to help himself, Jeb looked up and locked eyes with the man who so casually threatened his life. He could feel the hatred of Weston's penetrating stare and felt as if his acid blue eyes were burning a huge hole in his body. He returned his stare, squinted his black beady eyes and contorted his face, intimidating Weston to flinch. Jeb was the first to return to his game, but a wicked smile formed on his lips as he did so. So deep in thought, was he that he didn't even realize he was losing his hand to Harley. The thought of seeing Weston's lifeless body was much more rewarding than beating Harley at poker.

That bitch, Lacy, Jeb almost said aloud. She'd pay for seating his deadliest enemy next to his table. After this hand he'd seek her out. A good threat always puts that bitch in her place.

"You boys take a break." Jeb said as he pushed his chair from the table and left in the direction of the bar. "I'll send a bottle over on me. Got business to tend to, but I'll be back to beat your ass Harley."

"Wes, what are you saying?" Rawlings demanded. "You can't be serious about a bet like that? What about Lacy? How would she feel if you take her husband's life?"

Rawlings knew that Weston could beat Jeb at cards blindfolded. Moreover, Lacy was one of their best friends. In fact, he had never seen Weston strike up a friendship with anyone other than with himself, and Lacy. In the years he had known Weston, he never deliberately sought out trouble, but it always had a way of finding him.

"I thought you considered her a friend," he continued, knowing that mentioning his friendship for Lacy would hit a raw nerve.

"Don't be so sure Lacy will be upset about it." Weston told him. "I have a feeling I'll be doing her a great favor, and besides I just might lose!"

"I have a feeling you know something, and I have a feeling I know who's giving you this information." Rawlings observed, as he saw Ruby spot Weston and start in their direction. "If my guess is correct my friend, she's headed this way."

"Weston darling!" Ruby squealed with delight. "I was hoping you'd show tonight. I was beginning to think you met with some sort of mishap, not showing your handsome face for weeks."

She turned seductively, revealing her almost bare bosom to Weston, whose response was to grab her by her waist, and pull her closer to him.

"Don't you think you should save your seductive games for your bed chamber, Ruby?" Weston said dryly, unperturbed by the expression on Ruby's face as she tried to keep from blushing. He could hear the stifled laugh of his friend across the table.

"Anything I can do for you two," she said, recovering her embarrassment with difficulty and refilling their shot glasses, "don't hesitate to ask, I'll be available all night."

Leaving the two men to their cards, Ruby hurried to the next table, silently praying that she would end up in Weston's strong arms tonight

"I think you have a problem, Wes. I have a feeling Ruby fancies herself in love with you. Too bad she doesn't realize that you're immune to that emotion."

CHAPTER 7

Jeb looked all over La Salone for Lacy, still seething from what she had done to him. To seat Weston Yates, of all people, next to his table was unforgivable. He could still feel Weston's eyes shooting daggers from across the table.

How could he have known that the whore he had picked up from the docks was a good friend of Weston's? Considering the condition he had left her in, he had thought for sure she'd keep her mouth shut, particularly since he had left her with a threat to keep quiet, but if she hadn't talked, why was Weston looking at him that way? He had heard from his cohorts that Weston aimed to take revenge on whoever was responsible. Maybe the slut hadn't revealed his name, or perhaps Weston was just waiting to catch him with his guard down. Whatever Weston's reason was, Jeb was certain he'd have to kill Weston very soon. But he would have to plan it very carefully, and for that, he would have to enlist the aid of his friend Harley.

"Where in the hell is that bitch," Jeb growled to himself standing in the foyer, looking in the gambling rooms once again. As Jeb's eyes rested on Weston's back, he visualized a large knife protruding out through his chest.

Born in Under the Hill, Natchez, to a mother who was a prostitute and to a drunken father, Jeb was known as a river rat as a child. Gossips had it that his father killed his mother after she tried to pimp her own son for a bottle of whiskey, putting a loaded gun to her head and then turning it on himself leaving a twelve year old boy alone to fend for himself in a ruthless city.

As a boy, Jeb had taken to hanging around the saloons, watching men play cards, soon realizing that this would be the profession he would eventually take for himself. Anger and fear made him survive, and he vowed to himself he would kill anyone who got in his way of survival.

Upon reaching adulthood, Jeb decided to move on to bigger and better things in life. He decided Vicksburg, Mississippi was the place to acquire the riches he so badly desired. Arriving in Vicksburg with only the clothes on his back, he soon became proficient as a card shark and began his sadistic practices, taking women to the shack he had once called home in Natchez.

Knowing nothing of this, however, Lacy's father liking the well-mannered young man, and had hired him as a card dealer. And when his daughter had come of age, he had welcomed him into his family with open arms. In his eyes, Jeb was the perfect son-in-law, a decent southern gentleman, and when Lacy found out the truth, as she soon did, she had never had the heart to tell him otherwise.

Lacy came to know the real Jeb soon after their wedding night, although she tried to keep as much distance as she could between herself and her new husband without her father becoming suspicious. The only way she could do that was to threaten Jeb that she would tell her father about his abuse. Knowing that that might well mean his untimely death, Jeb decided to seek his pleasure elsewhere.

Jeb harbored a deep resentment for Lacy, but nothing compared to the hatred he felt for Weston. His hatred was based on jealousy. Despite his lack of a formal education, Jeb taught himself to read and write, but what he really wanted, was to be rich and respected, like Weston. And, although his refined manners and uppity airs could fool almost anyone, he knew that Weston recognized him for exactly what he was, a low life thug.

In his evil mind, Jeb was plotting the torturous way he wanted to kill Weston. Now, however, he needed to talk to Lacy.

Reaching her chamber, Jeb was surprised to find the door unbolted and slightly ajar. Walking in, he was quick to notice that the room had been redecorated. The four poster mahogany bed was massive in size and ornately carved with leafs and roses. A cameo carving and fluted pilasters appeared on the armoire, and the vanity featured an elaborately carved frame with beveled glass and brass pulls. How long had it been since he'd been in there? He himself couldn't recall the times when, in a drunken stupor, he would beg for his own wife's favors only to find himself thrown out and the door bolted quickly behind him. Luckily Lacy knew he wasn't himself and hadn't called on her father. But since then, Lacy had made it very clear that the door would be locked against him. And everyone else, for that matter.

Hearing her voice in the adjacent room, Jeb walked quietly to the door which, also was partially open and saw Lacy standing at the edge of the bed fluffing a pillow under a girl's head, and smoothing out her blue-black hair.

"Don't worry yourself honey, I'll make sure you're never hurt again," he heard Lacy say as she gently removed the strands of dark hair that had fallen in the face of what appeared to Jeb to be a child.

"How touching," Jeb said, his voice dripping with sarcasm. Entering the chamber, his eyes widened as he saw the bare breast of the ravaged beauty.

Pulling the sheets over her patient, and tucking the ends under the mattress, Lacy turned to Jeb in anger. "What the hell are you doing in here?" she demanded, leading him back into her bed chamber and closing the door of the adjoining room behind her.

"Who, may I ask, is that beauty?" Jeb said hoping that this was one of Lacy's new whores. The look of lust in his eyes was undeniable.

"No, you may not ask, and what the hell do you think you're doing coming into my chamber?" Lacy said, furious at herself for forgetting to bolt the door.

"It's your fault I'm up here," he told her, grabbing her by the arm and pulling her close to him. "Why the hell did you seat that bastard Yates next to my table? I'm warning you, bitch, keep that scum away from me, or all the nursing in the world ain't gonna bring a dead man back to life. Do you understand me?"

Lacy felt a chill, knowing all too well what he meant.

Flinging Lacy away from him, Jeb composing himself. "The girl in the next room is going to make lots of money," he told her sardonically.

"That girl is not to be touched," Lacy snapped. "Do you hear me, Jeb? If you so much as lay one finger on her, I'll have your black heart cut out and thrown to the vultures."

Lacy's anger did nothing to move Jeb. He slammed the door as he left.

Walking to the stairwell, Jeb had visions of the girl lying in his arms. He had never seen her around before, he would have remembered such a lovely face. Whoever she was and how she came to be here, he didn't care. One thing for sure, he would have to have her. He could see himself now, biting her nipples, and digging his fingers into her soft flesh. He would be close to the brink of fulfillment, as her screams would echo through the room. Hearing her pleading and begging for him to stop, would only make him continue leaving a trail of torn flesh and blood.

In the mean time, Lacy's protective attitude could only mean that she was a virgin, a flower that had never been plucked. Old Jeb would take care of that, he thought. He would enter the tight walls of her cave with such force that he could feel the delicate muscles tearing around him. He would wrap his hands in her hair, pulling hard as he rode her to sheer exhaustion or near death.

Reaching the bottom of the stairs, Jeb had to quickly find privacy to relieve the aching bulge within his trousers, wishing that the hands with which he stroked himself were those of the girl upstairs instead of his own. "Soon my little virgin," he whispered to himself before going

back to resume his card game with Harley. "Soon."

CHAPTER 8

La Salone was now crowded with men waiting for a glimpse of Ruby as she sang. Although she was talented as a singer, it was the way she moved her body that had the crowd cheering for more. No one in the room seemed to notice that Ruby's eyes were fixed on only one person as she sang her love songs.

She knew all too well, that she captivated her audience, but the one person whose attention she wanted to attract had not so much as glanced her way. And so every word she sang was directed at Weston. Because he had to notice her. He must.

As she finished, the whistles, clapping and pleading for her to continue even drowned out the noise from the thunder and lighting bolts that had suddenly descended on the city.

"Well Wes," Ruby asked, joining him as he sat with Rawlings in the back of the room, concentrating on the hand of cards he was holding. "How did you like my singing, could you tell that I was just a bit nervous pouring out my love to all those men?"

"Actually, I was surprised to hear you have a beautiful singing voice," Weston said with one of those sly grins on his face, which made

Ruby desire him all the more. "And to think the only talent I thought you possessed was between your satin sheets."

"You are a rogue, Weston Yates, I have a good mind to let you seek favors from someone else." Ruby said, trying to look injured and seductive at the same time.

She did, in fact, look lovely. Her hairstyle was arranged so perfectly, that in the way her natural curls were wrapped around on her head made her look more sophisticated. The lip tint she used was that of the same color that brushed her perfect cheekbones made of beetroot and berries. The jewels she was wearing, mother of pearl on her ears and around her neck, had been given to her instead of coin for services rendered from some smitten bastard, had complimented the dark rich colors of her gown.

Every man in La Salone had propositioned her as she sauntered to Weston's table, only to be disappointed when she told them she was taken for the entire night. She knew Weston's virility well enough to know that he would want to claim her for the entire evening.

Throwing in the last card of his winning hand on the table, Weston finally looked up at her and pulled her onto his lap, not caring if she wrinkled the satin material of her gown. "Make no mistake about who claims you tonight," he said huskily, taking her chin between his huge fingers and forcing her lips down to meet his.

Uncomfortable at seeing the way Weston was devouring Ruby, as if he were going to take her right then and there, Rawlings coughed to catch their attention and Weston broke away, a devilish grin was on his face.

Ruby, who was still clinging to him possessively while toying with the strands of hair on his neck, turned to Rawlings and threw him a look of hatred.

"Why don't you get us a bottle of champagne and wait for me in your chamber?" Weston told Ruby. "I want a few more rounds with Rawlings here. The man doesn't know when to quit."

"Don't be too long." Ruby replied as she tried to smooth out some of the wrinkles in her satin gown.

Straightening her bodice, Ruby turned and smiled in triumph as she left the smoke filled room to go to the bar to get one of the most expensive bottles of champagne Lacy had to offer.

Meanwhile Rawlings was expressing his concern to his friend. "If you could have seen the look on her face, Weston, you'd know why I believe she's in love with you," he said as he dealt the cards. "I don't know why you continue to pay for her favors when you know you have

every woman in this town begging to be loved by you."

Rawlings knew that, in all probability, Ruby genuinely loved

Weston, but there was something about her that he did not like,

something disconcerting.

"Don't worry about Ruby," Weston told him. "She realizes why

I pay for favors. These girls know better than to get emotionally

involved. It's bad for their business. As for the other women in this

town, I don't particularly care to be called out by some hot headed fool

protecting their honor when I refuse to make them respectable. As I

recall, my friend, the last relationship I had was one that you and your

conniving little mistress set up, and need I remind you how that turned

out?"

"I won't say another word." Rawlings managed to reply between

hiccups.

"By the way, what the hell has gotten into you lately," Weston

demanded. "You can't even concentrate on card playing. This must be

the tenth hand you've lost already, and I won't mention the dazed state

you've been in as far business had been concerned lately."

"There's no fooling you Wes, so I might as well come out with it," his friend told him. "I'm thinking about asking Beth to become my wife."

Rawlings dreaded what Weston might say. It was no secret that he detested Beth. Indeed the two were currently not speaking. He relaxed a bit when Weston smiled.

"So, that's why the strange behavior," Weston said with a grin. "Well congratulations, Rawlings, I wish you and Beth well. Does she know you're going to pop the question?" Weston was not at all surprised about Rawlings' announcement. He had known for some time that Beth would eventually trap him, he just hoped Beth wouldn't come between Rawlings and himself. Their friendship was too good to let a self centered, selfish woman like that destroy it as well as their profitable business. The bitch, Weston thought to himself. She didn't even bother to hide the contempt she now felt for him, and it was no fault of his own.

There was a time when Beth Jackson had thought Weston was the most gorgeous man she had ever laid eyes on. That had been when she had first been introduced to him by Rawlings, and had been impressed enough to introduce him to her friend. Victoria Blackstone, a favorite friend of hers with whom she had gone to boarding school with had instantly fallen in love with Weston, haunting the docks,

accompanied by her little maid, hoping to see him. Invading Weston's

privacy was unforgivable so Weston decided to put Victoria in the same

category with all the others he had his fill with, soiled and unattached.

Victoria flew into a rage when Weston discarded her as if she

were a common trollop. "One day you'll pay, you bastard." Victoria had

called after him as he had rode his stallion away from her plantation in a

gallop after having broken her heart.

"I'm pretty sure she knows and I know what the answer will be,

so it looks like I'll be a married man soon." Rawlings said now with a

drunken slur to his voice.

"Well in that case let's have a drink to you and Beth." Weston

said holding an unsteady hand to his lips. "I wish you happiness and lots

of luck." Downing the shot of whiskey, Weston started laughing as he

imagined the look of Beth's face if, some day, he literally threw her out

of his and Rawling's office.

Rawlings began to laugh as well, not knowing what he was

laughing at but was just relieved that he seemed to have Weston's

support.

"Why don't I pay for your last tumble before you become betrothed," Weston suggested. "You know Ruby's ready and waiting upstairs."

"Thanks for the offer, Wes, but Ruby would probably claw my eyes out if she saw me enter her bedchamber instead of you," Rawlings told him, "although if I were you, I would definitely take my business elsewhere. And I'm not just referring to Ruby, I noticed the way Jeb was looking at you earlier, and I could swear he was plotting something behind your back."

"Good God Rawlings," Weston said rising to his feet unsteadily, "you already sound like a married old man, you're too paranoid. Just to prove to you that nothing is going to happen to me, I'm going to go upstairs and bed Ruby and I'll see you at the docks tomorrow morning." Making his way through the noisy crowd, he climbed slowly up the stairs, holding onto the wooden banister.

"Take heed of my warning my friend," Rawlings said, toasting his friend as he disappeared around the bend a the stair case. "I hope to see you tomorrow morning in one piece."

CHAPTER 9

La Salone was so noisy below that Lacy couldn't concentrate. She was still terribly upset over the confrontation she had had with Jeb earlier, but her concern was more for the woman in the next room than for herself or Weston. Jeb's eyes had had that evil faraway look when he had mentioned that the girl could make them a lot of money. Lacy determined that she wouldn't let any harm come to the innocent girl she had rescued even if it meant killing Jeb herself. Somehow she would find the courage to do it.

On her way downstairs, she saw Weston making his way to Ruby's chamber. The way he was weaving told Lacy he was well in his cups, and in no condition to take her warning seriously. Besides, if Jeb decided to harm Weston, and she was fairly sure he already had, someone else would do it for him. He would probably hire thugs from Under the Hill to do his dirty work for him, particularly since he must know that he was certainly no match for Weston Yates. The blatant way Weston shows his dislike for Jeb could only mean that he wants Jeb to call him out. In fact, Lacy suspected that that was Weston's ulterior motive in coming here to gamble. It dawned on Lacy that Weston's table was almost always next to Jeb's, and that he was intent on intimidating him for some reason. Weston also has taken the whore that Jeb had been accustomed to bed. Poor Ruby, she thought. She doesn't even realize

that she's being used by both men.

When Ruby had first been hired by Lacy, she had set out to

catch Jeb's attention, thinking no doubt that he was very wealthy given

the way he gambled and lost heavily, always behaving as if he had

money to burn. She knew he was married to Lacy, but it was clear she

didn't care. Not knowing Jeb's situation, she probably thought Jeb was

the owner of La Petite Salone and had deliberately set out to destroy

their marriage, hoping Jeb would fall in love with her and lavish her

with his riches. Well, she had paid dearly for her treachery when she

found out the truth about Jeb's nature. Lacy thought now, and not for the

first time, she had seen the bruises.

Lacy had never bothered to stop Weston as he went to Ruby's

chamber. But she would definitely scold him tomorrow morning for

threatening Jeb and then drinking too much to defend himself if that had

been necessary. However, she'd seen Weston under similar

circumstances, drunk one minute and totally sober and in control the

next. And Jeb had seen it too, Weston had made sure of that. Jeb knew

that Weston was not a man to trifle with. His size alone made him a

dangerous person to meddle with, not to mention the fact that he had a deadly aim with a pistol. Jeb knew that, in order to pose a threat to

Weston, he would have to strike like a snake, with no warning.

CHAPTER 10

Brana slowly opened her eyes to unfamiliar sights around her. The last thing she remembered was the endless walking and fear. She had been walking with other homeless families for so many months she lost track. They had been trying to find shelter for the ill and destitute, but to no avail. Their last stop would be New Orleans, where at least there would be decent work available at low wages, or so they were told by other vagabonds.

Brana always stuck with the crowd and never wandered off by herself for fear of starvation or rape. When they finally reached their destination, however the ill and homeless crowd slowly began to go their separate ways, and Brana was left all alone to fend for herself in a city full of cutthroats and thieves. Murder was committed before her very eyes, just for a shiny bauble that, catching a glimmer of light, was mistaken for a valuable gem. She was never afraid to roam the city during daylight, but when darkness came, Brana would find the narrowest alley and try to hide, terrified to be mistaken for one of the whores who swarmed the docks, selling themselves for a mere trinket or two, rutting like animals on the dirt road. Looking up at the stars, Brana tried to forget the fact that she had to fight for the little food that she ate.

She knew that she was ill but she was certain that she had the determination to survive, if only she could fill the void in her heart as well as that in her stomach. She had no memory of the life she had lived before the war, only the poverty and uncertainty of her future. Her last thoughts before slipping away into unconsciousness were of the memory of a soft voice calling her name. But there was nothing else to remind her of the past except the gold locket she wore hidden under her rags.

Brana awoke to the moonlight beaming through the lace curtains of her bed chamber. The yellow and orange flames in the fireplace greedily licked the wood that had been piled there. The cotton sheets carelessly slipped around her body as she sat up to take a good look around her. It was a lovely room. The wooden table next to the four-poster bed was as shiny as the river itself on a moonlit evening, taking on the reflection of the flames that danced wildly in the fireplace. The polished wooden floor was scattered with oriental rugs.

She did not know what this placed was, but she heard the sound of men's voices and the odor of strong cheroots. In the next chamber, a woman laughed. It was a strangely wild sound. Slipping out of bed, raising her hand to her throat, she sighed with relief to find that her treasured gold locket was still there.

It was the only thing that had given her strength and the courage to survive as long as she had. She never once doubted that her name was Brana or that someone named Cam loved her. Whoever he was, she had to find him, her only link to her past. Deep down inside she feared she would never find him, but hope kept her alive. She couldn't give up without knowing who he was and what had befallen him. Every place she had stopped on the long trek to New Orleans, she had asked for him, hoping someone might have heard of that name and knew his whereabouts. But because she couldn't even give a description of what he looked like, her behavior frightened most of the people she tried to question. "Oh, Cam, please help me. I need you," she would say over and over again, at the same time wondering if everybody was right in saying she had become touched.

Slipping off of the bed, she winced as she tried to take a step and had to sit back to examine the bottom of her bare feet where the blisters were still very tender. As she rubbed them gently, she realized that someone had rubbed them with perfumed salve. She longed to see the face that belonged to the gentle hands that had cleaned her body and brushed her hair with such care. She remembered the way the woman's voice had sounded when she cuddled her in her arms as if she were a babe and sang her sweet lullabies. Her voice reminded Brana of birds in chorus on a hot summer day. She could still feel the soft touch of her hands as she tenderly removed the stray strands of hair from her perspiring brow. Brana had thought it was all a dream but it was true that she was clean and wearing a cotton nightshift which, although so large that it slopped off her shoulders, was comfortable. Brana sighed contentedly as, outside the narrow window, the silver light from the moon disappeared behind the thick darkness of clouds and the sound of rain pelting against the glass drowned out the sounds coming from below. At last, at long last she was safe.

CHAPTER 11

"It's been near three weeks and that child still hasn't waked up enough but only to get liquids down her. She's touched for sure, Miz Lacy, that fever done burned her brain." Cook told Lacy, as she took some broth from the kettle and poured it into a bowl.

Kassie, Cook's granddaughter was on her way up to Brana's room with a tray of broth and bread when Lacy took it out of her hands.

"I'll take the tray, Kassie," Lacy told her, ignoring Cook. "I need a break from the ledgers now anyway."

Now, taking out her ring of keys with one hand while balancing the tray with the other, Lacy slowly opened the chamber door. The first thing she saw were those big violet eyes staring at her and a chin was held up in defiance. Lacy was startled to see how beautiful Brana looked, with her eyes wide open, dancing with life. Lacy had been totally unprepared for the beauty of this girl she had once called "her waif," with her pale skin and blue black hair.

When Lacy came into the room, Brana saw for the first time how badly her face had been marked by the pox. Her face was heavily powered trying unsuccessfully to hide the holes that marred her beauty. What a pity Brana thought. If it hadn't been for the scars, she would have had quite a lovely face. Although it was still morning, she was already dressed in a satin gown the color of Brana's beautiful gold locket with a plunging neckline, her ample bosom covered with delicate black lace like that which adorned her long sleeves. Although, her hair was pulled severely back from her face, a few black curls had managed to escape the tight coil at the back of her neck.

"Good morning." Lacy said. "I was beginning to worry that you might not ever wake up." Setting down the tray, Lacy added more logs to the fire and turned to face the young woman she had saved, breathless with relief that she finally seemed to be all right.

As for Brana, she was beset by uncertainty. Given the sounds she had heard from the next room the night before, she had some concept of the sort of establishment she was in and she was determined that, although she owed this woman her life, she would not sell her body to repay her kindness. She couldn't tolerate the thought of being taken like the trollops she had seen on the docks. She would be the one to choose who would have her, and it would be out of love that she would surrender.

"I awoke last night to the sounds of mating and gambling around me," Brana said as Lacy set the tray in front of her and unfolded a napkin. "Why have you locked me in this room?"

Lacy was startled to hear a delicate voice with a deep southern drawl sound so harsh. Realizing that Brana was afraid, and guessing the reason for it, Lacy determined to reassure her.

"Don't worry," she said. "I expect nothing in return from you, only a speedy recovery." Lacy said with understanding in her voice.

Brana give a gentle sigh as if a heavy weight had been lifted from her.

"I'm sorry if I sounded ungrateful, truly I am," she told Lacy. "It's just that I can't trust anybody. I've been through so much I've forgotten what it's like to be human again."

Huge crystal tears formed in her eyes and Lacy sitting on the bed beside her, hugged her tightly.

"Don't you worry now," she said, gently brushing the tears off of Brana's cheeks. "Everything is going to be alright. Lacy's here to help you get through it."

"Oh Lacy, how could I ever repay you?" Brana asked her. "You've been so kind to me I surely would be dead by now if you hadn't helped me."

She took the scented lace kerchief Lacy offered her and wiped the steady flow of tears from her face.

"Any decent person would have helped you," Lacy assured her. "I was just lucky enough to happen on you when I did. But, for me you were a prayer answered. I prayed every night for something in my life besides running this establishment. The demands it's made in my life have me no better off than the girls that work for me. You see, we're all caught up in the same greedy web we have spun for ourselves. Money, never wanting to be without it, and never having enough of it. La Petite Salone is one of the most profitable establishments in Vicksburg, Mississippi. I can't spend the riches it gives me freely, knowing that there are homeless and starving people around me."

"You have an unselfish heart, Lacy," Brana told her. "I've seen and been a part of the cruel world out there. Yes, I can understand your dilemma. Perhaps it was fate that brought us together."

"What about your family?" Lacy asked Brana.

"I have no memory of my family," the girl told her. "The only thing I remember is the constant walking and fear. I feel certain my name is Brana. It's here in the locket. See, and Cam whoever he is, he must have been very dear to me. I was hoping to find him as I walked trying to find shelter, but with only a name and no description, it was useless."

"What you need now is a good hot breakfast," Lacy told her. "We've been gabbing long enough. I feel certain you will regain your memory after you've fully recovered. Now what we have to do is fatten you up. You're skin and bones. But my Cook will see to that in no time. Now let me go take this tray back and bring you some real food."

As Lacy left the chamber she thought about what Brana said. Had their meeting been fate? Indeed.

"I need a breakfast tray, with one of the best meals you have ever prepared." Lacy told Cook, as she went to the cabinet where the fine china and good silver were put away. Fixing a new tray, Lacy used her finest delicate china trimmed with solid gold around the edges. The long stemmed crystal goblets she took out to toast with Brana on her recovery were etched with the pattern of tiny diamonds. As Lacy held the beautiful cut glass up to the light and twirled the long dainty stem between her well manicured fingers, she could see sunlight dancing there. Wrapping the sterling silver utensils in a crisp linen napkin she headed for the cupboard where her favorite Champagne was kept. Today was a day for celebration she thought. Brana had survived against the odds. She had made a difference in the world. She had saved a life.

The noises Brana had heard and dreamed about last night were gone, having drifted away in the wee hours of the morning along with the dark clouds that covered the silver moon. The clouds were well on their way to Natchez no doubt, but she knew the other sounds would be in full swing again tonight. She wondered about the girl in the next room and the kind of man that would take advantage of her plight. Brana had no compassion for the scoundrels that had preyed on the unfortunate circumstances of the South and its victims.

Brana's eyes widened when Lacy entered her chamber carrying a huge tray laden with food fit for a queen. She spied white fluffy eggs that must have been folded over more than a dozen times to look like the white clouds in a clear blue sky, their centers oozing with cheese and tiny pearl onions. The smell of the mushrooms sautéed in white creamy sauce tantalized her taste buds. The jam and jellies were right next to a delicately toasted miniature sized tart garnished with oranges and cream. The coffee steamed in its cup. And then there was Champagne!

The sound of bubbles dancing as they were being poured into genuine crystal glasses made Brana tear her eyes away from the feast before her and she took the crystal glass filled with the delicious sparkling wine that Lacy offered her.

"To Brana," Lacy said, her voice cracking with emotion as she held up her crystal goblet to toast with Brana. "May you have a long and healthy life."

Brana was touched by the emotion in her benefactor's voice. "To Lacy," she managed to say trying desperately to control her tears. "I owe you my life. Your kindness one day will be rewarded and you have my friendship and respect as long as I live."

They looked at one another, the stout, middle-aged woman with the pockmarked face and the young beauty with blue-black hair, each of them wondering what they would come to mean to one another.

CHAPTER 12

"Good morning Simmons" Brana called on her way to the kitchen.

"Good morning Miz Brana, morning Miz Lacy," he replied knowing Lacy was never far behind. He, too, had become very fond of Brana in the months she had been there.

On the first day she was able to walk about the premises, she had sought him out to thank him for all his help. At first he hadn't recognized her, no doubt because her face and figure had filled out, thanks to Lacy's care. And she was embarrassed to recall that it had been he who had seen her unclothed.

All of Lacy's servants loved Brana. She would spend hours in the kitchen with Simmons and Cook gossiping about the activity around them when Lacy was in her study going over the accounts of La Petite Salone. She had even accompanied Simmons to the stables to take a look at the "friends" of which he spoke so fondly. As for Simmons, he wasn't at all surprised to see Brana warming the heart of his orneriest steed. When she cooed and whispered an endearment in the horse's ear, the animal would nudge her gently, as if they alone shared a special secret. Simmons never once complained about the long hours he had to wait in front of Estelle's dress shop when Lacy took Brana to be fitted for new gowns. His reward was the beautiful smile Brana would give him as he carried the boxes filled with silks and satins to the carriage. Even Cook was taken in by the newcomer's child- like innocence and cooked her special meals, eager for her to look healthy.

The female entertainers at La Petite Salone were told by Lacy that Brana was in no way a threat to them. She was her personal companion and had nothing to do with business. In fact, Lacy did not want Brana wandering around anywhere near the gambling rooms during the day, or night because she didn't want her running into Jeb, remembering all to well the look in his eyes the first day he had laid eyes on her.

When Ruby first caught a glimpse of Brana, she felt a jealous rage inside. She knew that being the prettiest and the most talented woman in La Petite Salone wasn't enough to guarantee that she would captivate the heart of Weston Yates. But she wanted no competition, planning, as she did, to enslave him with her lovemaking, and hopefully be lucky enough to get him bewitched so he would want no other.

Ruby didn't care that Brana was sleeping in the bedchamber next to hers. She wanted nothing to do with her. As long as she stayed out of her way, Ruby could pretend she didn't even exist.

"Simmons, bring the horses around," Lacy said quickly, seeing that he was just about ready to leave the kitchen. "Brana and I are ready for our picnic."

"Yes Miz Lacy." Simmons replied on his way out the back door, shoving a tart in his mouth and smacking his lips.

Lacy took the picnic basket Cook had packed for them and went to wait for Brana in the foyer.

"It looks like we're in luck today." she said when the girl joined her. "The sun is shinning and this basket is filled with delectable treats and a bottle of exquisite Champagne."

"Thank you," Brana told Lacy, "for sparing the time. I know how busy you are during the day. But this should be a real treat for you too."

"I'm happy you suggested a picnic," Lacy smiled. She knew she could not deny Brana anything she desired.

"You work so much," Brana informed her. "It's high time you started to enjoy yourself."

"It certainly is," Lacy agreed.

The day was glorious and the grounds of La Petite Salone were green and filled scented flowers. Lacy couldn't remember the last time she had relaxed and enjoyed the sun beating down on her. As they ate a meal of fried chicken, greens and overstuffed blueberry tarts, Brana chatted about everything and poked fun of some of the strange customers she had seen in Estelle's dress shop.

"Brana," Lacy managed between gasps, trying to control her laughter, "you are a breath of fresh air."

Simmons returned after a few hours to take them back to La Petite Salone. On the way back Brana was unusually quiet, letting Lacy do all the talking. Now, however, although she didn't want of offend Lacy, she had to speak her mind. And now once they were back at La Petite Salone, she would be ushered up to her chamber for the rest of the evening since Lacy never wanted her up and about when the customers started to arrive. Brana never even saw the girls while they entertained at night, although once, passing one in the hallway, she had been thoroughly snubbed. Brana had even spoken to Cook about it, and Cook told her not to pay attention to them, that they were just jealous.

One person Brana didn't want to know was Jeb. She'd heard the gossip from Cook about Lacy's estrangement from her husband and although curious, Brana would never be so bold as to ask Lacy about it. When she was ready, she would tell her. Until then, Brana would not pay any heed to the gossip. But, Brana often caught Jeb looking at her with a sinister leer on his face, a look that made her want to avoid him as much as possible.

The insolent way Jeb talked to Lacy made Brana's blood boil even though Lacy's cool composure kept him in place. Brana could swear it was Jeb's voice she sometimes heard in Ruby's chamber. And she knew that Ruby somehow acted different with him than with the others that bedded her. When it was Jeb's voice, Brana heard Ruby cry out in what was almost a stifled scream. But often Brana heard another man's voice, deep and penetrating with a husky laugh. When he spoke, it was, Brana thought, like a master speaking to his slave. Whoever it was, he bedded Ruby at least four times a week. Brana wondered why a man who sounded so confident needed to pay for favors. He must be disfigured, or missing a limb. Whatever his reasons, he certainly has Ruby smitten.

"Absolutely not, Brana!" Lacy said a bit too harshly now. "I won't have you out and about La Salone during business hours."

"I think I understand your reasons," Brana told her. They were sitting in the carriage waiting for the horses to come to complete halt. Lacy gathered the blanket and the picnic basket without bothering to look at Brana. "I'm not a child, I can take care of myself. All I'm asking is to let me repay you for the expensive gowns you bought me. It's not like I'll be in the gambling rooms for heaven sakes, I'll be helping cook."

Brana hoped she didn't sound as indignant as she felt. She was tired of being cooped up in her bedchamber and treated as if she were a child. She was starting to feel like a prisoner in La Salone. During the day she literally saw no one except for the servants and when Lacy would allow herself time away from her ledgers they would visit. But, mostly it was so quiet during the day that she couldn't stand it. Brana wanted to see faces, hear laughter and music like everybody else, not just behind her bedchamber walls. She wanted to feel alive and work for her room and board. Lacy had saved her life and she was not about to take advantage of her kindness.

The look on Brana's face melted Lacy's heart. Her bottom lip pouted, but the sparks in her eyes danced with defiance. Lacy thought maybe she was being a little unfair to Brana in sheltering her from what was going on around her. After all, it couldn't be any worse than hearing the moans of pleasure escape from Ruby's lips every night.

"Honey, I'm sorry," she told Brana, taking her hand. "I guess I'm just being a little over protective. But are you sure you're up to it? You know Cook can be as bossy as I am."

"Oh Lacy, you won't be sorry," Brana said, smiling broadly, her hair had become unbound and a massive mass around her face. The thick mane made her look fragile and vulnerable. "I promise not to be any trouble."

"Don't thank me yet, luv, you know Cook hates anybody invading her kitchen. Are you sure you're up to this? Cook is pretty busy you know. Let me talk to her while you take a long, leisurely, scented bath. And I will update you at dinner."

Gathering her skirts, Lacy hurried to the privacy of her study, not wanting Brana to see the worried look on her face. "Damn" she said aloud, banging her clenched fist on the polished wooden desk. She thought of Jeb.

Simmons noticed the mischievous look in Brana's eyes as she followed him to the stables, chattering his ears off. He knew too well what she was up to. He had been sorry when he had given in to her the first time the week before. If anything had happened to her he would have hell to pay from Lacy and Cook.

"Please Simmons," she said now. "Lacy's busy in her study." Brana pleaded, knowing full well that he would give into her.

"Now don't you go makin that face Miz Brana," he said, trying to sound stern. "Effen something happens to yous, I'd be hung fer sure."

His ploy was lost on Brana, as she pleaded with her big violet eyes for him to saddle Tiger.

"Effen I did saddle him, you can't ride in that there fancy gown." Simmons said, hoping that she had forgotten the breeches he had taken from Cook's grandson the first time he had let her ride..

"Don't be silly Simmons, I have a special hiding place in the stables. All you have to do is saddle Tiger and stop worrying. I'll step into the other stall and change into my breeches."

At this point Simmons didn't even try to argue. Taking Tiger out of the stables to saddle him, he heard the rustle of petticoats being removed.

"Don't forget to keep that there long hair under that cap I gave you," he warned her. "You don't want to run into any varmints!"

Simmons, already regretted his decision. The pit of his stomach was burning, and he knew it wouldn't let up until Brana was back safely.

The minute she was out of Simmons sight, Brana grabbed the cap from on top of her head and let her hair flow freely. Horse and the rider seem like one as they raced through the trees, and jumped over the brush that stood in their way.

Although she knew Lacy would be upset for going riding without asking her, Brana knew that this was something that she had to do. Lacy wouldn't understand that she and the horse had become one, that they had a special bond that Brana couldn't explain. The beautiful black stallion seemed to have been made just for her. And yet, as they trotted back, Brana suddenly felt saddened. She hadn't remembered anything about her past, yet some things seemed familiar. She had felt completely familiar with the expensive satins and silks from Estelle's. And it was as though she remembered seeing the fine china and crystal that Lacy sat before her.

Lacy assured her that she had sent inquiries about the town to see if anyone had any information on the whereabouts of a person named Cam. To this date no one has yet responded.

"Well Tiger," Brana said aloud, as the wind started to pick up slightly. "I can't wait to tell him the new name I've picked out for you. What do you think of Beauty?"

Tiger stood on his hind legs and whinnied as though he were in total agreement with his new mistress and something in the way she so easily reined him in, made Brana confident that she had ridden just such a horse before. But where? And When?

CHAPTER 13

Jeb was well in his cups, thinking of ways to bed Brana. Ever since he had first seen her, he could think of nothing else. He had kept his distance, biding time, waiting for Lacy to forget the reaction he had had when he first saw her. He had been careless in showing an interest for the girl in front of Lacy when he had first seen her. Now he could only admire her beauty from afar, and undress her with his eyes as she roamed La Salone. The thought of seeing her body writhing underneath his made him burned with desire.

Now, in his drunken state, he lost total control and sought out Ruby to release the spill of his seed. "There you are spitfire," he said as he stumbled toward her, not bothering to notice who she was sitting with at the gambling tables. "Come here to old Jeb."

"Not now, Jeb, I'm with a customer," Ruby spat back at him with a pleading look in her eyes.

"Now whore! When I'm calling you, get your ass over here now!" Jeb was too much into his own thoughts and liquor to have noticed that Weston and Rawlings had arrived at La Salone earlier.

Jeb never knew what hit him as he fell, crumpled, to the floor at Weston's feet.

"Get this lecherous vermin out of here before I forget he can't defend himself," Weston told Jeb's brutish friend, Harley in a deadly tone. Harley jumped at the sound of Weston's voice and carried Jeb out of the gambling rooms to sober him up.

"Well you got that out of your system for now," Rawlings told Weston calmly, uncomfortably aware that, given the possessive way Ruby was smiling, she apparently thought all this had been done in her defense. "What happens when he wakens?"

"I hope the bastard calls me out." Weston replied. "Lord knows I've been waiting long enough."

He was tired of antagonizing Jeb and getting no response, but he kept remembering the look on Serena's face as she told him the horrible way Jeb abused her body. He had to be stopped, and Weston was just waiting for the right opportunity to put a bullet between his beady eyes.

"Don't you use up all your energy on Jeb, Weston," Ruby purred, while licking the tips of her painted fingernails. "Don't forget I promised you a night you would never forget."

She and Weston had been just about to leave the gaming room when Jeb had interrupted them, but now that Jeb had been taken care of she grabbed Weston by the arm and pressed her hot body against his.

She had been dressed more seductively than usual tonight in a deep red velvet gown with a plunging neckline that showed a hint of light brown delicate nipples, a soft bustle in the back that accentuated drapes on her hips. Throwing her over his shoulder, Weston headed for the stairs.

Meanwhile, upstairs, Brana was remembering what Lacy had told her when they had dined in her chamber earlier, Lacy had explained why the door had been bolted when she was recovering and why she was a little overprotective of her. Jeb, it seemed had shown an interest in her and had been in a foul mood ever since because Lacy was protecting her so well. Lacy never went into any details as to why she should stay clear of him, but somehow Brana knew Lacy's warning wasn't exaggerated.

Having already donned her cotton nightshift, Brana laid on her side and she stared into the flames. Every time she stared long enough, she seemed to hear a voice calling her name, a voice that was so familiar Brana knew she had heard it before.

Turning around to face the wall with her back to her past, Brana realized that she was exhausted. The hot bath she had in her chamber after her exhilarating ride with Beauty and her internship in the kitchen had relaxed and soothed her.

She was almost to the point where sleep was about to consume her when she heard the sound of Ruby laughing. Brana tried turning the

other way and pulling the bed covers over her head to drown out the
noise, but it didn't help. And the man's voice was familiar. He was, she
was certain, someone who often came to Ruby's chamber.

"Ooh that feels real good," Ruby said in a horse whisper that
made the hair at the back of behind Brana's neck rise. Ruby giggled and
Brana heard the sound of water splashing. Tiptoeing to the door, she
turned the knob and was startled to find it open.

Through the flicker of candlelight, Brana couldn't believe the
scene before her. The most handsome man she had ever seen, covered
with a thin veil of mist, he stood in a porcelain tub, the firelight bringing
out the rich gold streaks in his light brown hair. His muscled body
glistened as tiny beads of perspiration formed on his brow.

As the veil of mist slowly began to disappear, Brana put her hand
to her lips to stifle her gasp of surprise. The handsome brown haired
Adonis was holding Ruby's head as she knelt before him.

Through the slow rising mist Brana could see Ruby's long hair
forming wavy ringlets around his legs, as though it was a magical vine
holding him in place. Nobody seemed to notice her intrusion as Ruby
covered his hardened member with scalding hot kisses, kisses that made
him cry out with pleasure as he gripped, her hair pushing Ruby deeper

and deeper into his body. Brana saw a flash of white teeth as he parted his lips and rolled his head from side to side, panting as if he were about to explode.

As she watched, Brana felt emotions stir within her that she had never felt before. Her skin tingled, and her stomach felt as if there were a million butterflies fluttering away inside. Without realizing what she was doing, she held her breasts with both hands, rubbing them gently. The beating of her heart was so fast Brana had to take in deep breaths, as though she had been running in the woods.

Caught up in the sexual scene before her, Brana never realized the door had opened until she felt a cool breeze cover her body. Regaining her senses, she quickly retrieved her fallen nightshift from the floor and saw a pair of startling blue eyes, dancing mischievously, staring mockingly right at her. Brana gasped at the look on his face and quickly closed the door shut.

Later, lying in her bed, she realized she had never felt so humiliated in her life. And by whom? By a man who was doubtlessly an insufferable cad. Tossing and turning under her bed covers, she tried to drown out the sound of his deep chuckles. She couldn't understand what had come over her. She had never felt that way before.

Remembering what she had seen in Ruby's chamber brought a crimson red stain to her cheeks. How could she have lost total control? But she could not forget the sound of his deep laughter and the way he had stared at her, eyes gleaming, aware of her humiliation and amused by it.

"Ooh!" Brana cried aloud pounding her fists on the feather pillow. The gall of him to show her a wicked smile as she closed the door on her shame. How could he be so cruel as to mock her with his eyes, doubtless knowing full well she had temporarily lost her senses?

Before finally drifting off to sleep, Brana determined to question Lacy about a man who was probably the most unscrupulous rogue she had ever had the misfortune of laying eyes on.

As for Weston, lying in Ruby's large four-poster bed with her nestled beside him, his arms behind his head, he kept picturing the beautiful woman's nude body moving seductively, her firm breasts standing at attention. The blue-black tiny triangle of ringlets made a startling contrast against her milk white creamy skin. He had thought surely she was a vision from beyond until her big beautiful violet eyes had met his. Weston could still see the shock that had registered on her face as she finally realized what she was doing, the crimson flush that had spread across her cheeks. What a pity he thought, he rather liked the idea of having two whores instead of one.

"Wes darling, you haven't heard a word I said" Ruby scolded as she lay her head on Weston's chest.

Weston never gave her an answer. He was still thinking of the sex nymph he had seen in the doorway. Ruby was right, this was a night he would never forget.

CHAPTER 14

"It sounds as if you are describing Weston Yates, honey. When did you see him?" Lacy asked suspiciously.

"Let's just say it was an accidental encounter," Brana said a little too loudly. She wanted to be casual but it wasn't working and she knew that Lacy had noticed her nervousness.

Lacy didn't want to interrogate Brana. When Brana was ready to confide in her, she would Lacy was sure of that. But she did feel obligated to warn her about Weston.

"Stay away from him honey," she said. "He's the kind of man a girl can break her heart over."

"Oh Lacy, I'm just asking what his name is and where he comes from," Brana protested. "You act as if I plan to fall in love with him."

Brana shrugged her shoulders in an effort to act as if it really didn't matter. But that couldn't be further from the truth. She had thought of nothing else since she awoke the morning after their fateful meeting to find that she couldn't even concentrate on the day's work. She kept seeing his face and hearing his deep laughter over and over again.

"Don't get me wrong Brana," Lacy said as she poured tea from a blue floral china tea pot. "There's a side to Weston that nobody knows. It's just that I know why he pays for favors instead of taking what all the women offer him freely. I personally pity the fools who lose their hearts to him, but I have to admit he is a handsome rogue. But a rogue all the same. Have no doubt about that."

"You two gonna yak all day or is my new helper gonna get ta work," Cook interrupted. She knew Brana had never worked the kitchens in her life. In fact, in her heart she was certain that this beauty was a true southern belle born and bred. Certainly she was no one who should wait on others.

"Cook's right, Lacy, I'd better get to work." Brana said, relieved that they had been interrupted. She could never tell Lacy what happened last night, just the thought made her quiver.

"Honey, are you alright?" Lacy asked as she put her hand to touch Brana's forehead. "You look a bit flushed?"

"I'll be just fine once I get to work," Brana assured her. "Really Lacy, don't worry. If I get too tired I'll go to my chamber and rest. I promise not to overdo it."

Lacy had been against the idea from the very beginning but she also knew that Brana was too proud to live off of Lacy's charity for long. Lacy knew that Brana would never be happy here, unless she could

repay her and wanted nothing more than Brana's companionship despite

the fact that when the headstrong chit of a girl took control, Lacy could

never refuse her.

Leaving Brana with Cook in the kitchen, Lacy headed for the

rooms upstairs. She thought she had better tell the girls that Brana would

be about La Salone and she wasn't looking forward to it.

Lacy saw the look of contempt in Ruby's eyes as soon as she

made her announcement about Brana. It had never been a problem

before because Brana posed no threat to anyone. But now they would

occasionally run into her, and given Brana's beauty, there was sure to be

jealousy, not only of Brana's looks but also the close relationship she

had with Lacy.

Ruby was the first to speak and when she did, it was in a tone

which Lacy didn't care for.

"You just warn her to keep away from my customers, Lacy," she

said. "Nobody takes from me what's mine."

"Don't worry," Lacy assured her. "She's not selling her wares.

Brana will be helping Cook in the kitchen. If she needs to leave for a spell and the customers get a little out of hand, you come and get me, is that clear?"

"We can't be babysitting her Lacy," Ruby said disapprovingly. "If she wants to work in La Salone, she'll have to look after herself. I for one think she should stay upstairs in the evenings."

"Well she's not," Lacy snapped, "and you really don't have any say in this matter so I suggest you get used to the fact. Now, does anybody else have anything to say?"

Nobody said a word, however, content to watch Ruby who was tapping her foot on the floor and staring defiantly at Lacy. When Lacy left the room, she felt eyes boring through her back.

"That bitch thinks she's so high and mighty," Ruby spat out the words. "Even if she does own this place she wouldn't make any business without me."

"Why are you so hard on Lacy?" Josephine, a meek, plain looking girl with big brown eyes asked. "She has always been good to us. We have the best gowns, food, and drink and I really think she cares for us."

"Well now, that's just none of your damn business. As for me, looking out for that virginal trash she has working now, I say let her get what she's asking for."

The girls knew Ruby was upset over the fact that Lacy had spoken to her in that tone in front of them. They had rather enjoyed it; Ruby needed to be brought down a peg or two.

"You wouldn't say that if Weston had his eye on Brana, would you, Ruby?" Santelle knew that would hit a nerve with her.

"You leave Weston out of this," Ruby snapped. "He's mine and I'll see that no one else has him, I'm the only one he needs as well as the only one who can satisfy him."

"I seem to recall a conversation I had overheard at his table the other night," Santelle persisted, "it was while he was talking to his good-looking friend. It seems to him you're just a whore like the rest of us. You're nothing to him. Can't you see that?"

On hearing that, Ruby threw herself at Santelle in a blind rage, and both women fell to the floor.

"You filthy, lying, jealous bitch!" Ruby screamed, pulling handfuls of Santelle's brown hair, her hands tightening around Santelle's neck.

"Josephine, get her off of me!" Santelle pleaded between gasps of breath. Santelle's eyes looked like they were about to bulge out of their sockets as Ruby's hold became tighter and tighter.

Mimi and Josephine tried unsuccessfully to pull Ruby off Santelle.

"Get off of her Ruby," Lacy cried. "Now!" Lacy had heard the screaming all the way down the hall. Usually, she let the girls work out their own problems but the screams were loud enough to require investigating.

Hearing Lacy's voice, Ruby finally let go of Santelle who immediately rolled over on her side, gasping for air.

"I'll have none of this fighting here as long as you're under my roof." Lacy told them angrily. "The next time it happens, you'll be out on the streets. Josephine help Santelle up and Mimi go get her some brandy." Ruby was, Lacy thought, not for the first time, a danger to have around, hot tempered and impulsive. But the customers liked her and she might as well give her one more chance.

Ruby waited for Lacy to leave the room before she spoke. "You're lucky Lacy came in, when she did," she told Santelle calmly. "She saved your life, because I would have killed you."

No one in the room doubted for one moment that she meant it.

CHAPTER 15

Weston was unable to concentrate on the work before him because he kept thinking of the beautiful angel who had stood nude before his very eyes. He had never seen that girl at Lacy's before. He would have remembered such beauty and would probably have bedded her as soon as introductions had taken place. The unusual color of her eyes kept haunting him and those sensuous lips were just waiting to be kissed. Best of all, the way she moved her flawless body told him she was an experienced seducer. Tonight he would find out all about his little temptress. Whatever her price was, he was willing to pay double just to feel her silken body under his.

"What's on your mind Wes?" Rawlings asked, from the desk opposite of Weston's. Ledgers were neatly stacked on the mahogany furniture waiting for Weston's signature. "You've been shuffling papers back and forth all day and you haven't even checked on the new accounts. That's not like you my friend, unless of course it has something to do a lovely woman I don't know about. She must be something special."

"Out with it Wes. Who are you thinking about? Do I know her?"

Weston smiled, knowing that if he didn't confide in his friend, he would never hear the end of it. "Well," he said, "If you must know, I haven't actually met her yet, but I will tonight. Care to come along?"

"Can't make it tonight," Rawlings told him. "Beth and I are dining with her family and if I cancel another engagement with them, I'll have hell to pay with Beth."

"What the hell do you find so amusing?"

"Sorry old boy, it's just that I couldn't quite picture Beth at Lacy's."

"Who in the world would you want to meet at Lacy's that you haven't already met?" Rawlings demanded, frowning.

"Actually, last night was the first time I've ever seen her," Weston admitted. "She's probably just a new girl being broken in."

"Strange, I didn't see anybody new last night?"

Weston cleared his throat to stall for time. For some unknown reason he wanted no one to know how they had seen each other.

"I saw her briefly in the dining area talking to Lacy before I left," he lied, going on to change the subject to the ledgers he had so carefully put aside, hoping his inquisitive friend would get the message.

Brana's first day in the kitchen proved to be more of a burden than a help. Cook tried to be patient with her but, after an hour, she was almost as the end of her rope. Brana was trying too hard to do a good job, but she knew nothing of cooking or even peeling potatoes.

Lacy would have never agreed to Cook's idea until she saw Cook chasing Brana out of the kitchen waving a sharp carving knife in the air.

"I'd much rather serve the customers, Lacy," she pleaded. "I might even see somebody that I would recognize, and that might help me get my memory back." She knew one thing for sure; she had never in her life before worked in the kitchen.

"Brana are you sure you didn't burn the apple fillings for Cook's famous tarts on purpose so you could work the tables?" Lacy questioned. She knew Brana wasn't the type to stay cooped up for very long.

"Lacy, how could you think such a thing." Brana answered with a smile, giving Lacy a hint that perhaps she was right.

"Listen to me Brana," Lacy told her in a serious voice. "The customers can get pretty tough, especially if they're well into their cups, and they just might mistake you for one to put out favors." She knew that was definitely going to happen. But Brana was adamant about working so all she could do was to be prepared for the worst.

"Don't worry Lacy," Brana couldn't hide the excitement in her voice. "I can take care of myself. Besides they might not even notice me in the plain cotton gown I plan to wear."

"Well Brana, I guess you'd better get to your chamber and rest up. Tonight's going to be a long one and you'll be standing up all night serving tables. After tonights over you're going to wish Cook had killed you with her sharp carving knife."

"You won't be disappointed in me Lacy, I promise you," Brana said as she ran toward Lacy and kissed her on her lightly powered cheek.

Before Lacy could reply, Brana was out of the study and almost up the stairs. Once in her chamber, Brana threw herself on her bed and smiled to herself. Her spirits were high. She hoped that she really might see somebody she recognizes, someone who just might jolt her memory back. Going to her cabinet, Brana picked out the plainest gown she could find, a simple, pale blue, cotton frock with a high neck, edged with white lace, and puffy sleeves that tapered thin from elbow to writs. She wore a blue ribbon in her hair and fine kid slippers on her tiny feet. Hearing a slight tapping at the door, Brana went to open it and admitted Simmons carrying buckets filled with hot water to start her bath.

"Miz Lacy thought you might want to relax in a scented bath, Miz Brana," Simmons said as he went to the door to Lacy's room where the porcelain tub they shared was kept.

"I should have thought of that myself, but leave it to Lacy to think of everything," Brana said. She was so excited that she needed to calm her nerves.

"Miz Brana, I don toll Miz Lacy that was a bad idea fer you to work downstairs during customer hours," Simmons said. "It gets ugly sometimes with the men carrying on the way they do. It's no place fer you Miz Brana." Cook had told him the mess Brana made in the kitchen and had even said it was her idea for Brana to work the tables. He was about to get angry at Cook until she quickly told him about the burned tart filling, his favorite.

"Don't worry, Simmons," Brana said. "I'm not worried a bit with you there for protection."

Simmons merely grinned and shook his head. He knew Brana was buttering him up, but he still didn't like the idea.

"Don't you worry none, Miz Brana," he told her. "I'll take care of any varmints that get outta hand. You jest comes tell me and I'll blacken their eyes for you."

"I knew I could count of you, Simmons," Brana said as she went to hug him. An embarrassed Simmons left the room, promising himself he would watch her like a hawk. Nobody would ever hurt her as long as he was around.

Deep in thought Weston, couldn't wait to leave his office. He had had enough of business for one day. After his conversation with Rawlings, he tried his best to forget the vision he had seen, but she still haunted his thoughts as the light of day began to turn grey.

Weston knew that tonight would be the only night he would be able to see her for quite some time. The new accounts to ship lumber to various places had just been signed, so needless to say, he and Rawlings would be quite busy for the next few months. Rawlings would oversee the lumber mill, pitching in with the crew to make sure the orders would be finished before the deadline date. As for Weston, he would supervise the loading of his ships at the docks, making sure the hold has no leaks to rot the lumber before it reaches its destination.

It had been decided that Weston would be the partner to set sail as captain. The crew members respected him and gave him their loyalty. The first time out, he had led the attack against a fleet of pirate ships ready for battle. That time they had been returning home after a successful voyage to the Orient with a ship laden with silks, satins, china and silver.

The battle had lasted several hours, until the pirates gave up in defeat, unprepared in the face of a merchant's vessel carrying more weapons than they. What the crew had admired most about Weston was that he had never risked their lives unnecessarily, preferring to out run and out maneuver the enemy.

Leaving his office, which was located near the waterfront, Weston couldn't wait to reach his home to bathe and dress for tonight. He had to make sure the lovely creature was not just a vision but a real wanton, eager to sell her favors.

Arriving at his brick townhouse on Pearl Street, Weston drew in a deep breath when he saw Beth's carriage. "What the hell was she doing here?" he wondered. He couldn't think of any reason why she would need to seek him out at his residence.

From his foyer, Weston spotted Beth sitting comfortably on the mahogany and inlaid satinwood paneled sofa with her satin skirts fluffed around her. She was wearing a green gown that made her look wan and sickly. Her face was so pale that you could see patches of brown freckles. As he entered the parlor, Beth looked up and gave Weston a practiced smile.

"Forgive me for the intrusion, Weston," she said before he could greet her, "but I must speak to you about Rawlings."

"What can I do for you Beth?" Weston asked not even pretending to hide the annoyance he felt at her intrusion. He tipped his head to her servant who was standing next to her.

"I want to speak to you about Rawlings," Beth told him stiffly. She hated having to turn to Weston, but she didn't have a choice. "He's been working much too hard lately. Why, he's been working so late he's exhausted and ill looking the following day. I'm starting to worry about his health and not to mention how upset Papa has been since he hasn't shown his face at our dinner table in a week."

"I fail to see what that has to do with me," Weston chuckled, not bothering to hide his amusement. So that was what Rawlings has been telling her, that he had to work while he went to Lacy's.

"What you could do, Weston, is stop working him so hard," Beth snarled and tightened her lips. "Everybody knows even though you're partners, you're the one that runs the business. He feels he has to do more than his share at the office and lumber mill because you take all the risks on the high seas. But from what I hear," she added uneasily, "you always have the time to spend with certain women of ill repute."

"Did Rawlings tell you that?" Weston asked as he folded his arms over his chest. Poor Rawlings, he thought. He'd betrothed himself to a meddling busybody.

"Well not exactly," she told him, flushing. "But I can see what's going on."

"See yourself out Beth." He said and then tipped is head to her servant, smiled and left the room.

"What are you smiling at?" Beth spat at her servant. "A time will come when the arrogant Mr. Yates will pay. Mark my words Minnie, you'll see."

CHAPTER 16

"Been holding out, Jeb?" Harley asked as he saw Brana serving the table across from his. "What a looker. Where did you find a beaut like that?"

Jeb turned to look over his shoulders. So Lacy was letting that girl work the tables. He winced at the pain in his jaw. Weston had nearly broken his jaw last night. Luckily he had been too drunk to feel any pain or notice that some of his teeth had become loose until this morning when he had sworn that Weston would pay dearly.

"Put your eyes back in your head, Harley," he said now. "That one's mine."

Harley knew better than to question Jeb's claim on the girl. If Jeb meant to have her, Harley knew that all he had to do was wait until Jeb had had his fill with her. After Jeb would break her in so that he would have an easier time of it. Besides he knew Jeb too long not to know the consequences of betraying him.

Brana couldn't believe how crowded La Salone had become in a matter of hours or, for that matter, the amount of coins tossed on the gaming tables, waiting to be claimed by the lucky winners. Ruby was sitting on the pianoforte with her skirts pulled up to expose most of her shapely legs. As Brana watched, Ruby started to sing her heart away.

The melody was something called *Little Tillie's Grave.* Her voice was deep and rich and she was clearly shameless, raising her skirts to show black net stockings and bending low at every opportunity, the better to show her breasts as they rose from the low cut bodice of her red satin gown. Beyond her, Brana saw a man staring at her. The expression on his face made her shiver with fear. Jeb had been staring at her with a glassy look in his eyes. Brana noticed his bruised and swollen jaw.

She would never have recognized him if it hadn't been for his beady eyes. Brana couldn't believe he didn't have the decency to turn away once she caught him staring at her. Whirling about, Brana left the smoky gaming room to go the kitchen where more orders were waiting for her.

"How's it going, dear?" Lacy asked her.

"No problems yet, Lacy," Brana assured her. "I just really can't believe how crowded the place is."

Brana couldn't believe the number of people that were still left with their riches after the war. Particularly since all she could remember was the poverty it left behind. Some customers, Brana noticed, played for small stakes, clearly not wanting to lose all of their life savings, but hoping they would be lucky enough to win a fortune. She understood why Lacy felt the way she did about her business, the guilt she felt on acquiring her wealth at the expense of someone else's misfortune. She's too kind not to let it bother her. That was why she couldn't spend her profits freely. She had a conscience and a good heart.

"It's going to be even busier as the night wears on," she told Brana now, "but if you get tired, don't hesitate to retire for the evening."

"Don't worry Lacy, I won't overdo it. Now I've got to run with these orders for Cook. I'll talk to you later."

Lacy shook her head in amazement. Even in her plainest gown Brana looked beautiful. The bodice was so tight it showed the dainty curves of her breasts. Brana might not have noticed the looks she was getting from the customers as they walked in, but Lacy certainly had. The only thing left to wonder about was who would be the first to proposition her.

"What's the matter Wes? Didn't you didn't have enough last night?" Lacy said as he appeared in the foyer, having heard about the fight he had with Jeb last night from Simmons. She has to find out what's going on with those two. It wasn't like Weston to start trouble in her Salon, not with so many witnesses prepared to say that Jeb had been defending himself if he had pulled out a gun to shoot Weston.

"I got more than enough last night Lacy," Weston assured her. "I just came in to relax a bit and ease away the day's tension." As Weston spoke to Lacy he quickly scanned the room to find his lovely vision.

"Well, in that case why don't you just have a seat and I'll pour you a drink myself." Lacy said, walking him over to the bar. This was the perfect chance to talk to him about what happened last night.

"What'll you have Wes?" she asked him." Whiskey or some of my best brandy?"

But it was clear that Weston didn't even hear her as his eyes roamed the gaming room.

"If you're looking for Ruby you just missed her about a second ago," Lacy told him. "She's been singing but she's upstairs now."

He shrugged his shoulders and looked at Lacy. He felt foolish that he had taken special care with his attire, something he had never done before to visit La Petite Salone. His black wool suit was unadorned but beautifully tailored. The look was casual without the usual cravat, but elegant. His shirt was bleach muslin with a bib front and the white pin stripes on his trousers were barely noticeable.

"I'll have that whiskey now, Lacy," he said.

"Here you go Wes; by the way, I wanted to talk to you about what happened last night." Lacy said as she poured whiskey into his glass. She was going to ask once and for all why the hatred for Jeb.

So the girl, whoever she was, had told Lacy what had happened. He couldn't understand why she would have wanted to do that unless of course she had lied and said that he had tried to invade her chamber.

"What about last night?" Weston answered as he gulped the entire contents of his glass in one swallow.

"Don't play innocent with me, Weston," Lacy told him. "You know what I'm referring to. I just wish you would confide in me and tell me what's going on with you two."

Why that little bitch! What the hell had she told Lacy? "I assure you, Lacy, there's nothing for you to concern yourself about," he said angrily.

"What do you mean Weston; of course I'm going to concern myself. I don't want your dead body on my conscience."

"Dead body? So she's threatened to kill me," Weston said with a hearty chuckle.

"I don't know who you're talking about, but I'm referring to Jeb." Lacy said with a confused look on her face. Who had Weston think she was referring to? And why was he laughing?

"Don't worry, Lacy, I can handle Jeb" Weston told her as he poured himself another drink.

"I want to know why you're after him," Lacy replied. "Does it have to do with a woman?"

"Does it really matter to you?" he asked watching her carefully. "I was under the distinct impression that you hate him."

"I should have known that you wouldn't tell me. All I'm going to say in the matter is to watch your back. Now, since I got that off my chest, have another drink and I'll have a meat pie sent over."

The look on Lacy's face told Weston all he wanted to know. Ruby must have been right when she told him Lacy hated her husband since Lacy did not seem to feel concerned about Jeb's well being. Weston's lip curled as it occurred to him that Jeb just might have abused Lacy. That could be one reason why she was warning him about Jeb's tactics. Could it also be that that Lacy had him working at La Salone because she was afraid to send him packing.

Brana couldn't believe how tired she had become just waiting for Cook to finish the new food orders. Still, she couldn't stop now. She was determined to keep serving until Cook closed the kitchen for the night.

Lacy laughed when she came into the kitchen to find Brana sitting on one of the straight back chairs, rubbing the bottom of her blistered feet.

"You've done enough for one day," Lacy told her. "You really need to tend to those blisters before they get infected."

"I'm fine Lacy," Brana told her, putting her slippers back on. "I just thought I'd rest a spell until Cook has my order ready."

"Very well, dear," Lacy said, shrugging her shoulders. "Will you take a beef pie to the bar? A gentleman there is hungry for one of Cook's specials."

Waiting for Cook to put the last pie on the serving platter, Brana realized that she was more disappointed than she had imagined she would be. She hadn't come any closer to finding Cam here than when she was with the destitute and the starving.

Weston helped himself to more brandy while waiting for Lacy to return. He felt a twinge of disappointment at not finding his vision here tonight. Perhaps, after all, she had been a just figment of his imagination. But he knew better. Nobody could conjure up the unusual color of violet in her eyes.

"Oh damn." Brana said aloud making her way through the crowd, uncomfortably aware that she had been using the words she learned in the streets more frequently of late. Once, in the stables, she had uttered an oath, and Simmons had given her a lecture on how ladies weren't supposed to know those words. He had, she realized, actually forgotten where he had found her.

As Brana came into the smoky room with the last tray of pies, a broad shouldered man waved her over to him and she went, thinking that there was something vaguely familiar about him.

Weston was just about to thank the servant for the meal, when he looked up and saw her. It was then that he noticed his beautiful vision right within his grasp, and he wasn't about to let her go. He managed to grab her by the arm and pull her close to him.

Brana had tried to wiggle her arm free, but his strength was too much for her. She had finally come face to face with the taunting blue eyes that had been haunting her thoughts all day and she was terrified.

"Let me go, you, you, despicable cad," she cried.

Weston laughed at the furious look on her face and he pulled her closer to him.

"I've been waiting all day to take you in my arms and taste the sweetness of your lips," he told her. And then he kissed her and her world exploded.

CHAPTER 17

Taken, as she was, by surprise, Brana felt as though she had lost control, just as she had when she had seen this man standing naked in the tub in Ruby's chamber. The male scent of him combined with the taste of whiskey as he forced her mouth open with his lips, played havoc with her senses. She realized she was responding to his kisses but she didn't have enough strength to pull herself away from him. The burning feeling in the pit of her stomach finally brought her back to reality.

"Get your miserable hands off of me!" Brana told him. "How dare you take such liberties?"

Although Weston was taken by surprise at her outburst, he tightened his grip on her arms. "Don't be coy," he told her, grinning. "Remember that I've already seen a good bit of you."

"How dare you!" Brana exclaimed.

"I do dare, my lovely," he told her, grinning. "I take what I want and I want you. And don't deny that you want me. Your reaction to my kiss tells me that. Let's not waste precious time playing virginal games. I intend to pay your price and much more if need be."

"OOOh," Brana tried desperately to release herself from his murderous grip in order to slap his arrogant face.

"If you think I would let you touch me, think again," she hissed. "I'd rather kill myself first."

Weston started to laugh when he saw her cheeks reddening and sparks flying wildly in her eyes. What a wildcat, he thought, as Brana freed herself from his vise-like grip. Suddenly, he felt the sting of a sharp slap across his face.

Santelle smiled as she watched Brana's attack. What a way to get her revenge on Ruby, she thought. But first, she must formulate a plan to get Brana and Weston together. Before she left La Salone, which would be soon, she'd see Ruby groveling on her knees begging for Weston to love her.

"Tomorrow," she said aloud. She knew exactly how she would do it.

"Hey darlin', aren't you supposed to be concentrating on me?" the bearded man beside her asked, putting an arm around her waist.

"I'm sorry handsome," Santelle said seductively. "Why don't we go to my chamber where I can really concentrate on you."

Weston was still rubbing his cheek when he looked down and saw the fallen blue silk ribbon from the fiery temptress's hair. Picking it up, he toyed with it thoughtfully.

"Weston darlin', how long have you been waiting for me?"

Ruby spotted him as soon as she came down the stairs. Deep down inside, she had been certain Weston would return to see her tonight. It was all she thought about all day long. Her obsession for him was becoming uncontrollable. Every waking hour, she fantasized about the life they would share together. Santelle had told her about the conversation she had overheard between Weston and Rawlings, but she took no heed of it. She knew Santelle had been jealous of her when she first started working in La Salone. Soon Ruby thought, she would be rid of all of them. Weston would take her away and lavish his riches on her. After she was accepted into the circle of the elite of Vicksberg, she would look down on all of them. They would soon see how much Weston loved her. She remembered how deep in thought he had been the night before and was certain he would take her away soon to be only his.

"Frankly, Ruby," he said now as she approached him, "I was just getting ready to leave. But I'm glad you're here. I need to ask you a question."

"Anything, Weston," Ruby purred. "What is it?"

Her heart was beating so fast she almost had a spell of the vapors. She had never thought Weston would propose to her like this. She had imagined him taking her to the finest restaurant in town where they would sip expensive champagne and dine under candlelight. He would take her in his arms and whisper endearments of pleasure in her ear.

"Who's the new girl?" Weston asked her still twisting the blue ribbon between his fingers.

Ruby wanted to scream. Instead she just looked directly at Weston and asked, "What new girl?" Her composure was complete, but she was seething inside.

"The beauty serving tables," he told her, holding the ribbon up to his lips so that he could smell the perfume of the stranger's hair. "I've never seen her here before."

"Oh her." Ruby shrugged. "She's just a trollop that Lacy picked up from the streets. I shouldn't tell you but she's diseased."

"What's her name?" Weston didn't notice the look on Ruby's face. He was too busy remembering Brana's lovely body moving seductively on their first encounter.

"Her name is Brana. Now no more questions. Let's go up to my chamber. I've missed you all day."

Ruby felt desperate. She didn't want him noticing any other woman. She swore that Brana would pay dearly.

"No thanks, Ruby, I have to be up early," Weston said.

Ruby watched him go with danger in her eyes. Did he really think that he could shrug her off this way for somebody like Brana and get away with it?

CHAPTER 18

"The nerve of him, Lacy," Brana burst into the kitchen, her hair unbound, sparks flashing from her eyes, her cheeks flushed with rage. "I've never been so humiliated in my life. Well, at least I don't think I've been. I'm sure I would have remembered the way I'm feeling now!"

"I told you Weston was a rogue," Lacy reminded her, amazed to see the girl in such a fury. "I'm sorry he upset you so. I should have told you he was the one that ordered from the bar. I'm sure he didn't mean any harm, honey. He just misunderstood your position here, that's all."

"Why are you defending him, Lacy?" Brana demanded. "After the way he spoke to me!"

"Well, dear, it's just that since I've got to know Weston, I kinda have a soft spot in my heart for him," Lacy told her. "He being so handsome and his devilish charm gets me every time. But, dear, I told you that being mistaken for one of the girls was bound to happen if you insisted on working downstairs. That kind of treatment just goes with the territory. Why don't you go up and get some rest. You'll feel better about this in the morning."

"Maybe you're right, Lacy,' Brana admitted. "I am a bit tired. But I know one thing for sure. I won't change my feelings about Weston Yates!"

"Would you like me to talk to him and explain your position here?" Lacy offered.

"I can handle him myself," Brana assured her. "You have enough to worry about without me adding to your problems. Now if you'll excuse me, I'm going to bed."

Brana was so drained that all she wanted to do was feel the soft mattress caress her tired body. Using the staircase in the kitchen, she hurried upstairs and bolted the door behind her. As she kicked her shoes off and began to rub her tired feet, she suddenly remembering that she hadn't checked to see that the adjoining door to her chamber was locked. She certainly didn't want any intrusions tonight. She felt a chill down her spine as she remembered the penetrating blue eyes that had held her captive all day in her memory. Remembering the way Weston had kissed her, the way he had pulled her close to him. She could feel the heat of his body, as it seemed to generate shock waves of lightening through her.

"OOOh," She screamed, as she threw herself on the bed and pounded the feather pillows. She knew sleep would not consume her tonight. No matter how tired she was those dancing blue eyes would haunt her very soul.

Downstairs Harley, having watched the exchange between Brana and Weston, turned to Jeb. "Looks to me that Yates dun beat you to the tasty morsel," he observed, grinning. He knows the time had come to dispose of Weston. The man had been thorn in their sides for too long now. Talk had it that Weston and some whore they had more than their fill with, were good friends, and he swore vengeance on Jeb for her abuse. Harley knew it was just a matter of time before Weston found he was the hooded figure who brought Serena screaming to her knees.

"Why do you say that?" Jeb demanded, as he flicked dried ash from a cheroot off the card table.

"Because I just saw him smack her a good one on the lips."

Harley could see Jeb's beady eyes bulge almost out of their sockets and a blue and green vein pulsating rapidly at the base of his neck.

"Did she return his kiss?" He said as he fought for control.

"Hell no," Harley chuckled, "she slapped him so hard I could swear I saw a red mark across his cheek."

He couldn't believe that he had had the good fortune to finally find someone who hadn't succumbed to Weston's good looks and charm. Now how could he use that excuse to talk to Brana? Hell, perhaps he would even offer her protection against the ruthless Weston Yates. Ruby would be more than willing to help him take Brana to his bed. She must be livid to know that Weston's attention has strayed elsewhere. Yes indeed, Ruby would be more than happy to help him plan Brana's abduction. He imagined Brana's frightened eyes as she lay on his soiled mattress. She would scream for help without realizing that his shack in Under the Hill, Natchez is almost in the middle of nowhere. The only living creatures that would hear her plea for help would be the animals that lived in the brush surrounding his run down hovel.

As soon as he saw Weston leave, Jeb went in search of Ruby. They would have to formulate a plan soon, before Weston became too interested in Brana. Already, Jeb realized that he wanted her more than any other woman he had ever seen. He also realized he would stop at nothing to possess her. He had kept his distance from her for weeks, but now he knew her every move. He had enjoyed seeing her ride out wildly, clad in men's attire when she thought no one was around. Just the thought of someone else's arms around her made him feverish with desire. He wanted her, and with Ruby's help, he will have her.

He found Ruby in her chamber, staring out into the cold night, her eyelashes glistening and tears staining her painted cheeks.

"Why the tears, Ruby," he asked, almost tenderly. "Yates turn you down flat?"

"Jeb, what are you doing here?" Ruby asked, not bothering to hide her heartbreak.

"I came to help you out with Yates," was his reply.

"What do you mean?"

"Just sit down right here and I'll tell you all about it."

For once, as Jeb motioned for her to come closer to the bed, Ruby had no fear of him. Weston was slipping from her grasp and if she had to enlist Jeb to help her, she would. Jeb wants Brana and she would sell her soul to Satan himself, for Weston. Whatever Jeb's plan was she'd help him. Together they'd succeed and Weston would finally be hers.

"What do you have in mind?" Ruby asked anxiously, as she sat on the bed.

They both knew it would be a long night, a very long night indeed.

The wind that was howling that night was almost as evil as the whispers that came from Ruby's chamber. All night long, Brana tossed and turned in the grip of horrible nightmares. Her dreams seemed so real she could actually feel her breathing becoming heavier and her body being abused by an unknown assailant. Her cries were that of a broken heart, not of the pain that was inflicted upon her by a sadistic monster. Figures dressed in black cloaks surrounding her, clawing her flesh. The laughter was mixed with men and women's voices as they tore at her clothing, pushing Brana closer and closer to a black pit. She begged and pleaded for them to spare her life, but a pair of scarred hands pushed her and, a scream tore from her throat as she sat upright on her bed to find that it was morning.

Brana was unaware of the eyes that followed her every move that day. Knowing that she had to get out of the confines of her chamber after her disturbing dream, she donned her riding costume and hurried to the stables. Riding Beauty would be the only way she could calm her nerves and sort through the emotions Weston had stirred up in her. Riding Beauty faster and faster might even erase all that happened last night.

When she had ridden miles from La Salone, she slowed Beauty to a trotting pace because it was useless to try to forget. The pit of her stomach burned as she remembered the way Weston had kissed her in a way that had told her that he would not rest until he possessed her, body and soul. Brana felt her body tingle as it had when those calloused hands had held her in a tight embrace. Before Brana had actually slept last night, she had felt the desire to be in Weston's strong arms. She wanted him to protect her from everything that frightened her. But of course she thought now, that had been absurd.

Riding Beauty, Brana realized she had mixed feelings about what happened to her last night. She realized why Weston had blatantly offered to pay for her favors. After all, how could he have known that she was not like the others? But she could never forgive him for humiliating her when they had first seen each other. He was a handsome rogue and under different circumstances, he might, she knew, have charmed her. But she could never forget his arrogance now. Never. And besides that, he belonged to Ruby.

CHAPTER 19

"Got a message 'err fer Mister Yates," the black child yelled at the top of his lungs. Dirty clothes, bare feet, he knew at the age of ten how to get sympathy and attention at the docks. He questioned the crew carrying pieces of fresh cut lumber to an anchored ship named Devils Fire.

"What have you there?" the captain's first mate demanded, as he directed the crew carrying loads of fresh lumber on board Devils Fire.

"Someone done paid me to give to him this right away," the child answered.

"I'll take that," Weston said taking the note and searched in his trouser pocket for a coin to give the street urchin, as he read the carefully written message, he lifted an eyebrow in amusement.

"Well, well, well," Weston said as he tapped the message with his fingertips.

His tight fitting leather pants hugged tightly to his long muscular legs, and the bleached white shirt with flowing arms was open down to the middle of his chest, barely covering his naked torso. A gun fit snugly against his thigh. Reading the message again, a smile formed on his lips.

"Harry," he said to his first mate. "I need to run a quick errand.

Take over for me, and make damn sure we're ready to set sail in the morn."

Within minutes, Weston was astride his stallion. It was early, the morning dew still lingering on the rooftops of the waterfront inns. Thoughts of Brana entered his mind as he saw men leaving the warm beds of their mistresses to be home in time to breakfast with their wives and children. His jaw muscle twitched as he remembered the times he had seen his father sneaking in before dawn, making sure the household was sound asleep so nobody would be the wiser. Weston knew, and it ate him up inside knowing the love his mother had for a father who was unworthy of that love. Weston had grown up defying and hating the man who fathered him until the day when he could no longer bear the shame and humiliation.

Weston was determined to confront his father, and he did so. After visiting the town saloon, a coward's way of getting courage, Weston had confronted his father as he was going over the accounts in his study.

"Don't deny it, father," Weston had challenged him. "I've known for years how you've shamed this family and made a laughing stock of my mother."

"Son, don't make any judgments until you know the truth," his father had said sadly, pain etched on his handsome, careworn face.

"What truth, Father? That you have an insatiable need of hurting this family?"

"How can I make you understand?" his father had said wearily. "You see, when I married your mother, it was out of honor and obligation, not love. I was fond of her, I don't deny that, but our affair was long over when she found out she was carrying my child. Her family found out she was with child and told your grandfather and he forced me to wed."

By this time the older man had made his way over to his favorite decanter and poured himself a drink.

"You mean to say you stayed with mother all these years out of loyal obligation and because of me?" Weston demanded.

"Your mother was determined to make the marriage work. She said she had enough love for both of us, but I still resented the fact that my freedom was taken away from me at a very young age. I tried to love your mother. But when your sister was born, the doctors told us that your mother could lose her life if she became with child again."

"So, honorable man that you are, you sought out the whores in the brothels for favors." Weston said sarcastically.

"For your information, Weston, it's only been one woman, the woman I wanted to marry before your mother ruined my life. In fact, after all these years, she has never married out of the love she felt for me."

"So why not leave Mother?" Weston asked him. "You're doing more harm than good as it is now. I'll take care of her."

"I couldn't do that to your mother, regardless of what you think. I care a great deal about her and I wouldn't want to hurt her."

Weston's father poured himself another drink as he turned his back to his son to hide the pain in his eyes.

"I hope to God, for your sake, that Mother never finds out." Weston threatened in a shaky voice. He couldn't believe the vows his father made to his mother were all a lie.

Weston couldn't wait to get away from his father, a man who now disgusted him. But as he turned to leave the room, he saw his mother, her face pale and glistening with tears. The last thing he heard was his father's voice calling his mother's name, as she ran to the privacy of her bedchamber, her face a mask of despair. Weston couldn't recall how long it had taken him to pry her chamber door open, but he had been too late. His mother lay on the floor, drenched in her own blood. That was the last time he had ever seen his father and sister as he left his family and fortune behind him. Anger and guilt made him vow to love no one and let no one enter his heart.

The family homestead on top of the hill, in California, remained empty, but the cries of anguish from the dead mother's only son was said to still haunt the mansion on the anniversary of Weston's beloved mother's death.

Through his solicitor, Weston knew that his father had disappeared and that his sister was being cared for by his spinster aunt who had become her legal guardian. He had always been very close to his beloved sister, and one day he'll find it in his heart to forgive himself and return to her.

CHAPTER 20

Brana's cheeks were flushed a scarlet red, and her blue black hair glistened as if tiny diamonds unveiled hidden treasure. Despite the fact that the trousers she was wearing were too large for her perfect frame, and stained to where a vigorous scrubbing would no longer help the garment look any more serviceable, Brana still made a beautiful sight. The tight fitting blue faded shirt whose cuffs almost came up to her elbow, showed the fullness of her breasts and her hourglass waistline.

Sitting astride on the black stallion's ebony back, Brana vowed to escape the turmoil of her own desires. She began to run her fingers thru the mane of her beloved Beauty.

Simmons had agreed to the name change of the giant steed, knowing full well the beast would want no other mistress than the beauty who tamed his ornery temper. Even the stable hand, who believed Beauty was the devil himself, was in awe of the girl who bewitched him with her magical powers. He spied them flying through the air with the morning mist, trying to reach the heavens above. Her unbound tresses transformed into delicate wings as he saw horse and rider chasing the demons that once controlled the ornery animal. Since that day, the stable hand never intruded on the goddess's privacy and cursed the animal for his stubbornness. Even if Simmons explained the bottle was playing tricks with his eyes, he knew better. The pair shared another life together. Was it possibly heaven or maybe hell? He didn't want to find out and told Simmons so.

Brana loved her early morning rides. Beauty had become a friend and confidant and she did not know what she would do without him. She had tried so hard to focus on her riding and forget what had happened with Weston, but she was getting a headache and her thoughts kept replaying the events over and over again. Brana had to admit that he was very handsome. But he was too sure of himself and she didn't like the way he treated women. Still, she couldn't stop thinking about him no matter how hard she tried.

Brana was startled when Beauty whinnied and threw her head back. "You!" She cried, seeing Weston. "What are you doing here?"

"My, my, my, aren't we a bit moody this morning," he said lazily, as he patted the head of his horse. "Is this how you treat an invited guest?"

"Invited guest, ha! How dare you spy on me!"

Riding closer to Brana, Weston leaned over and before she could strike him with her riding crop, Weston grabbed hold of her hands.

Everything happened so fast, that later Brana didn't remember being lifted off her horse and into the tight embrace of Weston Yates.

"I let down my guard once with you," he said in a husky voice. "And it shall never happen again."

The anger that flashed from Brana's eyes and the red flush on her cheeks fanned Weston's desire out of control. Before she could speak, he brushed her throat with one kiss after another, each leaving a blazing trail of desire.

Before Brana could come to her senses, Weston laid her gently on a soft bed of leaves and was on top of her removing her riding clothes, quieting her protests with searing kisses that set her limbs aflame. The cold air nipped at Brana's bare breast, hardening her rose pink nipples. Weston's tongue left her panting as he circled the pink rose tips gently, while rubbing the soft flesh of her inner thigh.

A moan escaped from Brana's lips as she arched her body upward unable to control the hot flames of passion that were consuming her body.

Weston knew that they were both ready to join together in heated passion.

"Please don't," Brana whispered. But Weston did not hear her whispers.

Spreading her thighs apart, he entered her gently, only to be startled by the delicate membrane of her maidenhead. His sharp intake of breath brought Brana back to reality and she realized what was about to happen to her.

"You little bitch," Weston growled. He had made it habit, to steer clear of inexperienced virgins. He had deflowered one years ago and still bore the scars on his back to prove it. The infatuated maiden had kept troubling him for months after that. Now, no matter how desirable virgins were, he figured they just weren't worth the trouble.

"Please don't," Brana begged, tears running down her face.

Weston's anger melted when he saw the fear in her eyes. His first instinct was to draw away from her and get some answers about her virginity, and her position at Lacy's. But he was at the crest of desire and, instead, he gave her a long, lingering kiss, feeling her lips tremble underneath his. He traced the trail of salted tears with tiny kisses and nibbled gently at Brana's tiny earlobe, as Brana shuddered involuntarily. As his hands touched her hair, he could smell perfume that was left lingering on the blue silk ribbon he now had in his possession. Losing himself in his own desire, Weston broke the barrier that defiantly stood in the way of his fulfillment.

Brana could not stop her body from betraying her as she responded to his lovemaking. As he thrust deeper inside of her body, she began to cry out with pain, and then suddenly noticed the pain was replaced with something that was indefinable. Her body took control as she arched herself upwards to meet Weston's thrusts over and over again, tasting the sweet scent of tobacco as it lingered on his tongue while he kissed her hungrily.

Brana was unprepared for the explosion she felt and the spasms of delight that took control of her entire body. She tingled from head to toe and was too weak to move until she saw those penetrating blue eyes dancing mischievously. But the ecstasy was short lived and, when she noticed the smug look on Weston's face, was at once replaced by anger. She sat upright immediately as he adjusted his shirt and trousers.

"Now that we both got what we want, tell me how you came to work at Lacy's with your virginity intact?" Weston drawled, his brilliant blue eyes emotionless. It looked to Brana as if he had become bored with the situation.

Brana tried her best to cover her nakedness with as much dignity as she could muster. Ignoring the blue gaze that roamed her body, she stood up and pulled her trousers into place. She then took the rumpled shirt from the bed of leaves and covered her exposed breast. Her hands trembled as her fingers fumbled with the tiny buttons. She whistled for Beauty, who had strayed and found a greener brush to nibble, and he came instantly. Brana looked over at Weston quick enough to see his brow quirk up in amusement. He was the first to break the deadly silence.

"Well now, it seems I've discovered quite a bit of hidden talent you seem to possess," he told her. "It makes me want to know more about you, little one."

As Weston moved closer to Brana, she reacted instantly.

"Get your filthy hands off of me," she told him. "Never, ever touch me again."

"You didn't seem to think my hands were filthy a few minutes ago," he reminded her. "Or did you already forget that these filthy hands now know every curve of your luscious body."

Brana felt her whole body flush. His hands had indeed roamed her whole body, awaking hidden desires that she had never thought possible, spurring the horse into a gallop, she welcomed the crisp air, fanning the flames of her passion.

Looking after her, Weston was surprised to find himself intrigued and interested in the slip of a girl who managed to stay a virgin, working of all places, at Lacy's. He wondered what game somebody was playing with him, since the girl genuinely seemed not to know about the note. He had plenty of questions, and was sure Brana had all the answers.

CHAPTER 21

"I really think you should consider the idea of taking over the business yourself," Beth whined. "Daddy said he would back you financially."

"The matter is closed, Beth," Rawlings told her, trying to hide his irritation. "Wes and I are doing just fine the way we are. Now I don't have all day to sit and chat so I'll see you tonight or have you changed your mind about the meal you promised me?"

He knew she had disliked Weston after she found out the summary way he had treated her best friend, Victoria. But Victoria seemed to have survived and already had been seen around town on the arm of several different men. Beth was the one that still held Victoria's broken heart against Weston. At every turn, she kept convincing him that Weston took advantage of the partnership. Usually he just ignored her barbs, changing the subject to the wedding plans.

"Of course you know I expect you tonight," Beth told him. "With Weston away I'll have you all to myself. Just until he returns of course."

Rawlings looked up from his ledgers in the direction of his betroth. Somehow he knew he would end up at Lacy's tonight. And he knew Beth would not like what he had to say now.

"Weston's not going Beth, I am."

"What?" Beth cried. "You told me yesterday that Weston would set sail at dawn this morning. And now you're going to go in his place. Do you really think you can leave me as easily as that?"

"I'm sorry, Beth," Rawlings said calmly. "But I'm going to set sail tomorrow at dawn. I was going to tell you tonight."

"How dare you do this to me?" she demanded, her face drawn with rage. "You knew how much I was looking forward to spending this time with you. What would people say if they knew you had left me all by myself just before our wedding?"

Rawlings fists were clenched under the polished desk as he waited until Beth had finished her childish tantrum.

"This is exactly what I mean about Weston!" Beth continued. "Why is it you have to go? I thought it was agreed he would always sail, leaving you to be the brains of the business? How dare he do this to me! And you. You could have stood up to him and told him no!"

It occurred to Rawlings that such outbursts made Beth ugly. It looked, now, as though every vein in her pale face was about to burst. He knew she wouldn't understand if he told her it was his idea, that he had been the one who stopped Weston from sailing the high seas this morning.

He had been lucky that Weston had been detained on an urgent errand and hadn't sailed on schedule. When he had reached the docks, Weston had been surprised to see him and just as surprised to hear his request. However, Weston had understood his reasons and had gathered his crew to notify them of their new captain for this voyage, a decision no one questioned, knowing Rawlings well enough to be sure that he was a good man, and that the first mate knew how to sail Devils Fire in his sleep.

"That's enough Beth!" Rawlings had tried to contain his anger long enough. "I'll not have you talk about Weston that way. You know as well as I do that he's responsible for our success. And you'll just have to resign yourself to the fact that we will always be partners as well as best friends. So in the future, refrain from these outbursts. They're so unbecoming, to put it frankly. Now my dear, if you'll excuse me, I have a lot to do today if I want to see you for dinner before sailing on the morning tide."

"How dare you speak to me in that tone?" she demanded, stamping one slippered foot. "But if you go, I never want to see you again!"

She waited impatiently for Rawlings to tell her he would reconsider and send Weston. She was not prepared for his reply.

"I'm sorry that's how you feel Beth," Rawlings said. "I shall respect your wishes and not call on you tonight."

"Well, I see you've made your choice then." Beth whispered and, bolting out the door, came face to face with Weston.

"You, you, you, cad!" she screamed as she ran to her awaiting carriage.

When Beth's carriage was out of view, he walked into his office and saw Rawlings sitting behind the desk with a scowl on his face.

"Sorry my friend, but you were right. She didn't take the news well. In fact, she said she never wanted to see me again."

"Don't worry," Weston replied as he lit a cheroot. "By the time you get back she will have cooled off."

"Thanks for the trade Wes; I really need the time to sort things out."

"Think nothing of it old boy. I have no doubt you'll have a successful voyage. When you get back you'll be a new man. There's nothing like the open sea to clear the head."

Weston had been puzzled at first when Rawlings had asked to take his place as captain on the next voyage out but now he thought he understood. He didn't question Rawlings, but he knew it had to do with his impetuous decision to marry Beth. In fact, it pleased him to know Rawlings had the good sense to think about the rash decision he had made. Weston knows Beth too well to be certain that Rawlings could never be happy with her.

"You know Wes; I thought it was going to be harder than it was to convince you that I could handle the voyage out West. You gave in a little too quickly. Did it have something to do with the urgent message you received at the docks this morning?" The smile on Rawlings face lit his eyes and Weston read amusement in them.

"Let's just say that, had I gone, I would have left some unfinished business behind." Weston told him.

Rawlings knew that his friend would say no more. "Well my friend, I suggest we finish our business here and head over to Lacy's." Rawlings mused, knowing that his friend would say no more.

"That's a very good idea." Weston replied. His mood was unforgiving and Lacy's was just the right place for him tonight.

CHAPTER 22

Ruby was singing. The smoke created a veil of mist, but there was no mistaking the painted face of Ruby, as she sat in center stage. All eyes were on her as she sang her second round of love songs, moved her body seductively with the beat of the music, her scarlet satin dress cut so low that, with each breath she took, it seemed that her bosoms would bare themselves.

The polished tables were laden with shot glasses and half empty bottles of whiskey or brandy and the crystal beads that hung on the doorway at the back of the room shone with a rainbow of colors, enticed the gamblers to the awaiting treasures above, if they so desired.

Laughter was heard everywhere throughout the evening, as well as shouts of joy from a few lucky winners. Even Lacy was caught up in the gay mood around her and generously provided Champagne for those who had acquired the taste for the light sparkling wine.

She had been a little worried about Brana who had taken to her bed chamber all day. It wasn't like her friend to sleep the day away with so much life about her. And it was strange to Lacy that Brana had refused to go out in the carriage as they usually did each afternoon, particularly since they had planned to stop at several of the different shops that had just opened for business. When Lacy had spoken to her this morning, she had felt that Brana was hiding something, but when she tried to coax it out of her, Brana turned defiant, and lifting her chin, her hair falling loosely around her shoulders, had assured Lacy that everything was fine.

Lacy knew differently, but respecting Brana's privacy, she promised herself not to pry any further. Lacy, did however, wonder if Brana's mood had something to do with the excellent mood that Ruby seemed to be in.

Indeed, Ruby was unusually cheerful and uncharacteristically friendly with everyone. She had even inquired about Brana's health. At first taken aback, Lacy had recovered quickly enough to assure her that she urged Brana to take the day to rest.

Lacy thought Ruby's concern for Brana was odd, very odd indeed. Even Jeb smiled at Lacy once or twice showing off those strange teeth, which were too small for his face. Could it be, Lacy thought, that Jeb and Ruby have fallen for one another. She shook her head to rid herself of the idea and shrugged her shoulders, resigning herself to the fact that she was wrong in thinking that she knew everything that went on in La Salone.

CHAPTER 23

"Just play your cards right, Harley, we'll have the girl soon." Jeb said, full of himself as usual.

"I think you're playing with fire this time, Jeb," Harley told him. "That sure looked like a determined kiss Yates planted on those rosy lips. He means to have her."

"Well, I'll just have to get her first," Jeb told him as he rubbed the thin veil of stubble on his chin. His black hair was long, wet and pulled back almost flipping at the base of his neck. Small beady black eyes were red- rimmed and overshadowed by thick, black bushy brows. His bleached white muslin shirt was opened at his chest, exposing pale skin, glowing with perspiration. "And I have a plan that should work."

Just thinking of Brana, forced Jeb to fight to control his passion.

"With Weston at sea, that should take care of all our problems," He continued, trying not to think of the Beauty that would soon belong to him. "To bad the mighty captain doesn't know he'll be ambushed in friendly waters. You have to hand it to me, Harley this time I thought of everything."

"Is Yates ready to set sail?" Harley asked.

"With any luck, Devils Fire left with the morning tide, and if it didn't, a sailor on the docks assured me it would be gone by tomorrow. He has a shipment with a deadline to meet and crew and shipment are waiting on his orders."

Jeb smiled. His plans were falling right into place. Not even Ruby knew that Weston would set sail, and he wasn't about to tell her, particularly since she might get discouraged knowing Weston would be at sea for months and not keep her part of the bargain to help him get Brana. Jeb smiled wickedly, knowing, as he did, that Weston and his crew would be at the bottom of the sea before the week was out.

"You ferget one thing, Jeb," Harley reminded him. "Lacy's just not going to hand the girl over to you knowing yer sexual perversions."

Harley laughed, but one look from Jeb's beady eyes told him he had gone too far.

"You leave the pocked marked bitch to me, Harley," Jeb said in a low voice. "And if you value your miserable life, watch what you say to me and how you say it."

"Err, you know what I mean Jeb." Harley whispered uncomfortably and poured himself another shot of whiskey and gulped it straight down. He knew all too well Jeb wouldn't hesitate to plan his accidental death. He's known too many men to have mysteriously disappeared or ended up in a river with their throats slit for crossing Jeb or cheating him out of what he considered his. Whether it is a woman or a card hand, it was always a fatal mistake to underestimate Jeb.

CHAPTER 24

"How could I have done it? What a fool." Brana scolded herself over and over again. How could she have let him sample her charms with such little resistance? Her own body had betrayed her as his calloused hands roamed every inch and curve of her. Fury consumed her as she remembered the way she had cried out in pleasure and arched her body upward to meet his.

When she had returned to La Salone, she had let out a sigh, relieved that no one was about as she climbed the stairs to her bed chamber. Going directly to the porcelain wash basin, she poured in a pitcher full of ice cold water. Then, dipping a clean cloth in the water, she began rubbing her cheeks vigorously, trying to wipe off Weston's touch. She shivered at the remembrance of the piercing blue eyes, so close to hers, eyes that she knew would haunt her.

"Miz Brana what are you doing in those clothes in here and your hare full of leaves?" Simmons asked her in a whisper as, she went out in search of Lacy, desperate for company. "Did you take a fall ridin' that devil?"

"I'm fine Simmons; I just tripped over a rotted tree stump," Brana told him nervously, hating the act that she had been put in a position in which she must lie.

Pushing her back in her chamber, Simmons let himself in and looked around before he closed the door shut.

"What were you thinkin' Miz Brana?" he scolded her, noting her bruised lips and flushed face. "Effen Miz Lacy saw you in those clothes you'd have a lot of explaining to do!" And then, softening, "are you sure you alright?"

"I'm fine Simmons, thank you." It took all the strength Brana could possibly muster to reply.

"Don't worry none," Simmons assured her. Whatever was wrong, Miz Lacy would take care of it. In the meantime, he had to help Brana compose herself. "I'll get your bath Miz Brana, and get this here fire going 'for you ketch yourself a chill."

Brana was too engrossed in her thoughts to answer Simmons or even realize he had left the room. She had seen it too often and it nauseated her to think that she had let herself be taken like a common trollop, shamefully submitting to a man she knew nothing about, a man who had humiliated her at every turn, a man who has no morals, and was as ruthless as the worst scum off the streets. How could she have swallowed her pride and given him the only thing she had to offer the man she would wed.

Brana had been staring out of the window when Simmons came in carrying buckets of steaming hot water. When he had filled the tub, the scent of lavender filled the room. She removed her clothes, still numb with shock only to be hit with full reality when she saw the dried blood on her undergarments. Then, letting her clothes fall to the floor, she slid her body in the tub, while tears spilled freely from her eyes. She caressed her gold locket and called the name Cam into the flames in the fireplace. Whoever he was, she needed him tonight. Somehow, she was certain that he would understand the turmoil she was going through. But would he understand as well that she felt love and hate for the man who had violated her. She wanted desperately to turn to Lacy, now that she was more composed, but she was too ashamed to admit what happened.

Donning her wrapper she dried her hair with a dry fluffy towel and began to brush out the snarls with the mother-of-pearl comb set Lacy had purchased for her. Then, feeling emotionally drained and physically exhausted, she covered herself with the patchwork quilt Cook had made for her and let sleep consume her.

When loud laughter and music from below woke her, she realized that she had slept the day away. Even in her dreams she had remembered Weston's piercing blue eyes dancing with excitement and the seductive smile that formed on his lips when looking, at her naked body. She remembered the pain and the pleasure he had given her and cursed a thousand demons on him. She knew he had possessed her body, but she vowed he would never possess her soul.

CHAPTER 25

Weston took special care with his toilet that evening. Normally he didn't care how he looked when going to Lacy's, but for some reason he wanted to look his best. The trousers he chose were the same style he had donned this morning, but were a little looser at the waist. His full front frockcoat was deep sea blue, a black velvet band at the wrist, showed off sapphire cuff links that adorned the cuffs of his shirt. His cravat was black silk, the same material as his shirt, and was tucked into the opening of his v-neck shirt. His boots were made of shining black leather, not a scar marred their workmanship.

Again and again, he kept going over the morning's events in his mind. Who could have sent the message? He hated the fact that he had been a pawn in someone's game. He would eventually find out who and why, and he would start with Brana first. He kept remembering her cries of pleasure and tears of pain. His jaw muscle twitched violently as he remembered that she had told him he had ruined her of the only thing she had to offer the man she loved. Could "that man" have given her the expensive gold locket around her neck?

Weston couldn't explain why, but he felt rage for this man. How could he possibly love somebody and let her work in a brothel.

Weston realized now that he had been obsessed with Brana ever since he had first set eyes on her, even though at the time he had thought she was just another whore, selling her favors. He had assumed she was playing the games of hard to get that most of the women had had know loved to play. But apparently, he had been wrong. He kept seeing her face when she left him this morning her expression had not been one of triumph. Rather it was a look of defeat and humiliation. And now the emotions he was feeling about this vixen were new to him and dangerous.

When it came to women, the rumors that spread throughout city were true. He was ruthless and unfeeling with each and every conquest, making it a point never to stay with one woman for very long to keep them form becoming too possessive. The last fling had had him swearing he would only pay for favors in the future. At least the prostitutes always keep business with business.

But now, why Brana? He kept asking himself. From the first time he had laid eyes on her, he could think of nothing else. Her beauty was undeniable, but it was the look of raw innocence that he had seen this morning, and the tears that she had shed in his arms that had made him soften towards her. He knew the unfeeling things he had said to her hadn't helped matters, but his nature always had been to strike first and ask questions later. Now he began to feel angry, knowing he had been careless. He could have been lured into a trap by a deadly enemy and it was unlike him not to be cautious. Someone had played them both for fools and he intended to find out who and why.

Leaving his townhouse where his evening carriage waited, Weston found himself joined by Rawlings, who ran down the steps of the adjoining building to join him, rain drops shiny on his black cloak.

"Well Rawlings, are you ready to set sail at dawn?" Weston inquired.

Rawlings hopped in the carriage and seated himself on the soft cushioned seat across from Weston.

"Looking forward to it Wes, my friend," he replied with excitement shining in his eyes. He would finally become a lover to the jealous mistress he had heard only stories about. He felt no regret about his decision to leave and put his marriage on hold. In fact, he was looking forward to the solitude the sea would be able to give him.

"Just do me a favor," Weston said, his voice expressionless. "If anybody asks you, we were a little delayed, and I'm still sailing at dawn."

"You got it Wes." Rawlings replied, smiling boyishly. How like Weston it was to be so secretive.

As the landau carriage pulled up in front of La Salone Weston, felt an urgent need to turn back. His knees were weak and his palms were sweaty. Scolding himself for acting like such a school boy, he lit a cheroot.

Once inside Weston quickly scanned the rooms and saw that Brana was nowhere in sight. Steering clear of the gaming rooms, he and Rawlings sat at the crowed bar near the foyer.

When there was no sign of Brana, Weston decided to go upstairs to her room.

"In case I'm not back when you decide to leave, take my carriage," he told Rawlings, shaking his hand. "I know you'll have a safe voyage. God be with you."

"I won't let you down Wes." Rawlings answered.

Weston gave him a wink and up the stairs he went. Rawlings smiled to himself knowing Weston was heading up to Ruby's chamber, or did he mean to visit the girl he had mentioned the other day? Was that why he had spent the evening looking around the room as if he were searching for someone. Rawlings now seemed to recall that Weston mentioned that she was new at Lacy's and come to think of it, he could hear Ruby singing in the gaming room. So maybe this was the unfinished business he had mentioned, he thought.

After a few more drinks, Rawlings decided to leave without his friend. As it is, he would only have a few hours of sleep until he became captain of Devils Fire. He knows now why Weston enjoys the excitement of the sea. He hadn't yet sailed but already he could feel the freedom that awaited him. He prayed that he would be worthy of the trust and the confidence Weston had put in him. Weston had gone over the map in detail, showing him the dangerous waters where pirate ships were likely to attack. Weston also told him which friendly waters would be the smoothest sailing, and Rawlings was looking forward to that. Just him and the crew and the defiant water goddess that he wanted desperately to tame.

"Well Jeb it looks like you were right," Harley said as he saw Rawlings going out the door. "Ain't that there Weston's partner leaving by his lonesome?"

Jeb smiled as Lacy closed the door behind Rawlings. He felt no pity for the man who just left, knowing he would grieve deeply for his friend. By the time word of the fate of Devils Fire reached them, Brana would be in his clutches and no one would dare be brave enough to confront him.

"See, what did I tell you?" he said to Harley. "We have nothing to worry about. Just remember our plan and you'll be well rewarded."

The only flaw in his plan would be Ruby. Once she received wind of Weston's death, she might be a problem. But certainly not one he couldn't handle. Just the thought of seeing her gasping for breath as his hands encircled her throat, brought him great pleasure.

Jeb raised his shot glass and toasted with Harley on their upcoming success. Brana would be his within days and he could scarcely wait.

CHAPTER 26

Standing by her window, Brana stared out into the night and listened to the rain batter the glass.

She felt entirely alone. How she wished she could regain some of her memory, but her past was just a blank. Suddenly she felt a chill and put her hands over her chest to rub her arms.

Behind her, Weston stood just inside the door, staring at the picture Brana portrayed. Her hair was so shiny he could almost see his own reflection in it. Her chin was held high, and as she turned slightly he could see the twinkle of tears on her long velvet eyelashes. The silk wrapper she was wearing fell in folds about her slender frame and the soft pink color of it seemed to reflect on her high cheek bones. Her eyes were closed as though the sounds of the wood crackling in the fireplace had put her in a trance.

Standing in the doorway, silent, Weston marveled at the beauty of her.

"Oh Cam, where are you?" he heard her whisper. Weston's jaw muscles tightened at the mention of another man's name. He couldn't believe the jealously he felt at the thought of another man bedding her. When he shifted slightly, Brana caught the movement from the corner of her eye and she turned to face him with the look of defiance in her eyes.

She couldn't speak. All her words seemed to be lodged in her throat. As he stood there with his powerful frame filling the doorway, she saw that he was much taller than she had originally thought, and his face was chiseled to perfection. She noticed the sea blue depths of his eyes, and the valuable gems at his wrists. Black trousers hugged the defining muscles of his legs.

She gathered her wits and made sure her tone was as serious and deadly as he looked.

"Spying on me, again Mr. Yates?" she mocked him. "First this morning. Now you've come into my bed chamber uninvited. One would think a man such as you couldn't handle rejection." Brana was surprised at how handsome and debonair he looked as his smile lit up his face.

"Rejection madam? You had a funny way of showing it this morning. Perhaps you do not know the meaning of the word."

Brana felt her cheeks redden at his words. But she was not about to let him have the upper hand.

"You took advantage of me this morning, in a way only a seducer and a cad would have dreamed of doing," she told him. "I would have thought an experienced woman like Ruby would have been more to your liking than an inexperienced virgin!"

Weston couldn't believe how her words stung him. Most women who had been used as she had been this morning would have tears in their eyes now and be begging for some sort of commitment. She was definitely no ordinary woman. Who in the hell was she, he thought to himself.

"Let's just say that I misunderstood your position here," he told her. "After all, you really can't blame me. When I first saw you, it seemed to me your position was clear enough."

Brana found she could not look him in the eye. She started to feel butterflies in her stomach, and it seemed the room was getting warmer.

"May I ask why you are here Mr. Yates?" she said. "No, wait. Let me see, you're going to tell me that you were invited, right?" Brana put even more distance between her and Weston as she spoke. Just the male scent of him clouded her senses.

"Well, actually I came to show you this." Weston pulled out a crumpled piece of paper from his frockcoat and handed it to Brana. Brana took the note, careful not to touch him, scanning the words written in cramped letters on a sheet of rough linen paper.

"What is this all about?" She questioned, with her brow raised, not quite knowing what to say.

"Well, it seems we were set up this morning," he told her. "As you see, I was meant to believe that you wanted me to meet you."

He waited for her reaction, more than ever convinced, given her expression, that she knew nothing about the note.

Brana looked at him suspiciously. "How do I know you didn't write this?" she demanded.

"I'm not in the habit of playing childish games, madam," he assured her. "And I certainly don't like being made a fool of. If it hadn't been for a delay this morning, I would be sailing the high seas by now."

"How dare you!" she exclaimed. "How dare you, you cad! You robbed me of my innocence and yet you have the gall to complain that you have been made a fool of, and how you've been inconvenienced. I think you're despicable. How could I have ever let you touch me? Why You! You bastard!"

Brana flung herself at him, pounded his broad, muscular chest with clenched fists. Grabbing both of her hands, Weston pulled her close to him. He was breathing heavily and she could smell the brandy on his breath.

They looked into each others eyes for what seemed like an eternity before Weston then lowered his head and met Brana's moist, trembling lips. Brana was lost in his arms as he lifted her up and carried her to the four poster bed, laid her in gently and nipped at the base of her neck. He could smell the soft scent of lavender on her creamy milk white skin.

Brana's mind raced with guilt and shame. What have I become, she thought as Weston penetrated her wanton body and took control of her senses.

CHAPTER 27

The lightning and thunder hit at the same time, but nobody seemed to notice. Ruby had been preoccupied when she had seen Rawlings leave by himself a few hours ago. She had scanned the room for Weston, but he was nowhere to be found. She thought it most unusual for Rawlings to have come by himself. Seeing Jeb at his usual table, she walked over to greet him.

"Jeb, have you seen Weston?" she purred.

"I saw him earlier, looking for you, but I heard he had to leave in a hurry," Jeb lied. " It had something to do with his ship."

An evil smile crossed his lips at the expression on Ruby's face when he told her that Weston was looking for her. He looked over at Harley and signaled him not to say a word.

"Why don't you sit down, Ruby, and I'll buy you a drink," Jeb offered smoothly. "We have quite a few things to discuss."

"Are you crazy Jeb?" Ruby whispered angrily, looking around, "anything you need to discuss with me has to be discussed in the privacy of my bed chamber. We wouldn't want our conversations to be overheard now would we?"

She was most anxious to take part in his plans to take Brana away from La Salone. Weston was hers and Brana deserved whatever fate Jeb had in store for her.

Santelle had been the only one to notice the three plotters sitting together at the other side of the crowded room. They had seemed to be plotting something but every time she had gotten nearer, their voices had faded to faint whispers.

She smiled to herself, knowing that her plan had worked. Weston had received her message and met Brana with no delay. She had known what had taken place when she had heard Simmons scolding Brana in the hallway this morning. Santelle had opened her chamber door just in time to see Brana's disheveled appearance. It had confirmed what she had guessed would happen if the girl and Weston were alone together. Santelle had taken in every detail before Simmons had ushered Brana back into her bed chamber.

With any luck, she thought, Weston would be back tonight. She knew Brana had captivated him when they had first kissed, and she also knew that it was not like him to show such an interest. She had seen the look on his face when he left La Salone that night holding a silk blue ribbon up to his lips. It was Brana's name that escaped from his lips as he walked out, and she knew it would be Brana that held his heart.

The earlier attempts Santelle tried to eavesdrop on Ruby, Jeb and Harley conversation were futile. But now it seemed Harley was voicing some sort of an opinion.

"Well now, ain't that the first time you've been invited to her chamber, Jeb?" Harley mused, well in his cups by now, irritated by the fact that they were talking about something that involved him, and yet never had once included him in the conversation. He was being treated like a mere servant, and he did not like it.

"Will you keep your voice down?" Ruby hissed, frowning at Harley. She looked around the room before she continued, unaware that Santelle had edged close enough to overhear everything that was being said.

"Can't you handle him Jeb?" she demanded. "His loose tongue could get us all into trouble!"

"You leave Harley to me," Jeb told her. "Lets finish this conversation in your chamber, where we have all the privacy we need."

"I reckon I'd better go, too, since I'm part of your plan to get rid of you know who." Harley said slurring his words.

"You just keep your trap shut, Harley." Jeb said in a threatening tone. "I'll let you know what you have to do later. And if I hear another word come from your mouth, you might find yourself without a tongue in the morning. Is that clear?"

"Yes sir, boss." Harley grinned. He rose to his feet unsteadily and left La Salone, disappearing into the blackness of the night.

"Are you sure we can trust that drunk?" Ruby asked Jeb.

"Just leave Harley to me." Jeb assured her.

Santelle saw the couple leave the gambling rooms through the door that held the crystal beads and wondered who they could possibly be plotting against. It seemed clear that something serious was being planned. In Harley's condition, all she had to do was to expose a little more of her bosom, and ask a few subtle questions, particularly given the state he was in.

The rain was being carried in different directions with the wind. Lightning left a jagged line in the distance, daring Harley to continue his journey. Just as he stepped off of the worn wooden platform, he felt a tug on his arm. It was Santelle, well wrapped in a woolen hooded cloak which was tailored to her body.

"Why Harley," she said, pressing herself against him. "You could catch your death going out on a night like this. Why don't you come back inside and let me buy you a drink, just until the rain lets up."

"I never turn down a purty lady." Harley chuckled.

"Why thank you, Harley. Let's go back inside and sit at the bar."

"After you, purty lady." Harley said unsteadily.

Santelle held on to him possessively as they made their way back into La Salone. Once in the foyer, she quickly glanced around to make sure Jeb and Ruby were no where in sight. Santelle ordered two whiskies from the bar. Harley drained his immediately and grinned, disclosing blackened teeth. Santelle shivered with revulsion. But she knew what she must do

"Jeb and Ruby seemed pretty upset with you tonight," she began. "They should know that they could trust you with the plans."

Harley looked at her and raised an eyebrow. "Which plans would you be referring to?" he asked her, teetering forward in his chair.

"You know," Santelle laughed and took another sip of her brandy. "The plans to get rid of you know who. I just couldn't believe how they treated you. Especially, since you're a big part of the plan. Don't they know how smart you are?"

"That high and mighty bitch Ruby, thinks she is better than me," Harley grumbled. "Always look'n down on me. I can't wait fer her to hear about Yates dying at sea. She'll be fit to be tied when she finds out

Jeb double crossed her. Yesiree, that bitch shor is goin' to get what's coming."

Santelle interrupted Harley abruptly.

"Did you mean Jeb is planning to have Weston killed!" Santelle exclaimed. "I mean, I'd love to hear how a brilliant mind like yours works. Tell me everything, Harley,"

"Well," Harley told her, filling his glass a second time. "I did kinda hint to Jeb what to do, but he took care of the details, you know him having friends all over and all. But one thing's for shore, Devils Fire will be at the bottom of the sea full of holes and dead bodies. Hell, it might even be happening as we speak. They should be long gone by now. Yes, sir, I planned it good."

Santelle stared at Harley in disbelief. She had to do something. If Weston had already left the docks, there was nothing anybody could do about it. Should she wait and pray that it was the liquor talking? No, somehow she knew it was the truth. Harley seemed too sure of himself. What see needed was to find Rawlings. And soon.

CHAPTER 28

Weston gently brushed Brana's dark hair from her cheek as she lay peacefully in his arms, so warm and soft, that he felt the familiar stir in his loins, but not waning to wake her from her peaceful slumber, he lay there, remembering all the things she had told him last night. Why had he promised her he would try to find Cam? He wondered. But he knew the answer. He couldn't deny her when she had looked at him the way she had, begging for his help. Without him, her past would be lost to her. He smiled to himself, thinking it was just like Lacy to take her in, ill with fever and half starved. He admired Brana for her courage and determination to live. He had felt such a sense of pride when she had told him how she had managed to survive against the odds, how she had fought with the other homeless and destitute for the scraps to eat.

What could have happened to his little one, he thought. Cam, he mused must have been someone very special for her to have deep feelings for him. He still couldn't believe the pangs of jealousy that had consumed him, when she had spoken of him.

Weston would never forget the look on her face when she had told him shyly that she knew he wasn't her husband. He had laughed and taken her again. For the first time in his life he knew what it was like to make love to someone he loved, kissing her softly. He waited patiently for Brana to be fulfilled, and when she clung to him arching her body upward, he entered her, glad to make her heated pleasure complete.

Feeling her stir in his arms, Weston kissed her gently and slowly lifted himself off the bed. Donning his trousers he went directly to the fireplace and added more fuel to the dying embers before going to the window. Through the morning mist, he could make out the tiny forms of street urchins looking in the garbage bins for food. It was difficult to believe that Brana had once been one of them.

Weston's heart went out to his little one, knowing the hardships she had endured before God had put her in Lacy's hands. She must have lost her memory immediately after the war. She might have been injured or possibly she might have witnessed something so horrible that she totally blocked it from her memory. He promised himself he would start inquiries today as to the whereabouts of a person name Cam, and he would start at the waterfront. New names were always heard there first as ship after ship docked there. Brana had told him that she had walked with the homeless to New Orleans. She could, he knew, be from anywhere in the south. One thing was certain. If Brana were to be his, he would have to confront any man that stood in the way of him possessing her.

Brana felt new feelings stir within her, as she watched Weston standing by the window. His muscled chest was bare and Brana could see the firm outline of his buttocks inside his leather trousers. When she had awakened in his strong arms last night, and known it was not a dream, she had felt a surge of happiness run through her. He was so caring and understanding, not at all like the ruthless pirate had she made him out to be. Lacy had been right when she told her Weston had another side to him that nobody knew about.

Brana still couldn't believe the genuine concern he had demonstrated when she told him how she came to be at Lacy's. He had uttered an oath and promised her that she would never be alone again, that he would be there whenever she needed him, to protect her, to love her. And then with that gentleness he had taken her. She cared not that he never spoke of love or marriage. She needed him and nothing would ever change that. She had given him freely something she had vowed only to give to the man she would love, her body as well as her soul.

Feeling her eyes on him, Weston turned and looked into her violet eyes. He smiled at Brana and walked over to the bed where she lay, letting the satin sheets caress her creamy, white skin. He couldn't believe how beautiful she looked, lying there with her silky hair covering her pillow.

"Good morning, my sweet" he said, kissing her forehead before cupping her face in his hands and devouring her lips.

"Yes Weston, it is a good morning," Brana replied happily.

"I guess we should be grateful for the person who brought us together," he told her with a smile. "Although I would still like to know who the culprit was who sent that note."

"I don't care who it was," Brana answered as she held out her arms to him. "I'm just happy being here with you."

Weston laughed as he hugged her tightly. He would not tell her he would start his search for Cam today. He didn't want her getting her hopes up until he at least had something to report. He had hoped, for the bastard's sake that he had been killed in the war, or he might contemplate killing him with his bare hands. Just the thought of him made Weston tense.

"Weston," Brana spoke softly as she pulled herself away from his embrace, "will you come back tonight?"

Rising from the bed, he went to the window again. If he were at sea this very moment, instead of his best friend Rawlings, he could clear his head and sort out his emotions. One thing he knew, he would not share her with any name from her past. She was to be his in past and present.

"What about Cam?" he questioned in a serious tone.

"I'm sure that whoever he is he would understand," Brana told him. "I can't explain why, but I know he would want me to be happy."

"We should talk about the future, my love," Weston said uneasily. "If you agree, I'd like to take you out of this place and have you move in with me."

"As your mistress?" she asked him, her heart slowly breaking.

Weston didn't know what to say. These emotions were all new to him. After all, he had always associated love with pain and heartbreak. Was this the kind of love his mother had had for his father? The kind of love she had killed herself for when he had betrayed her? Was he ready to say the word he had never used before to Brana? His thoughts were running in several different directions. He kept asking himself if he was ready to commit himself to the emotion he thought he had become immune to. Yet the joy he felt in having made her happy made him realize she meant more to him than anybody he had ever been with. All of a sudden his palms became sweaty and suddenly it seemed as if he couldn't breathe. He realized he needed fresh air and a strong drink to clear his senses.

"Let's talk about this later," he said, pulling his shirt over his head and taking his jacket off the chair. "I'll be gone for the first part of the morning, but you can bet I'll be back tonight."

As he pulled on his leather boots, Brana remained silent, aware of emotional turmoil he was going through even though he tried hard not to show it.

My poor darling, she thought. He couldn't say he loved her. But she knew in her heart, that he would sort out the truth.

Weston left La Salone unseen and still a little shaken. He wished he could have made a firm commitment to Brana, told her he loved her. But first he must know who Cam was and what he had meant to her.

CHAPTER 29

"How dare you come here, you trollop! Throw this tramp out into the streets where she belongs!" Beth called to one of the servants.

"Listen you snobby bitch," Santelle said, trying not to let anger get the better of her. "I've have been all over town since this morning. I need to know if you know the whereabouts of Rawlings?"

No wonder the servant who had opened the door to this woman had looked so flustered when she had announced her, Beth thought, shocked to find herself in the presence of a woman who was so clearly a harlot, dressed as she was in a low cut red satin gown showing off her bodies' assets, and reeking of cheap perfume.

"What do you want with Rawlings?" Beth had said, eyed her suspiciously.

"Don't worry," Santelle said, losing what little patience she had come here with. "I'm not after your betrothed. I would just like to know where he is. It's a matter of life and death!"

"Well I don't care if it is," Beth retorted suspiciously. "Why should I tell you anything?"

"I said it was a matter of life and death!" Santelle repeated, tightening her lips in anger.

"Well, I don't care what you said," Beth told her as she looked and played with her well manicured fingernails. "Now get on your way before I have one of the servants escort you out!"

"You're a cold ugly bitch." Santelle retorted and turned on her heel and left. "Rawlings is too good for the likes of you!"

Where could Rawlings be? If he wasn't at home or with his betrothed? She asked herself as the door of Beth's house slammed behind her. She was almost about to give up her search when she decided to try the docks for directions to his office. She knew it was too early for him to be there, but she would wait there for him all day if she had to. She turned her buggy in the direction of the docks, slapped the reins on the horses' buttocks to go faster. She hoped she wasn't too late to save Weston. He had always been kind to her and had given her extra coin whenever she waited on his gaming table. Once he had even defended her honor when a customer got out of hand.

Santelle had the docks in sight. The hustle and bustle was not uncommon at the docks this hour. A seaman caught her eye and was obliged to give her directions to the offices of the waterfront.

Pulling her carriage in front of the wood framed building on Vicksburg Street, she hurried inside and was stunned when she saw Weston sitting behind a desk writing in a ledger.

"Weston!" she exclaimed "What are you doing here?"

"I might ask you the same question, Madam?" Weston asked with his brow quirked.

Without bothering to take a breath, Santelle told Weston about the conversation she had overheard between Ruby and Jeb and what Harley had told her about the plot against him.

"I don't know what they're up to," she concluded, "but Harley did say that Ruby doesn't know that Jeb double crossed her. He said something about your death. That's why I'm here. He said that Devils Fire would soon be full of holes and dead bodies."

"Good God!" Weston exclaimed, jumping to his feet. "Nobody but the crew knew that we had a change in plans. They must have sailed hours ago."

Weston banged his fists on the desk and Santelle saw a murderous look come into his eyes.

"What are you going to do?" she demanded.

"With any luck I can hire a ship and crew and pray that I can catch up with them." Weston told her. "You might have saved a lot of lives today, Santelle. How can I ever repay you?"

"I don't need any repayment," she told him, her eyes misty. "You and Rawlings always treated me good."

"Santelle," Weston said earnestly, "don't tell anybody about what you just told me. Just keep your eyes and ears open for anything unusual. Remember, they still have something else plotted."

"Good luck!" Santelle called, but Weston was already gone.

CHAPTER 30

The open field was damp and muddy, but Brana didn't care. Her woolen cloak kept the frost from nipping at her.

After Weston's departure, she had not been able to fall back asleep at once and when she had her dreams had turned into nightmares and she had risen with a cold sweat all over her body to find that Weston's scent had lingered behind him. She remembered how safe she had felt in his arms the night before. Today, she felt so happy that she couldn't wait to share her news with Lacy. Realizing that it was still so early that everyone else would be asleep, Brana decided to go for a ride. After dressing in the trousers and shirt that she now kept in her armoire, she ran to the stables and quickly saddled Beauty and rode through the sleeping country.

Riding with the wind, her silken tresses tumbled around her. Her thoughts were far away, leaving Beauty to take control and manage his trotting pace back to La Salone.

Confiding in her friend, she heard the sound of pounding hooves behind her and the clasp of a strong arm around her waist. She screamed and struggled and then, suddenly, there was nothing but darkness. Little did she dream that back at La Salone, another woman was being abducted and that they would soon meet in a horror that neither of them could ever

have imagined.

CHAPTER 31

His hair tossed by the wind, his eyes eager with anticipation. Rawlings stood at the rail of Devils Fire watching the waves toss their white foamy heads around the ship, at times almost washing over the deck. In his new position of great importance, his excitement was masked with a calm mind, determined to govern the crew with confidence and courage. The wind made the sails clap together, and the crew chattered with ease, wonderful sounds, that only a Captain would appreciate. His thoughts suddenly turned the Beth. Why did she always have to make things so difficult? The memory of the hatred in her eyes when he told he would set sail disturbed him. The ugly scene was played over in his mind as he began to ponder what his future with her held.

"Hey, there Capt'in," the second mate, an older man, with years of sun on his weathered face, said "Noth'in like choppy waters to welcome your sea legs."

As a large wave suddenly smashed the railing, Rawlings jumped back and laughed, sea water dripping from his hair. "I am thoroughly wet," he said. "I've been baptized, a true seaman."

The second mate laughed and nodded his head in agreement.

Rawlings smiled and slapped the first mate on the back. He knew these men were good men, hard working and trustworthy. All of the crew had sailed with Weston for many years and knew the regulations on board Devils Fire and the strict policies regarding neither drunkenness nor uncleanness, which suited Rawlings just fine.

"Guess I'll go change these wet clothes," Rawlings told him, pulling the Le Capatiane waist coat away from his body. "I should also log my baptism in the ships journal."

By this time, other crew members were roaring with laughter, Rawlings looked as if he had just been plucked out from the sea. He joined in the chorus, made his way to the captains' cabin located to the aft of the main deck, a low ceilinged room with a single bunk built into one wall and an ideal table that served as a desk. Carpets covered the polished floor, and an assortment filled the surprisingly spacious room. The bulkheads were paneled and pictures of various war ships were hung. On the desk, maps of latitude and longitude were neatly stacked and various compasses sat on top. He was just about to remove his coat when he heard light tapping on the door. It was the first mate.

"Looker spotted two vessels in the distance," he said. The first mate, a young man, but despite his years, he was no stranger to the sea.

He had proven invaluable in numerous dangerous situations, saving the ship, and crew of Devils Fire on more than one occasion.

"This is supposed to be friendly waters." Rawlings replied, frowning. "Maybe they're just in a hurry to get to their destination."

"Maybe so captain, but something about this just ain't right. They're near caught up to us and we're going ten knots. Devils Fire has got lots of enemies everywhere and what better opportunity for them to strike when there's a different captain on board."

"I see your point," Rawlings said as he looked around the room. "Gather all the men on deck and I will be there shortly. Whoever it is, if there's a fight they want, we'll be glad to oblige."

When all the crew was gathered on deck, the first mate whispered something in Captain Rawlings ear.

"Men!" Rawlings shouted in order to be heard as the waves crashed against the ship. "'They have been following us for sometime now and have gain speed on us. We will set a different course and try to outmaneuver or out run the bastards. I want no unnecessary bloodshed, so only fire on command."

"Aye, aye captain," the crew shouted with pistols raised high into the air.

"May God be with us all!" Rawlings shouted to his crew.

In that instance, his romance with the sea was quickly eclipsed.

Hours had passed and despite the change of course, the two ships continued to trail closely behind.

The sunset, a fireball of light submerged slowly, until the last tip wavered and then sank into the sea like a decrepit ship.

The icy waves that hit the deck flayed the sailors, scattering them about the deck. And then there was a roar as a cannonball struck the mast of Devils Fire. The wooden splinters shattered everywhere as the mast slowly came tumbling down onto the deck. The deafening sound hid the screams of the unfortunate caught below it.

"Fire!" The voice of command shouted.

Their fate was almost certain as they were trapped and out gunned. Smoke assailed their nostrils, and fire blinded them as the crew fought to survive as one cannon ball after another tore into the belly of the ship. Some were thrown into the depths of their blue goddess as she rose and greedily wrapped her arms around the men she loved.

Weston noticed the waves were enormous and felt no sympathy for a young cabin boy who had been swept overboard. The sudden storm's fury was rising but was still no match for the burning rage Weston had felt.

"You might have to face the fact that we might not reach them in time," The captain told Weston grimly, holding a spy glass to his eye. "If that is Devil's Fire we've spotted, she is traveling at a fast speed, and the sea is against us. We'll be lucky if we even make it back to port. Strikes me we never should have set out in the first place."

Weston took the spy glass and held it up to his eye. He could see three vessels in the distance, tiny spots against the horizon.

When he stepped on board the Lizzy the welcoming was hospitable. He had known the Captain, Bruce Hancock for many years and at times played a game of poker or two. Weston could see the pity in his eyes, both knowing the odds that were stacked against them.

"Knowing my best friend and crew might meet their deaths, I had to do something." Weston's voice was hard, and his lips were set in a grim line.

"You sure the information that was given to you came from a reliable source?"

"Even if there was a doubt, I still wouldn't be able to rest until I knew for sure."

Weston had paid handsomely for the use of the captains' vessel and crew, telling him only that he had heard of a plot to have someone killed at sea, and wanted to prevent it if he could. The captain had agreed on the condition that he command his own vessel.

Weston put the spy glass up to his trained eye again and spotted only two vessels.

The captain noticed the look on Weston's face and took the spy glass from his hands. Looking through the glass, he had confirmed what Weston already knew. The captain shivered, as he thought of the fate of any man who Weston would seek revenge upon.

CHAPTER 32

His morning chores finished, Simmons had just had breakfast with Cook and was making his way through the heavy mud to feed the horses. As he walked in, he noticed that Beauty, was saddled, out of her stall, stomping his hooves against the straw covered stable floor. Simmons called Brana's name over and over again, but received no reply. Knowing that it was unlike Brana to leave Beauty saddled when she finished her morning ride, fear gripped him as he thought of Brana lying unconscious in the muddy field. After he put Beauty back in his stall, he went directly to Brana's bed chamber. When there was no answer to his knock, he turned the knob and found the door unbolted.

"Miz Brana" he called softly, quick to notice the embers in the fireplace were blazing."Probably gone to fetch one of those lazy chamber maids to draw her up a bath," he mumbled, promising to scold her about being so eager to comfort herself that she would leave Beauty saddled and not rubbed down.

In the next room Ruby had just settled herself on the soft feather mattress, and let the warmth of her bed covers erase the brutal touch of Jeb. She knew he would no longer have the need to seek her favors now that his obsession was about to become reality. She imagined that Brana and Santelle would be a good distance from La Salone by now, that is, of course, if Harley didn't stop to indulge his thirst for whiskey. But surely he would not risk Jeb's wrath. Besides, too much was at stake. Even Harley must realize that.

Hearing the knock on Brana's chamber door, Ruby sat up using her stained sheet to cover her nakedness, tiptoed to the adjoining door, and put her ear to the door. Hearing Simmons voice she gave a sigh of relief.

"Old fool" she muttered and made her way back to the warm and inviting bed.

Her dreams were the same. Over and over again she saw herself as wife of the notorious Weston Yates, waking up every morning in his strong muscled arms. She would be mistress of the manor he would buy her, with plenty of servants to cater to her every whim. She could see herself in the latest fashions from Paris, her body adorned with expensive baubles. She herself on his vessel, Devils Fire, visiting exciting and exotic places all over the world, with Weston by her side. She dreamed of Weston taking her in his arms and kissing away her very breath before lifting her in his arms and caring her to their bed chamber, where he would feed the burning fire of her passion, crying out with pleasure and confessing his love for her again and again.

CHAPTER 33

Perspiration trickled between Brana's breasts and her hair had become a tangled mass covering her face. She winced with pain as she tried to remove rope that bound her hands. Her mouth was dry, her lips swollen and chapped. The filthy, foul smelling rag in her mouth made it impossible to swallow. The coarse wool of the blanket that covered her body felt like tiny pine needles pricking at her skin and she could hear her heart pounding as if it would burst. She moaned as the wagon jolted her shoulders against the hard surface. It was becoming harder for her to breath with the heavy blanket pressed down on her face. Turning her head, she saw the limp, blood stained form of Santelle lying beside her, her hands and feet bound with the same gray rag that had been shoved into her mouth. Black ringlets of hair surrounded her face, but didn't hide her jaw, which had been badly bruised. Blood was oozing from her lips and had it not been for the slight rising of her chest, Brana would have thought she was dead.

Brana wondered how this could have happened. How could she have completely ignored the malevolence of Jeb? And why would anyone want to hurt Santelle? Confused, she kept thinking about Lacy. Lacy, she knew, would somehow find out about their abduction, and gather up a search party for her rescue.

Brana tried to nudge Santelle to waken but was unsuccessful at her feeble attempts. She decided to concentrate on saving her strength; Santelle may need her when she became conscious.

As the hours passed, Brana felt every bump, every turn, and every hidden rock that came in contact with the turning wheels. Her body ached and the pain was so intense that she began to slip in and out of consciousness.

Brana closed her eyes and shivered as she remembered the look in Jeb's beady eyes, eyes that had roamed her body with thoughts of insatiable desire. The things he was saying echoed in her mind.

"I knew the day would come when you would be all mine," he had told her twirling a lock of her hair through his fingers.

"I've waited until the time was right. I planned it perfectly. If I hadn't been a fool when I first saw you, I would have had you long before this. But that bitch Lacy kept watching me like a hawk. I bet you didn't know I saw you naked when Lacy first took you in. You were right there just for the takin', but I wanted it to be perfect. No one will ever know I had anything to do with your disappearance. You'll belong to me until I tire of you. And then, of course, you will belong to anybody I choose to give you to."

Brana couldn't believe the look of greedy lust in his eyes. She had kicked and scratched, but she was not a match for a mad man. Who laughed in her face and grabbed her by the shoulders. She fought back the bile in her throat as his open mouth came within inches from her quivering lips.

"Oh, and one more thing before you're taken to my paradise," he told her, laughing like a madman. "Don't get your hopes up about Yates. He's probably in a watery grave by now."

The wagon jolted and Brana heard faint moaning coming from Santelle. It had been hours since Brana had tried to wake her but now she was stirring back into consciousness. Brana wondered what Santelle had done to deserve this. Perhaps Harley would only agree to go along with Jeb if he would get Santelle for himself.

She thought of Lacy and of Simmons and Cook, certain she would never see them again. Tears blinded her eyes as she thought of her dear friends and how much their friendship meant to her. Her heart felt as if it had been ripped out and torn apart into tiny little pieces.

Her heart cried out for Weston but she could only see a vision of Jeb laughing and leering at her. She tried to nudge Santelle's leg again. But Santelle's breathing only became heavier. Clearly she was unconscious again or close to death.

Exhausted, Brana let sleep consume her.

Meanwhile Harley was whistling and singing to himself as he drove the wagon down the path to Jeb's hideout, Under the Hill, Natchez, trying not to think of the bottle of liquor he had stolen from La Salone to drink later that night, when the wind would chill his bones. He chuckled when he remembered the look on Santelle's face when he had grabbed her in his arms. He had seen the fear in her eyes as he had towered over her. It had pleased him to strike her. And now she lay quiet with the other, as women should.

He had felt lucky when Jeb had found him at the bar last night before he had left to the waterfront for cheaper pleasures. That was when he had found out that Santelle had played him for a fool. Jeb was more than happy to change the plans and let him take her to the secret hideout where many women had been before. He sure thanked his lucky stars that Santelle made it easy for them to take her.

"Yes siree!" Harley said now, thinking of the ways he would bed her. Maybe he would find satisfaction in the way Jeb bedded his women.

He would ride her till the juices felt hot and sticky and he would know it was her blood. Harley reached for the bottle of whiskey and tilted it to his lips.

"Ooh," he whispered as he licked his lips, trying to sooth the burning sensation. He tossed the cork out into the darkness of the night and decided to finish the burning liquid between the trees off of the road which offered some privacy. He felt his member burning for release and wanted the flesh that was waiting in back of the buckboard.

Santelle felt Brana's body pressed against hers. She had no doubt that it was Brana and that Jeb and Ruby had planned her abduction. That's what had been intended all along and now she feared for her life, tangled up in a web of passion and lust. She had heard the horrible stories about Jeb and his satanic hovel. She knew they were headed there and prayed for her life and Brana's. Even though they might kill her in the end, Brana, an innocent, should be spared.

When the woolen blanket was pushed aside, Santelle knew what was about to come. She silently prayed for Weston, but knew he would be long at sea and she would have to endure the brutal assaults that would undoubtedly befall her.

She heard the drunken slur of Harley's voice as he came closer and she could smell the alcohol on his breath. Thoughts of her childhood came easily to mind. Visions of her family, her mother, kissing her when she was injured or sad, broke her heart. The thought of never seeing them again was painful. Revenge on Ruby was not as sweet as she had thought it would be. Closing her eyes, she pretended to be in her mother's tender embrace. In her trance, she could almost smell her sweet perfume and feel her cradling her in her arms just like a newborn.

"I'm gonna want you, girl," Harley said, lifting Santelle out of the wagon. Throwing her to the ground, he pulled her to the side of the road by her hair, while fishing in his filthy trousers for his pocket knife. He hurriedly cut the tight bounds that held her captive.

"Stop your moving girl," he hissed. "I want you real bad. You're going to pay for what you did to me, tak'in me for a fool. This here is a part of my plan and I'm going to enjoy every minute you scream."

After untying her, he kicked her.

As he undid his breeches, Santelle almost retched as the smell of urine reached her nostrils. Grabbing a good sized rock, she waited for him to make his move.

Harley came closer and threw himself on Santelle. Then, before he could react, he screamed in pain as something sharp struck his eyes, blinding him.

Santelle scrambled from underneath him and started to run for her life. She heard his screams of revenge, but kept running, trying to find safety.

"I'm going to get you girl and you're going to pay." Harley kept shouting, "You can't hide bitch. Harley's going to get you and kill you!"

Finding a heavily wooded area, Santelle hid near a huge oak that she thought offered safety, holding her breath as she heard brush being crushed by heavy feet, passing her, moving on until she could no longer hear his cries. Thinking herself safe, she ran toward the open field, only to be thrown to the ground, Harley's thick hands circling her throat.

"No," she croaked.

"I enjoyed your little game, bitch," he growled. "Now it's my turn."

Santelle's life flashed before her eyes, finally resting on the image of her deceased father, who lovingly held his arms out to her.

CHAPTER 34

Debris was everywhere. He had seen the bodies and the flotsam of wood and sail that was all that was left of Devil's Fire. The horror of it was so great that he could not speak. And it was his fault. He had sent Rawlings- he had sent them all to their watery graves. He should have been the one to face Jeb across the surging waves.

Dizziness swept over him and he tightened his grip on the rail. When at last he opened his eyes he read the name of his ship on the side of some flotsam drifting by. It was as if his vessel was saying one last goodbye.

Weston slammed his fists on the rail, his complexion was as white as sheet. Nobody dared to intrude on his grief.

As night fell, the waters seemed much calmer and through the darkness they saw that the sea was taking on the reflection of the lantern and the silvery light of the moon. The wind seemed to carry the voices of the dead crew of Devils Fire and it seemed to some, that crashing of the waves striking their vessel sounded like echoes of the cannons' roar. The smell of death road with the sea breeze and the sea goddess slowly brought bits and pieces of Devil's Fire, under the iridescent light of the stars, to taunt and torment Weston. He stood shaken, by the rail showing the blue goddess he had defied her and still lived. She showed no displeasure as they seemed to come to mutual agreement, all the lifeless bodies and debris disappeared into the unknown depths of her kingdom within seconds. The sea was in control now. He knew that. And she was too powerful for him.

He continued to stand at the rail, looking out to sea. He thought of his crew, friends for many years and what the loss would mean to their families. He ran his fingers through his hair and anyone that was standing close enough to him could hear the sharp intake of breath but couldn't see the mist in his eyes. Taking blue silk ribbon from his pocket, Weston caressed the fine material and thought of Brana and her beauty. She had actually saved his life. He would never have let Rawlings sail without him, had he not wanted to see her, unknowingly sending Rawlings and his crew to their deaths. Putting the rich material up to his lips, he breathed in the fresh scent of her hair. This ribbon would, he knew, always be a reminder of his beautiful vixen. The defiant temptress, who had melted the ice cold barriers of his heart. Now that he had lost so much, he felt the need to hold her in his arms, kiss her, and love her in a way he had loved no other woman.

On the other side of the vessel, crates rescued from the sea were being put to the side. "Men," Weston shouted. "Anything you find whether it be a crate of food or gold coins, belongs to whomever defies

the sea goddess and fishes it out of her domain."

The crew cheered and Weston felt a slap on the back. Turning, he

saw the Captain looking at him with respect.

"Are you sure?" he said.

"Aye, I have no need for anything that will be salvaged."

"But, what about the personal effects of your crew? Shouldn't they

be given to kin?"

"For what, captain?" Weston replied. "The reminder of heartbreak

to pass on to their sons and grandsons. Gazing at the sea, will be enough

pain for them to last their lifetime. I find the best way to deal with grief is

to lock it up and throw away the key. It's the only way to go forward with

you life."

The captain saw sadness deep in Weston's eyes and knew that he,

too, had lost a loved one, that he, too, knew the ultimate pain of loss.

"Besides," Weston added, "my men never kept anything of great

value aboard. Your men will find mostly food and supplies, maybe a gold

coin or two, nothing more."

Weston looked at him with a strange glint in his eyes. Because in

his heart he knew that nothing they might salvage would ever make up for the great loss he and others had suffered today. And he would never, ever

escape the guilt he was feeling now.

CHAPTER 35

Lacy kept going over the cash she had taken in the night before, growing more and more certain that hundreds of dollars were missing. It was now well past the noon hour and everyone had been told not to disturb her. She knew that last night had been very profitable, but now the cash she had on hand seemed to be much less. Just at one table alone a rogue lost a fortune on a bad hand and had left swearing revenge on the card dealer. Lacy knew the cash box had been locked and put away when she retired for the evening last night. When she returned to it this morning, she was certain more than half of the money was missing. She put her hands on the well polished desk; she faced the fact that she had been robbed. Someone had had to have come into her study after she left, someone who knew the combination of the safe. The question she asked herself was, who?

Her thoughts went instantly of Jeb, his behavior last night was usually friendly and chatty. He didn't bother himself to get upset after losing a tidy sum to the house. In fact, he was in a very good mood.

Simmons was just finishing the remainder of his noon meal when Lacy interrupted him.

"Simmons, have you seen Jeb?" She demanded.

"Why no, Miz Lacy," he shrugged. "You know how lazy that scum is. He'd be sleeping off all that expensive champagne he don had last night."

Simmons continued devouring his favorite tart until he heard his mistress's foot tapping rapidly against the polished floor.

"Well then, find him!" she said sharply. "And when you do, send him into my study immediately. And do it now!"

Simmons had never seen Lacy so angry.

"I'll be waiting, Simmons, and I assure you my mood won't be any better soon!" she added and stormed out of the room.

"You heard Miz Lacy," Cook told him. "You best find him fast. If I were you, I would look in that harlot Ruby's chamber first."

Simmons muttered and shook his head on the way out.

Back in her study, Lacy paced, back and forth, her lips set in a grim line. All night she had been thinking about the money she had made and would use to try and purchase an old abandoned building on the waterfront certain she wouldn't be turned down this time. Her dreams of establishing a homeless shelter had almost been reality until somebody betrayed her. She had to talk to Jeb but, at the same time, she wouldn't be surprised if he wasn't found. He was the only one besides her to know the combination. It had to be him, she thought, as she banged her hands violently on her desk. She was just about to leave, when Simmons ushered Jeb into the room.

"You wanted to see me dear wife." His voice dripped with sarcasm.

"Don't you ever use that term with me again," she snapped.

"My, my, aren't we testy this morning," he raised an eyebrow. "After all, you invited me here, remember."

"I want to know where you were last night after closing?" she told him.

"Why, Lacy dear. Don't you think it's a bit late for you to become the jealous wife," he drawled. "As your husband, I might ask you the same question?"

"Oh, shut up, Jeb. Do you think I enjoy even being in the same room with you? Do you really think----"

"What the hell is all this about, Lacy," he interrupted her. "You can ask Simmons where he found me. I was in my chamber sleeping off the ill effects of last nights over indulgence."

"You were there all night?"

"Are you going to tell me what all this is about?" Jeb demanded angrily.

Lacy observed him closely. His eyes were a bit blood shot and he seemed to be wearing the same attire he wore last night. But she wasn't going to be taken in by the look of innocence on his face.

"I was robbed last night," she said, keeping her voice even with an effort, "and you're the only one who knows the combination to the safe."

"I'm going to overlook the fact that you blatantly accuse me of such a thing," he told her, assuming an injured expression. "If I had robbed you, do you think I would be standing here now?"

Lacy walked over to her desk and sat down gracefully on the leather chair facing him. It occurred to her that for once he just might be telling the truth, but she still had her doubts.

"Well, what am I supposed to think?" she asked him. "With your past history and conniving ways, naturally I assumed you were responsible."

"You just said the key words Lacy. The past. My past which I have tried to make up to you. I'm deeply wounded by your accusation."

He turned his back to her as he made his way to the crystal decanter and poured himself a generous amount of brandy.

"Well, I suppose if it had been you, you wouldn't be here now," Lacy admitted. "I just don't know who could have done such a thing."

She was puzzled as to why all the money hadn't been taken. Had she been robbed by somebody with a conscience? That would certainly rule Jeb out.

"Why don't you gather everybody right now and ask them if they saw or heard anything unusual. Somebody is bound to know something."

"Good idea," she told him. "I'll have Simmons gather the girls. But don't think you're off the hook just yet!"

Jeb smiled in triumph as he left the study. Lacy had fallen into his trap. She had actually believed his story. Now all Ruby has to do is play her part perfectly. Tonight he would be able to leave and never be suspected of a thing.

"You'd better have a good reason to wake me up from a good sleep." Ruby said yawning, wiping the sleep from her eyes, her wrapper hanging loose about her, leaving little to the imagination. The others gathered about her in various stages of dishevel.

"Simmons, where is Santelle?" Lacy asked.

"She weren't in her chamber, Miz Lacy. Nope, I didn't find her anywhere."

"Lacy, what's this all about?" Ruby demanded. "We girls need our sleep."

"Well if you must know," Lacy told her, "we were robbed last night. The culprit took several hundred dollars."

"Mondeiu!" exclaimed the French woman, Mimi.

"You don't think we had anything to do with it?" Robbie asked shyly.

"I asked you girls down here to see if you heard anything unusual or saw anything out of the ordinary. And I need to see all of you, including Santelle."

"Come to think of it, Santelle has been acting a little strange," Ruby told her. "I could swear it was her voice coming from Brana's chamber last night. They were both whispering.
Probably conspiring against you. I'll wager you didn't even bother to check to see if your little princess was in her chamber!"

It did not take Lacy long to determine that the girls, even Ruby, knew nothing that could help her. Sending them on their way, she asked Simmons to stay behind.

"I knew your precious little Brana was staying this long for a reason." Ruby said just before she left. "She probably had planned to rob you all along. It's my guess Santelle certainly helped her. They're probably aboard some ship this very minute laughing at the fool they made of you."

"Don't you listen to that filth, Miz Lacy," Simmons told her. "You don't think Miz Brana would do that to you Miz Lacy?"

"Did you check Brana's chamber?" Lacy's voice was soft and she held her breath until Simmons replied.

"It wasn't Miz Brana, Miz Lacy. I knows it."

"Simmons, you know I love Brana. But you need to tell me everything you know."

CHAPTER 36

Brana shivered. Not even the blanket kept the wind from seeping through the places that were worn and threadbare. Every bone in her body ached and her head was throbbing from hitting the buckboard with every violent turn. Her teeth chattered and her fingers were numb and stiff. The moon was shining brightly and the stars seemed to twinkle playfully. She thought of how long she would have to endure this torture. Where was she being taken? Her stomach turned at the thought of being held captive by Jeb. She shivered more violently at the thought of her never seeing Lacy again.

And where was Santelle? She reached out and felt nothing but the jolting buckboard floor. The only sign of Santelle that Brana could make out through the light of the moon were the torn fragments of her scarlet red dress. Fear gripped Brana as she struggled with the tight bonds that barely let the fluid of life flow through her veins. In her panicked state she could scarcely breathe and the palpitation of her heart rang loud in her ears, as she wrestled from side to side. She felt the wagon turn sharply, and come to an abrupt halt.

"Ere we are." His voice was slurred. "Well now ain't that something, Miz high and mighty seems to be a trifle scared."

"Stop that squirming, bitch," he told her, almost tripping over his own feet as he carried her up dilapidated stairs to what appeared to Brana to be an old shack. She heard the door creak loudly, squinted her eyes to adjust them to the darkness. She could see a ray of light from the moon which shone through an unveiled window and danced off of a huge fireplace. Harley roughly shoved her onto a bed in the corner and staggered to the table where he lit a lantern. In the blaze of light, Brana saw scurrying creatures run for cover.

"This is your new home now," Harley told her. "I suppose I should take the gag from your mouth and untie you. But I need a drink first." He noticed between the dirty dishes and empty bottles a full bottle of whiskey. He reached for a bottle of whiskey which sat among a pile of dirty dishes and empty bottles on the counter, he pulled out the cork with his rotted teeth. Taking a large gulp, he wiped the dribble with the back of his swollen hand and winced at the pain.

"Do you see what that whore done to me?" He shouted as he shoved a bloody hand in Brana's face. ""That bitch done bit me!"

All Brana could do was stare wide eyed with terror.

"I guess you noticed you little friend was gone," Harley said. "You better not give me trouble like she did if I untie you. Effen you do, I might not wait till Jeb gets here. I'll take you myself."

Brana just stared at him, blind with fear. She remembered fighting with the street urchins and them falling under her mighty blows, but she knew she could never overpower these mad men.

Pulling a pocket knife from his trousers, Harley grabbed her hands and cut the tight rope roughly. She tried to rub the life back into them as he unbound her feet, as well. Yanking the filthy gag from her mouth, Brana threw it to the floor.

"Water." she choked.

"Ain't got no water inside, and I ain't going outside to the well. Here, drink this."

When Harley shoved the whiskey bottle into her hands, Brana grabbed it and held the bottle up to her swollen lips. Only to spit the burning liquid out on the floor. Coughing and sputtering, took another drink and let the burning liquid warm her body.

"You bitch, get down and clean that there mess you done made," Harley shouted as he pulled Brana to the cold wooden floor by her matted hair. Falling to her knees, she pushed Harley back and when he stumbled and fell, tried to make her way to the door. But before she could open it, Harley had her by the hair again.

"You little slut!" he shouted and struck her.

Brana flew to the dirty floor, her senses rattled by the powerful blow. She tried to stand up but Harley came at her again and kicked her viciously on her side, sending her sprawling again. She tasted blood in her mouth. To continue to try was a losing battle, but Brana mustered all her strength and lifted herself on the bed. She could smell the rotting straw from the heavily soiled mattress. The coldness she felt earlier was now replaced with excruciating pain. Each breath turned into a whimper as she tried to curl up on her side, turning her back to Harley. She could hear his laughter but it sounded miles away. Her body was drifting as if she were floating in the air trying to reach the clouds for comfort.

"Weston," she whispered before she fell into a state of unconsciousness.

CHAPTER 37

Santelle was gulping for breath, teary eyed and in excruciating pain. Her throat felt as if it were burning in the depths of hell. Pain between her legs kept her from sitting up against the oak tree for support. Only partially clothed, she shivered uncontrollably as the night's chill penetrated her broken bones. Gently caressing her swollen throat, it was hard to swallow, she felt the outline of Harley fingers, whimpering as she began to remember how he tried to squeeze the life from her body. She struggled to focus her eyes, as the darkness of night engulfed her. And in desperation, cried out for help, but her whispers could only have been be heard by the animals hiding in the undergrowth.

Frightened and trembling, Santelle propped herself on an elbow, ignoring the pain and tried to sit up. Resting against the tree, she tired to cover her body with the rags Harley left her. After what seemed like eternity, she saw the glowing eyes of some sort of wild animal that happened upon her path. His growl was throaty, low and seemed to indicate bared teeth. Paralyzed with fear, she held her breath and sat very still. The animal inched closer, and then suddenly sauntered away. Having seen him, she could be hardly indifferent to the danger she was in and decided she must find shelter as soon a possible. Having overcome obstacles before, she knew she would find the strength to do so again, particularly once she was determined to not die in the hands of the likes of Harley and Jeb. Dizziness swept over her, as she stood and held on tightly to the branches of the old oak. Her knees were shaking with every step she took, but she continued in the direction which she thought was toward the road. Resting every few minutes, in order to save her strength, she continued forward. Stumbling over a branch, she fell to the ground and found what looked like a remnant of her scarlet gown. There was just enough material to use it as a cape, which she did and thus was able to shelter her body from the cold. The pain in her body was somehow masked by the anger she had felt in her heart.

Clouds started to cover the moon, almost obscuring the path to the road. The night was still and brooding, but she continued to walk, at times absent mindedly stroking her neck. Knowing now, the animal respected the storm to come and had retreated to the warmth of his lair.

Ultimately sleep became inevitable, and while she rested, having been awakened by a faint breeze, she saw the break of dawn on the horizon. She shivered as her makeshift cloak was damp with dew, but knew she needed to rise and continue her journey. Far in the distance, Santelle could see a frame house, with lighted windows. Smoke rose from the chimney. She stumbled toward it, rocks bruising her slippered feet, and bushes tearing at what remained of her gown. Once she fell and it was then that she remembered Harley's abuse vividly as if she were experiencing it again. Almost close to delirium she had visions of Harley laughing at her, remembering when his tongue violated her mouth, every bruise and wound on her body made her relive the pain he inflicted on her. And then, finally, she reached a clearing.

The shack was old, fronted by a sagging front porch, and next to it was a corral inside of which were two mares. Next to the fence was a buckboard covered with a tarp. There was a tin wash basin set on the rim of the well and she could smell bacon and coffee.

Santelle made her way up the steps to the door and banged her fists against it. Suddenly a man threw it open.

"You!" Santelle cried, and fell limp into his arms.

CHAPTER 38

"I can't believe she didn't tell me about her morning rides on that devil," Lacy said, shaking her head.

"She jest didn't want to worry you, Miz Lacy."

"Something just doesn't seem right here," Lacy insisted. "You say she left that beast saddled which was something she had never done in the past?"

"Yes Miz Lacy. I got worried and went to look for her think' in she might have taken a fall off the ornery devil, but she was nowhere in the muddy field. Then I went to her chamber. It was unbolted so I done poked my head in and a fire was going sure enough, but Miz Brana wasn't in her chamber."

"Why didn't you come and tell me?" Lacy demanded.

"I figured she was getting a chamber maid to draw a bath,"Simmons told her, "so I went about my chores!"

"Something's up," Lacy said, almost as though she were talking to herself. "I know in my heart Brana would never leave without telling me, even if she had regained her memory that I'm sure of. Something disturbed her the night before and she didn't want to talk about it. I should have insisted. One thing we both know for sure is that Brana certainly was not responsible for the theft. But Santelle could be. Do you remember when you saw her last?"

"I done saw her last night sittin' at the bar in the foyer talking to that trash, Harley."

"Yes, so did I. Santelle did seem a bit friendly with him as I recall. I know she would never bed him even if he could afford the coin for her services."

"Then I didn't see her no more when Jeb was talking to Harley."

"That was the last I saw of her, too, but she might have been in her chamber entertaining."

"Are you going to the authorities, Miz Lacy? We gots to find Miz Brana 'for somethin' happens to her."

"Them Yankees!" Lacy said, remembering her last visit in town without Brana. "Ha, they wouldn't help the likes of me. As it is, whenever I go into town, they threaten to close me down!"

"No Simmons, we'll wait," she continued. "Somebody's bound to slip up. What I want you to do is keep your eye on Jeb and Ruby. Their stories were a little too convincing, as if they contrived them. Don't be obvious but come and tell me right away if you see or hear anything. I'll question Mimi and Robbie privately to see if they might have forgotten to tell me anything. Don't let on that you suspect anything and do be careful. Let's not underestimate Jeb and Ruby at this point. I know they're capable of anything."

"Don't you worry none about me, Miz Lacy," Simmons assured her. "I'll do whatever I can to find Miz Brana."

It touched Lacy to see the love for Brana that shone brightly in Simmons eyes. When Simmons quietly left her study, she kept going over the turn of events. Puzzling over Santelle's disappearance and wondered if perhaps she had conspired with Harley in the theft. But she also thought that it didn't have anything to do with Brana's disappearance. Jeb and Ruby had something to do with this she felt certain, but until she could prove it, she would have to keep her eyes and ears open and wait for Harley tonight. Somehow she would manage to loosen his tongue and hopefully get some answers about the strange disappearances.

In the meantime, all she could do was to pray for Brana's safety.

CHAPTER 39

"Jeb, what the hell are you doing here?" Ruby hissed. "If Lacy saw us, you could ruin everything!"

Jeb closed the door quickly behind him and saw Ruby pacing up and down nervously.

"If your behavior is any indication of how you carried off your interview with her, you're probably her number one suspect," he said rudely.

"I was as good as you, no doubt!" she answered hotly.

"Then why are you so nervous. Just think of the rewards we'll both have."

"Speaking of rewards, I want half of the money."

"My dear, that money has already been spent. I had to pay Harley a tidy sum. The rest I will need for supplies." Jeb wanted to laugh aloud. If she only knew that the money had been spent to rid the world of her precious Yates.

"Well, I suppose I don't need any money," Ruby said confidently, twirling a loose curl between her fingertips. "I feel certain Weston will propose at any time."

"I'm sure he will Ruby," Jeb said with a grin. Later, making his way down the hall, he chuckled at his cleverness. His plans were very carefully thought out. By the time Ruby heard about Weston's fate, he would be far away with his prize possession at his side. She would know he lied about seeing Weston the night before in La Salone and would suspect he had something to do with his death but he felt sure she wouldn't go to authorities; after all if she did, she would have reason to fear for her life.

That evening, Lacy dressed in one of the latest fashions from Paris. A couture design, an embellished apron style top skirt spun of golden silk that draped above her contrasting underskirt, the color of dark brown satin, which made an exceptional look of elegance.

Taking special care and time on her toilet as her maid, Ella coiled her hair into elaborate curls at the back, she remembered the conversation she had had with the French girl Mimi.

"Madam Lacy," Mimi had said in a heavy French accent. She was adjusting her wrapper and offered Lacy a seat near the polished table. Lacy noticed her chamber was a bit untidy. The dress she had worn hours ago was now a heap of satin material thrown on the worn carpet that donned the polished floor. Her armoire was open and Lacy saw a rainbow of different colors in shiny silks and satins. She knew she was generous with her girls, but surely she would have remembered purchasing a gown for every day of the year.

"Well," Lacy said, looking directly at the French woman, "it seems you have enough gowns to put Estelle out of business."

"Oui. Now you can see how generous a man can be when you whisper the words of passion in French. It makes them feel as if they were in Paris, making love in an expensive chateau."

Lacy saw mist cloud her eyes, and knew the French woman had painful memories that she knew nothing of.

"Well I suppose it doesn't hurt to pretend you're miles away. Anyway, the reason why I'm here is to see if you remembered anything about the disappearance of Brana and Santelle." Lacy looked into her eyes and read sympathy in them.

"I'm sorry I cannot be of any help, Madam Lacy," Mimi told her fingering the shiny bauble on her finger that was given willingly as payment for her services.

"Ah, but wait. There is one thing you might be warned about. Ruby and Jeb have been very close lately. And remember, Ruby did swear revenge on Mademoiselle Santelle after the scene they made not long ago. Maybe that had something to do with Santelle's disappearance. But in any case, talk to Robbie. She and Santelle seemed to be pretty close friends."

And indeed, Lacy learned quite a bit from the shy young girl. Apparently Santelle had let it slip once, in a conversation they had had while dressing for the evening, that she had planned to leave La Salone, although she did not say where she intended to go. Robbie did say in Santelle's defense that she didn't believe Santelle could have robbed Lacy or that she would leave and not say goodbye.

After talking to both girls, Lacy headed down the hall to Santelle's chamber to find her bed neatly made. Opening her armoire door, Lacy saw that it been emptied. Santelle's prized collection of scents were gone. It seemed clear to Lacy that Santelle had no intentions of returning. Now all that she could think about was how Brana tied into all of this.

Sitting on Brana's neatly made bed, Lacy stared at the ashes that were all that was left of Brana's fire. She had never believed Ruby's accusations about Brana being the thief, and she really didn't want to believe that about Santelle. The mother of pearl encrusted comb set that Lacy had purchased for her, was gone. Lacy remembered Brana's words upon receiving the exquisite gift.

"Oh Lacy," Brana had murmured with misty eyes. "It's beautiful! You shouldn't have spent the money. You'll need every cent."

"Don't you worry about my finances. There's plenty more where that came from." Lacy had replied.

"Oh Lacy!" Brana told her again with tears spilling down her cheeks, hugging her tight. "I can never repay your kindness."

"You already have, my dear," Lacy murmured in reply.

Lacy's tears ran down her powered cheeks as she remembered the touching scene.

Brana might be gone, but in her heart Lacy knew there was an explanation as to why. It might have been the reason why Brana had been acting strange the night before. Again she thought of Jeb. Lacy hadn't forgotten his interest in Brana when he had first seen her. But subsequently he had seemed to take heed of her threat and had kept as far away from Brana as he possibly could.

Taking a last glance in Brana's mirror, Lacy told herself that Harley would succumb to the charms that she planned to use on him. Because if a crime had been committed, you could depend on Harley to know something about it. "Don't worry Brana," she murmured as she left the room, "wherever you are, I'll find you!"

By the time Lacy went downstairs, someone was pounding out a tune on the piano loudly enough to be heard over the general uproar. Jeb was at his usual table, dealing out cards to the hopeful. As she came into the room, Ruby was arranging herself seductively on one of the love seats, no doubt waiting for Weston to appear. Lacy wondered where Weston was. Most nights he was at La Salone, receiving the attentions of Ruby, but she had failed to see him the evening before. If he came tonight, she would question him about Brana. Brana knows him somehow, and Lacy intended to find out how.

Lacy saw Simmons, his wrinkled face and his mop of a white beard a welcome sight, and motioned to him with a wave of her hand.

"Well, anything unusual?" she whispered.

"No Miz Lacy. They haven't said a word to each other since they been down 'ere," he replied, shaking his head.

"Well, just continue watching. I'll keep an eye out for Harley."

As the night wore on, Lacy began to feel disappointed. Harley hadn't shown his drunken face, and neither had Weston. She poured herself a drink, which was something she had never done during business hours before and drank it quickly. An uneasy feeling was starting to prickle down the base of her spine.

Simmons had given up his watching on Ruby and Jeb, who hadn't said a word to each other all evening. Jeb had been dealing a steady hand, and Ruby had disappeared more than once behind the crystal beads. Even

Lacy was too tired to continue keeping her eye on the swinging doors at the bar. At this late hour, she knew Harley was elsewhere, possibly with Santelle, drinking himself to oblivion. She started to realize that maybe she had been wrong about Santelle. The girl might have been the one to deceive her after all.

Lacy saw Simmons walking through the foyer and called out to him.

"Nothin' Miz Lacy," Simmons informed her when she called him over to her. "They'd be working all night."

Neither of them saw Jeb slither his way through the hanging beads and sneak out of La Salone through the back way. He smiled in triumph as he reached the stables unseen. Saddling his horse, he left in the darkness of night. His beautiful Brana would soon be his. And no one could stop him.

CHAPTER 40

The clean up effort and its agonizing slow pace took more time than anticipated. Tension radiated from the men who had not yet discovered a live body or anything of great value. Filled with dismay, Weston continued to look in the spy glass, standing erect, grim determination etched on his face as he watched with a sinking heart, the bodies and debris floating by. At times, a string of curses came from his lips as he remembered the disastrous turn of events. In no mood to socialize, he kept silent and vigilant, looking through the spy glass. Some said, he stood, watching for forty eight hours straight, with no signs of surrendering until he knew for sure, not one man survived.

The captain, a man who drank too much whiskey and was overly fond of tobacco, showed no expression, even though Weston suspected that inside he felt a considerable degree of compassion. He barked orders to crew that were that were starting to grumble and turned to utter a few words to his long time friend, the ships Doctor.

"Can you blame' em Capt'n?" the cantankerous, old doctor told him. "'They been at it for two days now, an seeing nothing but dead bodies, they want to go home and see their loved ones."

The Captain could smell whiskey on his breath, although the doctor showed no signs of intoxication. He never did.

"Seems to me," he said, taking the sort of liberties no one else could, "that there is nothing here to salvage. What don't we head back to the harbor?"

"This is not a decision for you or I to make," the captain told him, "Weston will be the one to decide."

"Young fool," doc said looking over at Weston. He had known the likes of Weston for many years, and knew the signs of revenge. He could see that Weston clutched a blue ribbon in his hands, and couldn't help but wonder if the owner of the silk cloth had anything to do with the tragedy.

The sea mist had dissipated and the sea was calm against the sharp blue sky. Weston thought he had seen something white flutter in the distance, shook his head and looked again. The vision was gone.

"Capt'n," a young seaman shouted as he ran towards the captain and pointed out to the sea.

"What is it sailor?" the captain asked

"I thought I saw a body hangin' onto a piece of driftwood, Sir, but now it's gone!"

"You aren't the first to see the mischief the goddess can play on a man's senses," the captain told him.

"I guess you're right Capt'n," the young seaman said. "I guess I was just hope' in too much, is all."

"We all hoped for the same thing, son," the captain said, shaking his head in despair. "I knew most of the crew on board. They were all fine men and good sailors. Most of them left young'uns and a good loyal woman behind."

"It's the risk we all take, sail' in the sea," the doc snorted.

"That's right my boy. Never underestimate the sea. She can turn on you when you least expect it. But this time someone had a hand in it, and I pity the fool. Captain Yates, without a doubt, will seek revenge for his murdered crew. Rest assured the bloody bastard will pay dearly for his treachery."

"The boy maybe right," Weston said as he walked over to where the captain stood. "I saw something worth investigating a few minutes ago."

"Humm," the captain grunted and shouted orders.

A boat was lowered into the water and headed in the direction of the sighting.

"Well, I'll be damned," the doc said as they saw the body drift away with the tide, anxiety mounted and the crew all rowed faster, faster as if their own lives depended on it.

"I knew he was alive, I just knew it!" the young sailor shouted with joy and yelled out to the sea and her deadly disciples, "we beat you!"

The man's body was ice cold to the touch, but his chest was rising and falling slowly. But his face was bloodied and bruised beyond recognition.

"We got to hurry up and get him to the ship," doc said taking his vitals. "He's in bad shape."

"Do you know who he is?" the captain asked Weston.

Weston shook his head.

"Tell me he's gonna make it, Doc!" the young sailor cried.

"He won't if we waste anymore time yakking," doc yelled. "Let's get!"

Upon reaching ship, all hands seemed to be on deck. Cheers roared through the crowd and moved aside for the doc and his patient.

"Captain Yates, I'll see to the clean-up, go with Doc," the captain offered.

Grateful, Weston shook his hand and thanked him but what the captain saw deep in Weston's eyes chilled him to his very core.

Weston followed the doc below deck to a room which had one small table, chair and a bunk that was attached to the wall. The room was sparse but clean, nautical maps hung on the walls, a bottle of opened whiskey sat on the table.

"Be gentle, now," the doctor told his helpers. "He's still alive and I intend to keep them that way."

Weston caught a whiff of whiskey in the air, and noticed the doc's eyes were bloodshot. He eyed the doc suspiciously when he pressed down on the man's abdomen and heard a groan.

"Is he going to live, Doc?" Weston asked as he studied patient and pondered who it might be.

"As you see," the doc said, "he suffered burns on his hands, cuts, and bruises on his entire body. Maybe some broken bones, but what we have to worry about is the fever. Hell, I can't be sure he'll make it through the night with this fever."

"If anyone can pull him through," the captain said as he entered the cabin, "It's you Doc."

"You otta know," the doc retorted, "I've saved your hide more times that I can remember."

"Aye, that you did," the captain replied. "Do you recognize the man?"

"It's hard to tell with his face swollen,"

Weston put has hands in his pockets and found the silk ribbon again. It gave him comfort to know that Brana's embrace was waiting for him. He absent mindedly put the ribbon to his lips, smelled her perfume as it wafted up his nostrils, could feel the softness of her hair, see the nakedness of her body.

"Captain, there is nothing left here for us. May I suggest we head back to port?"

Weston put the ribbon back in his pocket and looked at the captain. "Yes, Captain, I believe we should head back," Weston said wanting nothing more than to hold Brana tightly in his arms.

At that instant, everyone inside the cabin heard whispers coming from the injured sailor. Weston leaned over the sailor as he tried to speak.

"I'm sorry, old boy," he gasped and Weston's heart began to race. Did he recognize that voice? He wasn't sure.

"Doc is going to take good care of you," Weston told him. "Please, save your strength."

"Wes, If don't make it, tell Beth that I love her."

At that moment, Weston bowed his head and sobbed.

The captain ushered him to the chair and poured them both a drink. Weston gulped and poured another until the bottle was empty.

The hours of light that poured through the porthole were dimming as time wore on. Weston had not left Rawlings' side the entire time. His fever seemed controlled but he had a long way to recovery. The ship's doctor had left a few minutes before, pleased with the progress.

"Why don't you come up for some air?" The captain said, as he slipped into the cabin unheard.

"I'd rather wait until he regains consciousness, again" Weston replied.

"That might not be for a few days." The captain said as he walked over to the bunk, looking at Rawlings.

"Doc said, he might come to for a few minutes at a time, and when he does I want to be here." Weston was adamant.

"I understand Captain." The captain replied, as he patted Weston on the back. He left as quietly as he had entered the cabin.

Once he was alone with Rawlings, Weston thought about his future. He had never really cared about where destiny would take him, but now with losing all his crew and almost his best friend, he was having second thoughts about his former recklessness. He thought of Brana and the future he might have with her. She was always in the back of his mind. He could visualize her face and her rosy lips. When her violet eyes looked at him pleadingly, he felt his ice heart slowly melt. He desired her more than any other woman he had ever known. He was intrigued by her innocence and defiance, and her spirit, the way she tamed the black steed to cater to her every whim as she rode him with the same fire that ignited her passion.

"Wes, I...," Rawlings moaned, turning his face to Weston. He winced with the pain it caused.

"Don't try and move old boy," Weston said relieved, "you're going to be sore for awhile. I'm going to take you to Lacy's. She'll have you up in no time."

"Sorry my friend, Devil's Fire and the crew...did anybody else survive?" Rawlings whispered and looked away.

"I was to blame for that," Weston informed him, "not you. You warned me about Jeb and I didn't heed your warning. Now the lives of my crew suffered for it."

"Jeb?" Rawlings exclaimed. "Two ships came at us. There was nothing we could do but fight back"

"Jeb hired them to kill me," Weston told him, his lips in a grim line. "He thought I was sailing. He wanted me dead."

"Are you sure, Wes?" Rawlings strained to speak.

"I'm sure of that, and one more thing," Weston added. "Rest assured, my friend, Jeb and all his cohorts will suffer a worst fate."

CHAPTER 41

With eyes too bruised for her to open them, Santelle felt herself being laid on a bed. Gentle hands removed what remained of her clothing and sponged her naked body. She felt salve being applied to her wounds and when she cried out at the pain of it, someone swore an oath, although whether it was a man or woman she could not be sure.

"Water" she whispered, her throat parched and burning. The man who, earlier that day, had given her directions to Weston's offices took a pitcher from wooden shelves that were neatly attached to the wall just above some wooden cabinets where dishes were neatly stacked.

"Don't you worry, you're going to be just fine," he told her, "I'll be right back with some fresh water from the well."

He poured water from a pitcher into a well worn tin cup and lifted her head gently off the pillow tipping the tin to her bruised and swollen lips. When she could no longer drink he walked away into a room that was hidden behind a huge braided rug. When he returned, a clean cotton nightshift was folded on his arm.

Santelle tried to smile, but any movement caused extreme pain. He lifted her head and her arms and dressed her as if she were a child. The nightshift was too large, but Santelle welcomed its comfort. The words she wanted to speak were lodged in her throat.

"Don't you worry," he told her. "You'll get your voice back once the bruises inside your throat heal, so don't even try to talk now. You're warm to the touch with fever and you're exhausted. You'll feel better once you've had some rest."

When Santelle had initially seen him at the docks, his hair had seemed black and curly tucked under his woolen cap. But now, in the light of the fireplace, it seemed to be light brown with a sprinkle of salt at the sides. His face and arms were tanned and he had the bluest eyes that she had ever seen. Or had she seen them before? There was something so familiar about him, with his distinguished, weathered face. He was, she was certain, a man who had sailed the seas. Santelle closed her eyes and thought of Brana. Brana's fate would be much worse than her own if they didn't save her in time. She tried to speak again but it was useless. And soon she fell asleep.

"Don't you worry, when you can talk again, you can tell me who was responsible for this and I'll make sure he dies a slow and painful death," the stranger murmured, pulling another blanket over her as gently as though she were a child. He knew Santelle couldn't hear him. She was already in a deep sleep.

When he had opened the cabin door earlier and she had fallen into his arms, he had wondered who she was. Now he was certain she was the same woman who had asked directions of him hours earlier on the docks. He thought she had looked much younger then, her brown hair pinned up, leaving a few loose curls dangling down around her face. Given what she was wearing and the amount of bosom she had exposed, there was no doubt about her profession but there was softness about her that he had found appealing.

Now, as he looked down at her, he felt something he hadn't felt in years. After the death of his wife he had not been able to live with himself. Guilt and shame forced him to leave his small daughter behind in care of a spinster sister, while he had taken to the sea, leaving the haunted memories of his past, changing his name and leaving his wealth. Signing on to different vessels, he had traveled around the world, but had always made it a point to visit his daughter once every two years, bringing her gifts from every port he had visited.

Disgrace was why he had had a desire to be at sea, and shame was why he never wanted to return home. Looking at Santelle, pain tugged at his heart. He longed to see his beautiful daughter, hear her sweet voice in endless chatter, she would love him unconditionally. The small child he had left behind had suddenly become an adult and understood his pain.

His wife and son were lost to him, but his daughter was waiting and

begging for him to leave the past, and start a future

Santelle stirred under the patched quilt that covered her body. At

the docks that morning, luck had been with him as he spotted an old

friend, ready to set sail aboard, Devils Fire. His friend offered the use of

his cabin until his return. Accepting the generous offer, he informed him

he would only stay a couple of days, deciding to return home to his

daughter, where ultimately he belonged. Tired of running, ready to accept

blame and responsibility for the death of his wife and estrangement of his

only son, he was ready to start a new future.

He pulled a recent letter, from his daughter, out of his trouser

pocket and re-read it.

Dearest Father,

I received your letter on the 28th of March. It had been a long time since we had heard from you, but I never gave up hope! I thanked the good Lord, hearing that you are in high sprits and good health.

I am happy to inform you that all is well here, with the exception of Auntie's troublesome cough. Doctor Jonas is not the least bit worried though, he continues to visit her regularly, as usual.

Derek came by last week and joined us for dinner. He asked about you, as always, and wondered when you will realize the sea is not a home. I'm afraid he had too much port, and continued to prattle on about the dangers at sea and that you should realize your family and friends would be happy to placate and support your troubled past. He mentioned he could use your help with the business, which apparently, is busier that ever before.

Things have changed around here, Father, since you have been gone, with regret, not for the better. The city politicians are now just as corrupt and ruthless as common thieves and thugs. The new Mayor has made false promises and the city has been in an uproar, yours truly included.

I long for the day you forgive yourself and stop your suffering. You are needed here now. My heart is heavy knowing that you could die alone, when you could be with family and friends who love you, here at home. I know one day, your son will open his heart and forgive you and we can be a family once again.

In closing, Auntie sends her love and is longing to see you again. Jessie and Isaac send you salutations along with all the staff. I miss you terribly; forever will you be in my thoughts and prayers.
I love you so,
Your daughter
P.S. I'm traveling to New Orleans with your future son-in-law with Auntie as chaperon. My betroth is meeting his solicitor to complete a legal transaction. I pray for you to be home upon my return.

Lighting a cheroot, he sat at the wooden kitchen table and thought

of his son, who has earned a reputation as a successful trader and import,

export shipper. A young man who walked away from family wealth, made

his own destiny in the world, had filled him with pride.

Folding the letter carefully, returned it to his pocket. Yes, he

thought home was where he wanted to be, but he certainly wouldn't make

it there before she returned since the letter was dated five weeks ago. He

realized he needed to wait until Santelle was able to be move and then he

would make preparations as quickly as possible. He was going home and

was ready to face the demons of his past.

CHAPTER 42

When he awoke, Harley was in a foul mood. His head throbbed and his hand was painfully swollen. It was already midday and Jeb was due to arrive at any minute. He looked over at Brana and could see the swelling of her face, her bruised lips. How was he going to explain her condition and what was he going to tell him about Santelle.

"Damn" he muttered as he threw the empty whiskey bottle into the fireplace. The sound startled Brana awake.

"It's all your fault, bitch. You and that dead friend of yours. I didn't mean to hit ya, but you were tryin' to escape, and that's what I'm telling Jeb."

"I'm starvin' and you're gonna fix us some vittles as soon as I get a fire goin," he sneered. "Do you hear me girl?"

Harley threw more logs in the fireplace and Brana started into the orange and yellow glow. It seemed that she could see a white mansion set proudly on a hill. Slaves were working in the cotton fields and a girl was riding wildly on a black stallion, through a meadow, her ebony black hair loose on her shoulders.

"Are you touched, girl?" Harley growled, shattering the vision. "I said get up and start cooking us some vittles!"

Brana winced at the pain in her side when she tried to sit up. Harley yanked her off the cot by her arm, whereupon, lightheaded and dizzy, she fell to the floor.

"Get up bitch!" Harley shouted and was about to nudge her with his foot when the cabin door creaked open and Jeb entered the room.

"What the hell is going on here Harley?" he demanded.

"She's been giving me a rough time, Jeb" Harley said, clearly startled.

Jeb scowled as, helping Brana up, he saw the bruises on her face. He helped her to the cot and turned to look at Harley.

"What the hell is the meaning of this?" he demanded. "I told you she was not to be touched. Where's Santelle?"

Harley swallowed the bile that rose in his throat. "I had some problems with that one," he explained. "Yes sir, she done tried to escape, and while I was chasin' her she fell and hit her head on a sharp rock. I had to bury her with my bare hands. Yes I did, 'bout a mile down the road."

"Santelle is your business," Jeb replied. "But I told you Brana was not to be touched."

"She was tryin to get away when we were here in the cabin, so I had to stop her. Here, look what she done."

Drawing his pistol, Jeb aimed it straight at Harley.

"Quit funning, Jeb," he stammered.

"No more games…"

Brana stared at Jeb in disbelief as he slowly cocked the hammer back on the pistol. Sparks flew as he fired and Harley fell slowly to the floor with a gaping hole on the side of his head. Brana screamed.

"Weston! Cam! Somebody!" and covered her face with her hands. When she looked up, it was to stare straight into the flames where she saw the face of a woman, a familiar face which somehow brought her peace. When she heard the cabin door slam, she looked up to find that Jeb had apparently dragged Harley's body outdoors. Would he, she wondered, bury him? And then what would happen? Would she, too, be in danger of losing her life?

Jeb's gun was left it lying on the wooden table, close to her reach, slowly she went for the it, ignoring the pain she felt all over her body. The vision in the flames have given her strength to hide the gun underneath the rotting mattress. Somehow fueling her strength, she continued to look in the flames, preparing to face Jeb.

"You won't get away with this, Jeb." Brana told him. "Lacy's probably reporting you to the authorities this very minute."

"My dear girl," Jeb laughed, "report me for what? I plan to cover my tracks very carefully."

"Lacy's bound to realize by now that I'm missing." Brana said as she tried to keep her voice from quivering.

"Yes, that's true," Jeb said walking towards her. "But her heart is probably breaking right now; thinking that you and Santelle deceived her and robbed her of several hundred dollars. Ruby and I planned that part of it perfectly you know."

Brana's hands balled into a tight fist thinking of Ruby's hand in this mad man's scheme.

"Don't worry my dear;" Jeb told her grinning, "Ruby will suffer even worse than you will. Once she hears about the death of her beloved Weston, there's no telling what she might do."

"I don't believe you." Brana told him. She didn't what to believe that her beloved Weston could be dead. It's just not possible, that he would die before she could ever be with him again. And Lacy, Lacy would find her; she would never believe Ruby's treacherous lies.

"Whether you believe me or not, Weston is at the bottom of the sea feeding the fishes." Jeb said, standing directly in front of her. "As for you, you can't run from me, Brana. When I want you, I'll take you and there's nothing you can do about it."

Reaching down, he ripped her shirt open and laughed as she tried to cover herself.

"Why hide it, my dear? Tomorrow I'll see it all and taste every inch of your body. In the meantime, I'm, putting Harley underground where he belongs."

Brana clutched herself and rocked back and forth, filled with despair. Weston, dead? It couldn't be and yet she knew Jeb was capable of anything.

"I'm sorry Weston" she said sadly, letting the tears spill down her cheeks. Suddenly, she knew Jeb had killed him. Jeb would never leave anyone alive that might come to her rescue.

Her heart broke into little pieces then. Weston. The man who might have come to love her, the man who had promised to help her find her past. And now he was dead because of her. The man who held her passionately and kissed away her tears was gone forever.

She thought of Lacy, and knew her friend would never believe the vicious lies Jeb and Ruby were bound to tell about her. She could only hope that Lacy would not try to find her. It would mean her death, just as it had meant Weston's. It was difficult to believe that the man who had held her passionately and kissed away her tears was gone forever. But in heart she knew that it was true.

Brana sat quietly as Jeb entered the cabin. She could feel the gun protruding through the mattress, hoping Jeb wouldn't notice it was missing, until it was too late. She saw how Jeb cocked the trigger, pulled it back shooting Harley on the side of the head. Playing it over in her mind, she knew she had the strength to do the same, but she would aim between his black beady eyes.

CHAPTER 43

Pouring herself a cup of strong coffee, Lacy was shocked to see sunlight already pouring through the windows of La Salone. Apparently staying up all night, she was, she found, a good deal bothered. She kept going over everything in her mind once again. Harley hadn't shown his face last night and neither had Weston. She could only hope that Weston would come tonight. She wanted to find out once and for all if he was the cause of Brana's strange behavior.

"Morning, Miz Lacy." Simmons said walking in the kitchen, and from the smell of him, Lacy knew he had just come from the stables.

"It's morning, and nothing's good about it, except maybe we have some sunshine for a change," she told him.

"You want me to go see if I can find Masta Yates?" Simmons asked.

"No," Lacy told him firmly. "I need you here just in case we get a word from Brana or Santelle. I was thinking of going myself, but I'll just wait until Weston arrives. He's bound to show up sooner or later and I'll ask him for his help then."

Going back to the stables, Simmons went directly to Beauty's stall. He spoke to the horse as if it understood him.

"You know what happened to Miz Brana, don't you, boy?" he said. Beauty stomped his hooves and whinnied.

"I ain't gonna hurt you, boy," Simmons assured him. "I just want to talk to you. I knows you miss Miz Brana and so do I. Maybe effen you let me ride you and you take me where you and Miz Brana rode, I might find something important."

"Miz Brana shore loves you and I know you love her," Simmons continued getting closer to Beauty. "That's why we hafta go back and see if I done missed anything when I first went out with that old nag. You could take me to where you was when you came back without her. I know she wouldn't have left the saddle on yer back. She always took it off and rubbed you down good when she done finished her ride. We know Massa Jeb and that evil Ruby told lies about Miz Brana, don't we boy?"

No one was more astonished than Simmons when the stallion allowed himself to be mounted. As Simmons rode out of the stable, the steed picked up the pace to a fast gallop. The stable boy came to investigate the hollering he had heard in the distance.

"Why, look who's riding the devil!" the stable boy shouted to Cook's grandson as Beauty galloped past them. "It's old Simmons and

look, I bet his eyes are closed and that ain't plain old hollerin'. He's sayin'
his prayers."

"He's probably going to meet his maker the way he's bouncing off
that saddle," the stable boy said laughing. "Why, I bet his head is going to
fall off 'for his body does."

"I wonder what made him do such a fool thing," Cook's grandson
shouted. "He knows that no one can ride that ornery devil but Miz Brana.
And she's got powers to make that devil listen."

Simmons heard them mock him but he paid no heed. Beauty was
going to take him to Brana. Letting the reins drop, he clung to the saddle,
prayed that they would find her safe.

CHAPTER 44

From the deck of the ship, Weston could see that the waterfront was dancing with activity even at this late hour. Lantern light was everywhere and a light wind carried laughter and voices. As they sailed closer to the spot where they would dock, he could make out the waterfront harlots standing in the well- lit doors of their brothels. He knew them all by name, but had never cared to bed them because of the diseases they carried to the customers. Serena, however, had been different with the face of an innocent child, and a body that knew well how to please. He had grown very fond of Serena. He knew that one of her customers was violent. He had seen the results of his brutality, even though she always tried to hide them from him.

When she had told him the name of the man in question, he had been amazed that he could be found at Lacy's establishment and after several discreet inquiries, he also found out that he was none other than Lacy's husband.

He had known Lacy a long time, often playing cards and drinking at La Salone, but never had he entertained himself with gossip about her or anyone for that matter. He liked Lacy and eventually they had become good friends, respecting privacy, her past or his had never come up in any conversation. But, now he had reason to pry, the reason was Serena and the pain she had endured. Weston made it a point, when at La Salone, he would watch Jeb. The more he knew of the man, it became obvious that Jeb was vermin. It was also apparent to Weston, that Lacy was extremely distant and appeared somewhat frighten around her husband. Ruby was just the person who would tell him want he wanted to know. She did. That's when he discarded Victoria, Beth's best friend and gave all his attentions to Ruby, which was, after all, his duty to please her.

"We'll be docking in just a few minutes," the captain told him, "there are plenty of hackneys for hire at this time of night; it's earlier than I expected we would arrive."

Weston looked at the sky and noticed twilight had not been marred by the dark clouds. The stars were peaking through, with just enough light, to let the shape of moon form. The closer to docking, the more anxious he became. Rawlings would have to be taken care of first, Lacy would, no doubt, mother him until his wounds would heal. Jeb would be next, Weston had waited for the very moment until his set his eyes on Jeb, and then he would decide a fitting demise.

Thoughts of Brana clouded his vision. He would take her away immediately, settle her in with him. Then the task of finding the elusive

Cam would be the next appropriate step. He would see that Brana would be his.

"I want to thank you for taking on what other captains would have thought an impossible task." Weston told him. "If it weren't for you and your crew, Rawlings would never have survived."

Weston stood still and heard the large chain splash in the water. On the dock several hackney cabs were waiting. He would hire one to take him and Rawlings to Lacy's.

"I have to tell you that, I had my doubts about us finding anything out there in those waters," the captain told him, clasping his hands behind his back, "the deep blue mistress had shown kindness in sparing Rawlings life, but rest assured she'll be ruthless and unmerciful to the next poor soul who falls prey to her waters."

"I have no doubt of it, Captain." Weston answered.

When the ship docked, the crew shouted with joy. Going below deck, Weston found the ship's doctor tending to Rawlings burns and applying clean bandages to stop any infection.

"I'll be hiring a hackney to take him to the person that will tend to his wounds," Weston said. "He should only be uncomfortable for a short time."

"He'll be fine with the proper rest," the doctor told him, "you'll need to change that bandage. If you're lucky, infection won't set but, you'll have a big scar. Your damned temper could have had your hand lame, you would have never been able to use that hand for anything except holding a bottle up to your lips."

Weston smiled for the first time since this terrible ordeal began. He looked at his battered and bloody hand and remembered the finished bottle of whiskey, drunk with the captain. His thought of Jeb's lifeless body under his vice grip gave him excitement! Clutching the bottle tightly, it shattered into a million pieces.

"Where did captain find such an ornery doc like you?" Weston told him with amusement dancing in his eyes. "I bet your tongue alone patches up his crew."

Ha!" The doctor retorted.

"I took the liberty of hiring a hackney," the captain said as he walked into the cabin. "He'll be waiting for you and Rawlings,"

"I was just about to do that, thanks for saving me the trouble."

"You're not going anywhere you young scoundrel," the doctor told him. "At least not until I re-bandage that ugly wound."

"You'd better listen to the old man, Captain Yates," the captain said dryly. "He'll have great pleasure amputating your hand once infection starts eating your flesh."

"Um, who are you calling an old man. If it weren't for your boyish tactics at sea, I wouldn't have aged beyond my years," the old doctor said in his own defense.

"Somehow, I believe both of you," Weston replied, unwinding the bloodied bandage.

Half an hour later, Weston carried Rawlings to the waiting hackney and gently propped him on the torn leather seat. He could see the old doc and the captain standing on deck as the carriage slowly drove away into the city.

"Come on doc, I'll buy you a drink," the captain said watching the carriage turn off the docks.

"How can you sound so casual, you know there's gonna be a murder tonight!" the doc told his friend.

"I know doc, but it is a well deserved one," captain replied. "We don't need to worry we both know who the victor will be. You could see the thirst for revenge in his eyes and he'll have it."

"You otta know, it's the same demons that almost drove you to your death," the doctor scolded, remembering all too well how he had met his best friend.

The carriage ride seemed endless at the slow pace they were traveling, trying to avoid ruts in the road but it was impossible. Rawlings moaned with agony more than once, while Weston uttered oaths under his breath and yelled at the driver.

"Where are we going, Wes?" Rawlings asked.

"Lacy's" Weston replied.

"Good, I can't wait to get my hands on Jeb!" Rawlings voice was a whisper and the attempt at those few words left him breathless.

"The only thing you're going to get from Lacy's is good food and some rest," his friend told him. "You leave Jeb to me."

"I can handle myself, my friend." Rawlings whispered.

"I know you can, old man," Weston replied." But I've waited too long for this moment and I intend to make him suffer for every man of my crew that died. And this time I don't intend to underestimate him. He'll have no time to even say his prayers when I call him out."

When he reached La Salone, the driver drove to the back near the kitchen just as he had been told and, pulling the horses to a complete stop, waited for his passenger to give him further instructions.

"Wait right here." Weston told him. And to Rawlings, "I'll be right back."

"Lordly, Massa Yates. Miz Lacy's been waitin' for you!" Cook informed him, unable to hide her excitement.

"Where is she?"

"Why she's in there," Cook nodded in the direction of the gaming rooms, while she stirred whatever was boiling in a black kettle with both hands.

"Where's Simmons?" Weston asked, looking around the room.

"That fool? He's in his chamber still shakin from that ride that devil gave him. He's lucky to even be alive!"

"Cook, I need you to get Lacy and tell her to come to the kitchen. If she asks why, just tell her to come and don't say anything else."

"O.K. Massa Yates," Cook said wiping her hands on a white starched apron. "I'll go and fetch her."

Weston could hear loud laughter and glasses clinking together, and the sound of Ruby singing. He wondered if Jeb and Harley were at their usual table. Jeb would be very surprise to see him, he mused, since Jeb had no idea his plans had been foiled.

"Weston, thank god you're here," Lacy cried, appearing in the doorway, her face was etched with worry, still the same gown from the night before. "I was hoping to see you last night. Something is terribly wrong."

"Before we get into that," he interrupted her, "Rawlings is in the hackney out back. He needs to be tended to. He's weak and has burns over his body. I thought maybe you could look after him."

"What happened?" Lacy asked shocked.

"I'll tell you all about it as soon as I see to Rawlings."

"Of course. We'll go up the back stairs to the rooms above." Lacy said already at the foot of the stairs.

Weston was surprised to see that it was Brana's chamber she led him to. As he lay Rawlings on the bed, Weston's mind was flooded with memories of when he and Brana had lain there together. But there was not time for remembering now. He watched Lacy cover Rawlings as tenderly as if he were her child and offered him some brandy. Only when his friends' eyes were finally closed did he address his main concern.

"Where is that murdering son of a whore?" he asked her in a low voice. "I'm talking about Jeb. He's responsible for the loss of my ship and my crew. He plotted to murder me thinking I was aboard my vessel, but

Rawlings set sail instead of me. I should have killed the bastard long ago, but tonight he's a dead man."

Lacy's paled, looking at Weston. She held on to a wooden chair and sat down quickly. Words seemed lodged in her throat but she managed to speak, her voice trembling.

"You'd better pour me a drink." Lacy said her mouth dry.

Weston handed her a drink and Lacy swallowed it in one gulp. She held out her glass for Weston to pour her another, while her hands trembled.

"I don't know where Jeb is," Lacy told him. "We haven't seen him all day. Last night was the last time I saw him. He was gone this morning. Are you sure he's the one responsible?"

"I'm certain it was Jeb," Weston told her. "He's the only man that I know who would pay others to do his dirty work for him."

"The money!" Lacy exclaimed, "Weston, it had to be him. I was robbed last night and he and Ruby made up a story about Brana and Santelle having taken it."

"Why would he accuse them when he knew they would defend themselves?" Weston demanded.

"Weston, Brana and Santelle have been missing since all this happened." Lacy told him. Her voice quivered and he saw now that she was shaking. "I don't know where they are. Brana apparently went for an early morning ride and that beast came back to the stables saddled, but Brana was nowhere to be found. I know she wasn't responsible for the robbery, but I fear that something might have happened to her and Santelle."

When Lacy told him that Brana had disappeared, Weston clenched his fists and kicked a chair which smashed against the wall.

"Santelle came to warn me about Jeb sinking my ship," Weston told her. "She said she, heard Jeb, Ruby and Harley conspiring about something but she also said Jeb had double crossed Ruby, so we know that something else was planned. It's my conviction that he intended to take Brana all along. He wanted me out of the way so he could have her."

Weston's rage was beyond control. When he heard Ruby's laughter as she entered her chamber with a customer, he walked slowly to the door and kicked the bolted door down, scattering debris everywhere.

Ruby was sitting, half clothed on the edge of her bed, and Weston caught a glimpse of a man scuttling out the door. Ruby smiled sweetly.

"Weston darling, you startled me. Where have you been? I missed you terribly." Ruby purred.

"Where's Jeb, Ruby?"

Taken aback at the look on Weston's face. "I-I, don't know what you mean," she stammered, putting her arms around his neck. "Surely you don't think that I would have anything to do with that scum."

"I'll ask you again, Ruby." Weston growled, pushing her away. "Where is Jeb and where has he taken Santelle and Brana?"

"How should I know?" Ruby said sullenly. This was not the reunion she had anticipated.

"You know and you're going to tell me or I'll choke it out of you," Weston said, putting his hands around her throat. "Tell me where Brana is, you whore, or so help me, I'll kill you."

Ruby paled under Weston's glare and wiggled away from him.

"Brana doesn't love you, I do!" She cried hysterically, "I've always loved you. Can't you see that! What I did, I did for us. Brana is where she belongs. How dare she try and take you away from me. You're mine, and no one else will stand in my way."

"I could never love you!" Weston spat out the words. "I used you as Jeb used you to try and kill me. Your lover wanted me dead and he killed all of my crew in the attempt. You conspired with Jeb to take Brana. You told Lacy those lies about the stolen money, when you knew all along that Jeb was responsible. Santelle found out about your plan and he took her, too, didn't he?"

"You're lying," she told him, weeping now. "Jeb didn't try to kill you. He just wanted Brana. And with her gone, you would love only me. Can't you see I did it for us? No one will stand in our way now!"

Weston grabbed her by the shoulders and shook her violently. "I never told you I loved you! I love Brana. Now tell me where she is!"

"I'll never tell you where he took her," Ruby wailed. "She's probably dead at this very minute. You'll never have her Weston, never!" Lacy appeared in the doorway.

"I know where Brana is Weston," she said softly. "Jeb has her Under-the- Hill."

"Tell me how to get there!" he cried hoarsely.

"Oh god!" Lacy exclaimed. "Look behind you, Weston. "She has a gun!"

"You'll never have her Weston" Ruby said as she cocked the pistol and pointed it towards Weston's heart.

At that moment Simmons appeared behind her, holding a pitcher high in the air. When it struck her head, she fell to the floor, her eyes frozen in an expression of horror.

"Thank you Simmons, you saved my life." Weston told him. "And now I need you to go with me."

"Weston, let me go with you," Lacy pleaded. "I might be needed, in case Brana or Santelle is hurt, or you might get lost and lose precious time."

"It's too dangerous, Lacy," he told her. "I'll bring Brana and Santelle back. They'll need you here. And Rawlings needs you now."

"Come on, Simmons," he said. "Hitch the team. We're going Under-the-Hill." Weston led the way out of the room without a backward glance.

CHAPTER 45

Daylight had come and gone and Brana was waiting for Jeb to make his move but he seemed content to terrorize her. Brana sat on the cot, her hand on the lump the gun made under the straw mattress. Looking out the window she could see that the night was clear but in the distance she could see dark clouds coming closer. A wind was rising, and she could hear it blowing its way through the cracks and crevices of the shack.

Jeb was sitting with his feet resting on the wooden table, watching her every move. He was, Brana knew, taunting her, delaying the rape that she knew must come, hoping to terrorize her into resisting with all the passion she could muster.

"You sure are beautiful," he said now. "No wonder Weston took a fancy to you. Too bad he will never know what it's like to bed your luscious body."

"I think you're all talk, Jeb. You've had me here for hours and all you do is stare," Brana taunted him. Her nerves were on edge. If she waited any longer the dark clouds that were closing in would cover up the light the moon would offer to help in her escape.

"Can't wait to have me, can you Brana," Jeb said in a husky voice. "Take your clothes off. I want to make you squirm."

Jumping to his feet, he tore the shirt from her body and laughed as he saw Brana try to cover her nakedness.

"Now them boy's trousers. Take them off or I'll have to rip them off too."

Seeing that there was no helping it, Brana slowly began to remove the riding attire she had once felt so free in and threw them at him.

"Well now you little spitfire, let's see how much of a woman you really are." Jeb grabbed Brana by the hair, forced her lips to part, kissing her violently, and then threw her on the cot, while he laughed.

Brana spat at him, wiping the vile taste of him from her lips. Beneath the mattress, she felt the outline of the gun, assuring herself she could pull the trigger.

"Well, my dear, in return for that childish tantrum, I'm going to make you suffer as I have suffered all this time waiting for you."

Brana wanted to scream. She knew he was toying with her. Her head was pounding and her hands were itching to grab the gun from its hiding place, but she knew she had to be ready.

"Thinking of escaping, Brana?" Jeb said. "You should know better. No one leaves here alive. There have been plenty of women here before you who tried to do just that, let me assure you. Now if you behave yourself I might consider taking you with me. I've decided to make a new life for myself, maybe out West. These towns are getting a little too hot for me."

"You'd have to kill me Jeb," she assured him. "I'd never go anywhere with you!"

"You wouldn't have a choice." Jeb told her.

"You would have to watch you back closely, because at every turn I'd try to kill you!" Brana told him.

"I sure love defiance in a woman," Jeb replied, "you're perfect for me Brana."

Glancing out the window, Brana realized that she could no longer see the moon, for the dark clouds that were now covering it. She would never find her way to the road without the moon's guidance, but she knew she would die trying.

Lying on the cot, Brana waited for Jeb's final assault before brandishing the gun. When Jeb had turned his back for a few minutes, she managed to move the gun to the edge of the mattress. She fought her impatience to end it all, by thinking of Lacy, Weston and the love they all shared.

"I can't wait any longer, my love." Jeb told her and undid the confines of his trousers. Seeing her chance, Brana and leaped off the cot, grabbed the pistol he had used to kill Harley with, cocked and fired it, all in a single move. Clutching his chest, Jeb fell to the cabin floor.

Slipping into her trousers and what was left of her shirt, Brana made her way to the door and ran as fast as she could. Hours seemed to pass as she tore her way though the underbrush, stopping now and then to catch her breath, exhausted, her only hope that she could somehow reach the road.

And then, finally, there it was, the stones flittering in the moonlight. Turning back, she saw smoke rising from the direction she had come. But there was no time to wonder about that now. Her eyes were fixed on the rode ahead when she saw a carriage in the distance, its lanterns swinging in the wind. Exhausted, she sank down on the road and waited, for what she knew not, just as the driver reined in the horses.

The driver of the carriage reined the horses to a halt when he saw the woman lying at the side of the road.

"Damnation," he growled, jumping down off the driver's seat. He took a lantern off the hooks of the carriage and walked over to the girl. He noticed the girl was in a state of exhaustion and as he comforted her and covered her with his cloak, seeing her eyes widened, she then fainted in his arms.

"Damnation," he muttered again as he held the lantern up to the woman's face. A chain around her neck danced and fluttered in the light. He noticed the gold locket and opened it slowly, squinting his eyes as he read the inscription. He looked at her face again, and then remembered.

"Oh my God!" he cried, falling to his knees and cradling her in his arms. "You're alive, Brana, you're alive!"

"Who is it darling?" It was a woman's voice.

"It's my sister," Cameron Prescott told her. "My god, she's alive!"

CHAPTER 46

Weston covered his ears with the lapels of his woolen cloak. The rain was coming down harder, plastering his hair to his head. He could see the lanterns glowing on a carriage ahead that had been stopped in its tracks. As they passed it, they saw a man carrying someone wrapped in the man's cloak. Weston had his eyes fixed on the road ahead. Neither he nor Simmons uttered a word since the news of Brana's death. Sitting alone in the back of the carriage, Lacy's tears had not stopped falling.

Weston could not keep Lacy from joining them as they left La Salone, in search of Brana. Now, he regretted that decision. Lacy almost fainted when Jeb told her how he had enjoyed killing Brana.

When they had reached shack, Weston kicked opened the door and immediately saw Jeb on the floor, hunched over, blood draining from his body. Lacy and Simmons ran in after and called out for Brana. Weston kicked Jeb in the stomach, and punched him square in the face, splitting his lips, shattering the bone in his nose.

"No! Weston," Lacy pleaded. "Brana's not here. We need to find out where she is."

"Brana!" Weston shouted, while Jeb struggled to stand.

Jeb clutched his chest and managed to sit on the cot, blood spilling from his mouth.

"Weston, Brana and Santelle aren't here," Lacy said frantically. "Where could they be? Could they be with Harley?"

"Harley took that whore, Santelle, and all the money I stole from you!" Jeb laughed huskily, pointing to his chest. "Look here, he shot me."

"Where is Brana?" Weston growled. "Simmons go out, look around."

"Dead." Jeb coughed.

"I don't believe you!" Lacy shouted.

"Come now, wife," Jeb said, trying to sit up. "Didn't you almost die? You pocked mark bitch. Come here and let me refresh your memory on how good it was."

Weston pushed Jeb down on the cot, pinning him with his fist, pressing down directly on his wound.

"Go on, finish me," Jeb teased. "Then you can go out back, take Brana out of the grave she's in. Your precious, beautiful Brana was mine until the very end and will continue to be mine, even when I'm dead."

Simmons came running in, shouting, "Miz Lacy, Massa Weston, a dug grave is out back. It look fresh. Lordy, please say it ain't so!"

"You bastard!" Weston said as his grabbed Jeb by the throat with one hand. He didn't let go until he heard it snap.

"Lordy, lordy, not Miss Brana," Simmons cried, as he paced back and forth. Lacy was on her knees, sobbing, praying for Brana's soul.

"Let's get out of here!" Weston shouted as he walked out of the cabin.

"Go to hell where you belong, you bastard!" Lacy cried, seeing a lantern on the table, she threw it at the lifeless body of Jeb. The flames surrounded the cot quickly, and started to engulf the cabin.

Weston paced, and couldn't bring himself to look at the grave. He heard the wails of Lacy and Simmons, saying their last goodbyes at Brana's gravesite. They waited, until the flames, of evil chased them away from the burning inferno.

They had been hours on the road and Weston could see the lighting in the distance. He knew they would not make it back to La Salone before the storm.

"We ain't gonna make it before the storm hits and there ain't a place for miles we could use for shelter," Simmons informed Weston.

"A mile off the road, there's a cabin that belonged to one of my crew," Weston told him. "We can stay there until the storm lets up."

Weston led Simmons off the main road to a cabin, and from the distance they could make out smoke that came from the chimney.

Surprised, Weston pulled out his pistol and rested it on his lap, underneath his cloak. His friend went down with Devils Fire and he was in no mood to meet up with the thieves that roamed these parts. As they came closer to the cabin, he could make out the warm glow of the lantern escaping from the unveiled windows. A buckboard partially covered with canvas was nestled next to a fence. The two horses that were fenced up were prancing nervously, unwelcoming the storm. As they came to a clearing in front of the cabin, Simmons came to a complete halt.

"Nobody is supposed to be in this cabin," Weston told Simmons firmly. "Stay put."

Jumping out of the top of the carriage, he ran to the porch clenching the pistol firmly in his hand. Moving to the window with his back against the wall, he looked inside and saw a man putting logs on the fire in the fireplace. Giving the door one swift kick, he burst into the room.

"Move and you're a dead man." Weston shouted, as the man turned to face him.

"Don't try it stranger. I can shoot faster than you can throw that burning log."

"My god!" he exclaimed. "Father, is that you?"

Weston stared at the man standing by the fireplace, the fire covered him with a warm inviting glow.

A woman, sleeping, lay bundled in blankets on the bed. It was Santelle. "How did this happen?" Weston demanded, dropping the pistol, his handsome face masked with amazement. "What are you doing here? How did you find her?"

It was at that moment that Lacy and Simmons came into the cabin.

"You could say she found me," his father said huskily.

"What is this?" Lacy demanded. "Who is this man, Weston? Her eyes narrowed. "You look too much alike not to be related. Is this man, is he, your father, Weston?"

Weston looked into his fathers' eyes. "Yes, he is," he said in a low voice. "I haven't seen him since I was seventeen, when I left home."

Weston remembered that day as if it was yesterday. He could still remember the look on his mothers face as she lay in the pool of her life's blood. And remembered the harsh words he had exchanged with his father before he had realized that she had heard everything, that she knew the truth. And then she had run up the stairs, his father following, calling her name.

"I know you're in pain, son," the older man said now. "I've lived with that pain since the day you left. I ran away as you did not wanting to deal with it. But, it was always there haunting me, tormenting me, robbing me of all the good years of my life."

Meanwhile Lacy had seen Santelle.

"My God" she said as she kneeled down on the floor beside her, seeing the marks around her neck. She also noticed that she was dressed in a clean white gown and that her hair had been brushed loosely.

"How did she come here?" She demanded. "What has happened to her?"

"She came from the woods to my doorstep." Weston's father said. "She was fevered and had marks on her body. Someone had apparently attacked her and left her for dead. I can't wait for her to speak so she can tell me who did this, so that I can rid the earth of his presence."

His voice was strong and determined and Lacy saw that his hands were clenched at his side.

"That man has already been taken care of, Father," Weston told him. "He's burning in hell this very minute."

As the story unraveled, Weston's father could see the girl, Brana, meant a great deal to his son, although only Lacy mentioned her name. But every time she did, he could see his son stiffen. Lacy spared no details, except for the meeting of Brana and Weston so that he was left wondering about the girl who had entered his son's heart, the girl whose death was clearly causing him so much pain.

When Lacy was finished, Weston rose from the table, went out into the dark night beyond. Lacy and his father just looked at each other, silently agreeing to let him be alone with his grief. Lacy settled herself next to the fire. The cabin was quiet now except for the cracking of the logs in the fireplace. It was as if each person was morning the deaths of those who had died in Jeb's hands.

Weston didn't hear his father behind him. The rain now turned into a light mist which meant that the worst of the storm was over.

"Son." Weston's father rested his hand on the younger man's shoulder. "You're tired. Maybe you should try and get some rest."

Weston didn't want to close his eyes. He didn't want to dream of the love he had lost. He didn't want to dream of her face and see those big beautiful violet eyes twinkling with defiance.

"I know how you're feeling, son," his father tried to comfort him.

"You're wrong father," Weston whispered hoarsely. "You never loved Mother."

"It took me all these years to find out just how much I did love her," his father replied. "All these I've been running away from the guilt of killing the only woman that I ever really loved."

"You didn't kill her," Weston told him. "I did. I brought up the subject and she overheard."

"No Weston, you're wrong. She knew all along, it destroyed her to know that you found out. You see, I was to blame for losing her. No one else."

Weston struck the post in front of the porch with the flat of one hand. No matter what his father had told him, he knew it was because of him that his mother took her life, and he was also responsible for the death of Brana, and the crew of Devils Fire. He knew his soul could never be the same again, his heart, would never love again.

Weston's father had noticed how pale Weston was earlier, but he hadn't realized what was causing it until now. "Weston," he said. "Your hand. It's bleeding badly."

"What the hell happened?" he asked as he held the blood soaked hand in his hand.

"Just a cut," Weston replied, leaning against him for support, as his father examined his blood soaked hand.

"Let's get you inside and look at this," his father had told him. "It seems to me you've lost a lot of blood."

"Don't tell Doc," Weston told him, lapsing into delirium, "the ornery old cuss will take great pleasure in cutting it off."

"No one is going to cut it off." Weston's father said holding onto to Weston while making their way to the door.

"You don't know, Doc." Weston muttered. He held his breath as he felt burning liquid being poured on his hand. He could make out the voices of his father and Lacy, but they sounded miles away.

"This should take care of any infection that might have set in," his father told Lacy. That's one deep cut. He probably reopened it when he was fighting Jeb."

"I noticed it earlier, but I plum forgot about it," Lacy told him, brushing a lock of hair from Weston's brow. "Pour some whiskey down his throat; it will probably help him sleep. Lord knows he needs it. Poor darling. He's really had it rough."

"Your son is one of the finest men I know. You should be very proud of him."

"I've always been very proud of him," he told her, "even when he decided to leave home. He did what he thought was right at the time and I can't say that I blame him. Lacy, if it's not too painful, can you tell me about Brana, I like to know about her? I'd like to know about the girl my son fell in love with."

Lacy's eyes grew misty. She already missed her friend terribly.

"I'd love to tell you about Brana if you don't mind me crying on your shoulder occasionally."

"I wouldn't mind at all. Come out on the porch with me so that we won't disturb him or Santelle and Simmons. He's dropped off in his chair in the corner."

And so they sat through the break of dawn, talking and grieving together. Although she liked this man, she also finally understood why Weston Yates was the most ruthless man she had ever known.

CHAPTER 47

Sunshine glared through the window of the inn where Cameron had stopped for shelter from the storm. Once having settled his betrothed and her aunt in one room and Brana in another, he had spent most of the night remembering a time long ago, when he had given her a gold locket, a birthday gift, before leaving for the war. He remembered her tears and the way she had pleaded for him no go. The last visions he had of his mother, father and Brana as they hugged him tightly and said their goodbyes were flooding back to memory.

He came out of the war physically unscratched and a high ranking officer but it was when he had reached Prescott Plantation that his world came crashing down. He had heard that father had entered the last stages of war and was seriously wounded. These wounds had sent him home without a limb and crutch that would always be at his side.

It seemed like an eternity, when the war was finally over, and he, for the first time since the war began felt happiness and excitement to reunite with his family once again and made an oath to God and himself that nothing would ever tear them apart. The long journey home had been painful, burying his countrymen along the way. Their lives ended on the sides of the roads clutching to any remembrance of their loved ones.

They had been strong enough to survive the bullets and cannon fire, but not strong enough to survive against the fevers and infections that sent them to their maker. He remembered the battlefield and would always be haunted by the screams and lifeless bodies of his childhood friends and fellow soldiers who had lost their lives, in the mist of smoke from the enemies cannon fire. It was when the smoke had cleared that he recognized the faces of the proud countrymen who fought bravely for their beloved homeland.

The untainted beauty of the fields that had once been clear with green grass and sprouting flowers had been filled with death and destruction. Young and old soldiers who had fallen under the mighty cannon fire, wanted to die, begged for someone to end their suffering. It was then, that the eldest Alden, his neighbor and friend had held onto him, the tears rolled down his blackened face.

"Cameron," he whispered, "when you get home, make sure you tell Miss Brana that I'll be calling on her. She would be of age now you know, so you can't make much of a fuss."

"Don't use your strength on talking," Cameron told him. "The doc's going to be here any minute. Be strong, think of Brana."

"Think Miss Brana would accept my marriage proposal Cam? I've always carried a torch for her even if she was too headstrong for her own good." Every word was a gasp and every breath was an effort.

"I think she'll be proud to accept your proposal." Cameron said had holding a canteen of water up to his friends' lips, cradling him in his arms until the last breath of life escaped from his lips. He buried his childhood friend that day and after that all he could think of was home.

He remembered traveling the worn road and passing the Alden plantation, seeing only charred remains. Panic had gripped him as he pushed his worn horse faster in the direction of the Prescott Plantation. Turning off the road familiar sights greeted him. The huge oak trees that he had remembered before the war, still stood tall and proud. Further down he stopped and rubbed his eyes, thinking his mind was playing tricks. The plantation should have come into view by this point, but it had not. Pushing the steed into a gallop, he rode like a madman until he was there, until he saw that Prescott Plantation had too, been burned to the ground, a scream tore from his throat. Nothing left but charred pieces of wood and some of the brick chimneys.

Cameron had the bile rise to his throat as he walked in the direction of the family cemetery. Behind the trees he could see the vines covering the wrought iron gate which squeaked as he pushed it open to see the raw dirt covering three new graves, the names of the dead carved on wooden crosses. One was his fathers, another Brana' and the third, his mother.

That night he had slept on his mother's grave, awakening to a dreary sky littered with darkened clouds. Saying one last goodbye to the three people he had loved most on this earth, he had ridden towards an unknown destination, a different man that day, heartless and cold. He hated the way the south had become. Unable to stand the blue belly bastards, blatantly reminding the southerners of their loss, he decided to head out to new territory were he wouldn't have the painful reminders of all that was lost to him. And it was there in the West that he had fallen in love.

Never leaving Brana's bedside, Cameron was relieved, the doctor finally arrived after hours of fighting against the wind and the rain.

"From what you tell me, Mr. Prescott," he said now, her unconsciousness is probably due to the shock of seeing you. The bruises on her body will heal in time. She'll be sore for a few days naturally, but physically she'll be fine."

"When will she regain consciousness?" Cameron asked him.

"You're asking a question that I don't know the answer to, Mr. Prescott," the doctor said, clutching his shiny leather bag.

"Damnation, what the hell are you trying to tell me?" Cameron demanded in a raspy whisper.

"What I'm saying, Mr. Prescott, is that I don't know," the doctor said stiffly. "It must have been quite a trauma for her to see you. She's had a terrible shock, and she's clearly exhausted. She needs time to get her strength back."

"What about the bruises, can she be moved?" Cameron asked.

"I really don't think that would be wise, she doesn't appear to have any broken bones, her mental state is what concerns me, at least wait until she regains consciousness. I've done all I can for her, Mr. Prescott. The rest is up to her."

After the doctor left, Cameron sat in the chair next to Brana's bed and drifted off to more memories of his past.

"Cam." Brana's faint voice brought him out of the past and into the present.

"I'm here" he whispered.

"Water," she murmured.

Lifting her head with one strong arm, Cameron held the cup to her lips.

"Cam, I can't believe it's really you." Brana told him when she was resting against the pillow again. "I remember everything now, it was horrible. The soldiers burned down our home. They killed mother and father. Mother made me hide in the family cemetery when she saw smoke coming from the Alden Plantation. I wanted to stay with her and father but she made me go. That's when they came. Father came out with his pistol in his hand and they shot him in cold blood!"

"Hush, don't talk about it now." Cameron told her pushing back the hair from her face.

"I have to, Cam," she cried. "I have to get everything out, it's been locked up for so many years. Mother heard the shots and came outside. The soldiers carried her inside and all I could hear were her screams. I could hear Lynnie's screams too. After a few hours, the soldiers came out carrying food and our valuables and started a fire with torches. The fire spread everywhere and before I knew it the house came tumbling down with mother, father and Lynnie in it. It was horrible."

She sat up and Cameron hugged her tightly.

"I took the secret path to the Alden Plantation and hid for days," she continued, sobbing now. "I hid in the burnt rubble. That must be when I lost my memory. Cam, I hadn't been able to remember anything about my past until I saw you."

Brana put her face in her hands and sobbed uncontrollably.

"Try and rest Brana," her brother told her. Nothing's ever going to happen to you again. I'm here now." He heard a slight tapping at the door and lay Brana down so he could answer it. Just then the door opened and Bonnie appeared, a petit figure wearing a Gabriel Princess gown, with a constrained buttoned up white collar and the skirt was draped, made of grey silk. Her blond hair was pulled up away from her face, with curls cascading down the back of her head.

"How is she darling?"

"She's been through a lot," Cameron told his betrothed. "She just relived the past. She saw my father shot down and heard my mother and her servant being raped. The bastards burned the house down with them in it. Whoever buried them probably thought the servants burnt body was Brana's. She suffered amnesia all this time, until she saw me, then she remembered the horror of my parents be murdered."

"Poor darling." Bonnie said to Brana as she sat on the edge of the bed and removed the stray strands of hair from her brow. Her eyes were closed now and she was sleeping.

"Darling, why don't you get some rest?" Bonnie said. "You look exhausted. I'll stay with Brana and call you the minute she wakens."

"No," he replied, rubbing his bloodshot eyes, "her mind is in a delicate state right now. I need to be here when she wakens. She's never seen you before and who knows what she's suffered. She just regained her memory, I will be better if she sees me here when she wakens."

"I'll stay too." Bonnie told him firmly. "She'll be my sister in a few months and I want to help in any way that I can." Bonnie told Cameron in a firm tone.

She knew the joy he felt at finding his sister but before the day was out he would also feel heartbreak and morn the tragedy of his past, one more time.

Cameron threw her a kiss as he sat down on the chair next to Brana's bed. Looking down at his sister, he saw the same child he had seen before he left for the war, her beauty ripened, matured. He clenched his fist when he looked upon the purple bruise on the side of her jaw, aware of a rising burning rage. She had been running from somebody and he wondered if it had anything to do with the burning fire he had seen in the field from the road they were traveling. But he would not ask her yet. Instead he would wait until she was ready to tell him. Something terrible must have happened to her and he felt helpless in not being able to help her cope with it. He decided to put his business on hold and take her to their home. He would book passage on a ship as soon as possible and take Brana away from here. She needed him and this time he would be there for her, vowing never to let anything bad ever happen to her again.

CHAPTER 48

"Well, at least the sun is shining today." Lacy told Weston when he woke from a deep sleep, head throbbing, a foul taste in his mouth. His hand hurt him even more that it had the night before.

"I've got to get out of here. I need to see to Rawlings and I need to tell the families of my crew members of their fate."

He sat up on the bed and dizziness washed over him. The color seemed to drain from his face.

"You're in no condition to go anywhere," Lacy scolded him. "You lost a lot of blood with that open wound. You're damned lucky you didn't bleed to death." Lacy was exhausted but she could not rest. Santelle, waking earlier, had managed to tell Lacy what had happened, warning her to get to Brana before Jeb did. Lacy relived the nightmare all over again, telling Santelle about their journey, holding Santelle in her arms as she wept for Brana. As for Lacy, she could no longer cry. The tears had simply been drained out of her leaving a hollow emptiness inside.

Weston determined to muster enough strength to stand on his two feet. He weaved as he stood but made it to the washbasin on top of a worn table that sat against the wall. Splashing cold water on his face, he ran his fingers through his hair.

"I'll be fine," he said as he pushed aside the rug that was used to separate the rooms. Sitting across from Lacy, in a chair that was next to the fire, he poured himself a cup of coffee. They both sat in silence. The creaking door was the only noise that was heard as Weston's father entered the cabin carrying more logs for the fireplace.

"Even though the sun is shining, there's a cold frost in the air," he told the two sitting silently. "How are you feeling Son?"

"My hand is not bleeding and after I have this cup of coffee, I'll be on my way."

"Want me to come along?" he offered.

"No, this is something I have to do by myself." Weston's said in an emotionless voice. "How's Santelle?"

"She'll be fine after some rest." Lacy said looking at the sleeping Santelle.

Weston put the empty coffee tin down and rose to his feet, grabbing his cloak that was hanging on a hook behind the door.

"I'll make sure that La Salone is closed down tonight." He told Lacy and headed for the door. Riding off on the muddy road, Weston took a deep breath and never looked back. Thoughts of Brana clouded his mind and he reached into his pocket for the silk blue ribbon he carried, but only to find it was gone. Only the horse could hear the oaths he muttered under his breath as he pushed his steed to a gallop, leaving Natchez behind him, he raced with the devil to reach Vicksburg by mid afternoon, trying to ignore the pain in his hand. When, finally turning on the road which led to his office, he noticed the Jackson's Phaeton carriage in front of his office.

"Weston," Beth cried as he leaped off his horse. "It's been all over town that Devils Fire is at the bottom of the sea. Is it true?"

Finding that he could not unlock the door, Weston kicked it open, startling Beth and her maid.

"Be warned woman, you're trying by patience!" he shouted.

"How dare you speak to me in that tone? It's your entire fault my Rawlings sailed to his death. You should be at the bottom of the sea with your men instead of him."

Weston turned away from her and took several deep breaths to try to control his anger.

"What do you want Beth?" he demanded. "As you know, I have a lot of work to do. I'm leaving right now to see the families of my crew."

Weston opened the safe and pulled out several pouches containing gold coins.

"Just what do you think you are doing with that money?" she cried, stamping one slippered foot. "I'm entitled to that money, no one else. My betrothed was killed on that voyage and I want what's due to me!"

Weston turned and stared at her in disbelief. A devilish grin formed on his lips and his laughter echoed throughout his office. "My dear," he managed trying to contain his laughter, "you would not even be entitled to bury his remains. He told me that you broke off the engagement when he decided to set sail."

"That's not true." Beth protested. "You're making it up so you won't have to compensate me for my loss."

"Even if it weren't true, I wouldn't compensate you for anything," Weston said in a serious tone. "The family of my crew deserve to be compensated, no one else."

Putting the pouches in the pocket of his cloak, made his way to the door, pushing Beth to one side.

"You can't do this, Weston," she warned him. "My daddy will see that I get everything. He'll prove you negligent by sending an inexperienced captain to sail. You sent everybody to their deaths."

Weston stopped in his tracks and listened to Beth, he shook his head at the greed in her voice and turned to face her.

"Don't meddle in my business, Beth," his voice was dry and deadly. "That could prove to be unhealthy."

"It would never need to get that far if you give me Rawlings half of the business," Beth was pleading with him now. "He would have wanted me to be taken care of. After all, no man would consider courting me now, knowing my heart had been broken."

"Don't worry, Beth; I'm sure you'll get what's coming," Weston told her dryly. He turned to leave and then turned back to tell her one more thing. "Oh, by the way," he said. "I hate to disappoint you, but Rawlings was the only one to survive the attack."

The color drained from Beth's face. Grabbing a crystal decanter off the desk, she threw it at the wall where it shattered into a thousand little pieces, liquor splattered everywhere.

"Oooh!" she screamed shaking her whole body. How would she ever explain her behavior to Rawlings? He would never take her back once Weston told him what she did. She didn't even know where he was, so she couldn't get there and explain her actions before Weston.

"Pox, on you Weston Yates!" she hissed before taking her little servant's arm.

Weston was on his way to Lacy's after finishing the terrible task of telling the families of his crew the bitter news. Darkness was beginning to engulf the city and he wanted to arrive before Lacy's customers did. He couldn't remember when he had had his last meal but as hungry as he was, he knew he knew he could not eat a bite. The bright lights that usually came from La Salone at this hour were dim and the outside doors were shut tight. Going around to the back, he found the door to the kitchen open and Cook was nowhere in sight. He continued his way to the bar area and saw Rawlings sitting on a stool, hunched over what appeared to be a brandy bottle.

"Should you be up and about?" Weston questioned as he helped himself to the bottle of brandy.

"Did you find Brana and Santelle?" Rawlings asked. He looked at Weston and could see redness around his eyes.

"We got there too late, old boy." Weston told him

"Jeb had already left?"

"Jeb's in hell and before he died he killed Brana." Weston took another gulp of whiskey. He tightened his lips as the liquid left a burning trail.

"Santelle, too?"

"She's lucky to be alive," Weston told him. "She's with Lacy."

"Sorry my friend," Rawlings said taking the bottle Weston put down on the bar and pouring himself another drink. Since he had overheard everything that was said in Ruby's chamber, he knew Brana was the girl that had been in his thoughts. Brana had been the girl Weston had fallen in love with.

"What are you doing out of bed?" Weston asked his friend.

"I wanted to close up the place, but don't worry about me. It's you that I'm worried about. What happened to your hand?"

"Don't worry about me, I'll survive," was all Weston could say before he took another drink. He needed the burning liquid to ease the lump he felt in his throat.

"I'm sure the town knows about the fate of Devil's Fire." Rawlings said, "I know how you feel about Beth, but if you could just get word to her that I'm alright, I'd be truly grateful."

"You really love her, don't you?" Weston asked quietly.

"I can't explain it, Wes" Rawlings said "I really don't think it's up to us to pick and choose who hold our hearts."

Weston listened, and nodded. He couldn't tell Rawlings about Beth, her behavior. "She was waiting for me when I rode to the office. She had heard about Devil's fire and knows now that you're alive."

"She must have been grief stricken when she found out about attack."

"She was grief stricken all right." Weston managed. He would let Beth explain her actions

He saw something in Rawlings eyes, he wondered if his eyes had shone that brightly for his true love, Brana.

"The authorities didn't question anything about Ruby's death," Rawlings informed him. "Simmons has no need to worry."

Customers were banging at the door, but both men ignored them, intent on their own affairs.

"How's Lacy handling everything?" Rawlings asked. "It seemed to me that she and Brana were mighty good friends."

Weston stiffened at the mere mention of Brana's name.

"Lacy's a survivor," he said. "She'll be O.K. in time. I guess I should go home since everything here is under control and you should get back into bed."

"Wes, if you want to talk about it, you know where to find me," Rawlings told him. "You saved my life, my friend and I could never repay you for it. If it weren't for you, I would have fed the sharks. I'll never forget it."

Rawlings clearly weakening had trouble lifting himself off the stool. Then, with Weston's help, he was on his feet, he looked directly at his best friend. "Don't blame yourself," he said. "You were against a mad man, Wes. You could never have known what he plotted with that bitch, Ruby."

Weston didn't speak as he helped Rawlings up the stairs, feeling that if he spoke he would lose all control. He knew Rawlings was trying to help him ease the guilt he felt. But Rawlings had been unsuccessful. He would live with the fact that he made one mistake, underestimating the man who was the enemy, that he should have taken heed of Rawlings warning about Ruby falling in love with him.

Rubbing the stubble on his face, he opened the door to Brana's chamber, although he couldn't bring himself to go in. He tried, not to remember the passion he and Brana had shared but her perfume lingered in the air, overcome with emotion, he hurried. All he wanted now was dreamless sleep.

CHAPTER 49

"Cam," Brana said "When Jeb kidnapped me, when I knew he was going to-to attack me, it was mothers' voice I always heard. I actually saw her face in the flames. I didn't know who it was then because I didn't have my memory. But now I know it was mother all along who gave me the strength to escape."

Brana was physically better after a week's rest at the inn but she couldn't bring herself to tell Cam about Weston. She had told him everything about Lacy finding her and taking her under her wing. And she told him about Jeb, what he had done and how he had conspired with Ruby and Harley. She told him, with tears in her violet eyes, about the ship he had sunk and the men who had lost their lives because of her. Cameron was ready to do battle for his sisters' honor, but Brana told him that Jeb and Harley were dead. Titling her delicate chin, she told Cameron that it was her fingers that had pulled the trigger and sent Jeb's soul to burn in hell.

Brana had not left her chamber at the inn taking her meals there with Cameron and Bonnie. The bruises on her body were fading but Cameron was worried about her mental state. Sometimes she just sat staring into space with tears running down her cheeks. They couldn't bring her out of her depression. She barely nibbled at her meals and at night he could hear her muffled cries. He felt helpless and raged at the thought of her suffering, and swore that she would never suffer again. He would take her home to live with him and Bonnie and they would be a happy family once again.

"Darling, I think Brana's holding something back," Bonnie told him as they wandered through the rose garden behind the inn. "I fear she might have lost the man she loves. I think he was on the ship that sank."

"What makes you say that?" Cameron asked her.

"When she told us about it sinking, I saw something in her eyes." Bonnie explained. "I saw pain and heartbreak. I'm fairly sure it was the captain she lost her heart over."

Bonnie could see the look of fury on Cameron's face. She still couldn't get over the resemblance the brother and sister shared. They had the same milk white skin and startling blue black hair color. Cameron's eyes being aqua blue and Brana's violet. Of course, as where Brana was petite, Cameron was well over six feet, towering over both of them. When in a rage, his eyes become cloudy and stormy, almost the color of the turbulent sea, and just as deadly. He was not a man to toy with and most who knew him steered clear of his wrath.

"I guess I'm lucky the sea took care of him for me." Cameron said now, suppressing his anger with an effort.

"What do you mean?" Bonnie hissed. "Surely you don't know what you're saying Cameron! We're talking about the man your sister loves. Why on earth would you want to harm him?"

"You heard what she's been through," he told her. "If the captain felt any love for her, he would have made sure that she was safe from the bastards that took her. Besides, she has me to look after her now. She doesn't need anyone else."

"Cameron, Brana is not the child you left before you went off to the war," Bonnie argued, cheeks flushed. "She's a grown woman and you have no right to treat her like a child."

"I have every right," he told her grimly. "I'm the only one she has left and I'll make sure she never hurts again. I wasn't there when she needed me most, and by God, no one or anything will come between us again."

"I know you love her, Cameron, but don't try to shelter her," Bonnie insisted "I can't believe you can be so pigheaded. She loved this captain, I hate to think what you would do once she starts receiving gentlemen callers. Your sister, my darling, is too beautiful and spirited to live the life of a lonely spinster."

"You leave Brana's welfare to me," Cameron said roughly, his patience running out. "I have decided to book passage on the next ship out of Vicksburg. I want her away from here as soon as possible. I intend to put my business on hold for a while. And now, if you'll excuse me, I want to talk to my sister alone."

And leaving Bonnie staring after him, he hurried inside and up the stairs to Brana's chamber, finding her sitting up in bed, staring at the quilted bedcovers, clearly miles away in thought.

"Cam, I didn't hear you," she said when he sat down beside her and took her hand. "I was just thinking about how safe I feel now that you're here." Brana attempted a smile, as she looked at her brother.

"I'll always be here for you, Brana," he assured her, taking note of the dark circles under her eyes. "I was thinking of booking passage on the next ship bound for home. Do you think you're up to traveling?"

"Yes, Cam. I'd like nothing better than to get far away from here," Le she replied.

"It's settled then. And I want you to put everything that has happened here behind you" Cameron told her sternly.

Brana thought of Weston. She would never forget him. He would always be in her thoughts as well as Lacy, Santelle, Simmons, and Cook. She would never be able to put her past behind her. It was burned into her memory and every waking hour she could see the piercing blue eyes haunting her. He had left a void in her heart that no man would ever be able to fill.

Cameron could see a veil of mist clouding her eyes and realized the truth of what Bonnie had told him. Brana was suffering and it was up to him to take her away from a place that clearly held so many painful memories.

"I'll be fine Cam, really," she assured him.

As soon as he left the inn to make arrangement for their voyage, Bonnie joined Brana.

"Now that Cameron isn't here to eavesdrop on our conversation, do you want to tell me about the love you lost?" Bonnie asked affectionately.

Startled by her openness, Brana covered her face with her hands and gave way to her tears. She felt Bonnies' arms wrap around her tightly and patting her back in comfort.

"Oh Bonnie," Brana cried between sobs. "I feel terrible. Because of me, the man I loved and other innocent people were murdered. How can I ever forgive myself?"

"Don't blame yourself, honey," Bonnie told her, handing her a lace trimmed handkerchief. You're not to blame for anything that happened under Jeb's hands. There could have been no way you could have known what he was planning. There now, dry your tears and tell me about the man you fell in love with." Bonnie questioned.

"Was it that obvious?" Brana choked out the words.

"I'm afraid it was, my dear. You might feel better if you talk about it."

"Well, there's really not much to tell. He was the handsomest man I have ever seen, besides Cam of course. I really despised him when we first saw each other."

Bonnie could see Brana's cheeks redden. She arched her brow and continued listening to the intriguing story.

"And that's when I found out he wasn't the rogue I had thought him to be." Brana told her. "Oh Bonnie, my heart aches for him. I never even knew what it was like to be in love until he entered my heart. He could have all the women he wanted, but I really believe he loved me."

"He sounds like quite a rogue, but probably as gentle as a little kitten. Tell me, what did he look like."

When Brana described Weston, Bonnie had a strange feeling that he was someone she knew.

"What's his name?" Bonnie asked.

"It doesn't matter," Brana told her. "He's gone forever.

Bonnie did not pursue the subject, not wanting to upset her new friend. Besides, it was impossible that he should have been anyone she had known. But something else occurred to her.

"Brana," she said. "Have you ever given it thought that you might be with child? Have you had your monthly?"

Brana put her hand to her lips and gasped. It had never even crossed her mind that she could possibly be carrying Weston's child. She felt a surge of joy run through her at the possibility that she might be with child. She would at least have a part of Weston to remember the love they had shared.

"There hasn't been time for me to even suspect something like that," she said eagerly. "Do you really think I could be carrying his child? Nothing would make me happier knowing a part of him still lives."

"If it is true, I don't know how your brother will react," Bonnie warned her. "He still sees you as the child you were before he left for the war. I understand why you might want a child but Cam won't handle the news well I'm afraid."

"He'll l just have to get used to the idea that I'm a grown woman now," Brana said defiantly. "He can't treat me like a child!"

Bonnie could see the resemblance of Cam, not only in her face but in her spirit.

"He just needs a little time," she told her, hoping that it was true. "After all, it was a shock for him to find you alive. You know how stubborn he can be, but I'm sure he'll come around." "Let's not worry about anything until we know for sure," Bonnie said, taking Brana's hand. "Then when the time comes, we'll handle Cam."

"You've been so good to me, Bonnie!" Brana held onto Bonnies' hand. "I know mama and papa would have been proud to have you in our family. I'm so happy he has found you. He told me you have changed his life. You gave him a reason to live and I'll always be grateful for all you've done for him. He really loves you Bonnie and I'm happy for the both of you."

Bonnie and Brana hugged each other, knowing the bond they shared would never part them.

Cameron had returned to the inn, the front desk informed him about a letter that was to be delivered to Lacy, in Vicksburg. A note was attached, thanking him in advance for the delivery. Brana's writing had never changed, he mused, and put the letter in his pocket. He would destroy it in the privacy of his chamber. Lacy and her brothel would remain in Brana's past, he would make sure of it.

Before entering Brana's chamber, he could hear Bonnie and Brana chattering noisily. The tales of his courtship were told, as he was able to ascertain upon hearing some of the conversation.

"I'm glad to see that you two are enjoying yourselves," Cameron observed. "I hope you're not doing so at my expense."

"Forgive me, darling, but Brana wanted to know about our courtship and I told about the times you made an utter fool of yourself," Bonnie explained.

"It's a side to you I've never seen before," Brana told him. "Did you actually sing love songs under her window? Cam, I never thought you were the romantic type."

"I only have to say one thing to say, it worked didn't it. Now before I leave you two," he said. "I have some good news. Tomorrow we set sail for home and it looks like we'll have a good voyage with the weather clearing up. Bonnie, make sure your auntie is ready. Brana, will you be O.K.?" he questioned.

Brana was silent, she would miss her life here, as tough as it was at times, and knew that she needed to be with Cam now. But one day, she knew in her heart, that she would find a way to return to Lacy and La Petite Salone.

CHAPTER 50

"Well Wes old boy, do you know when you'll be returning?" Rawlings asked his friend. "I kinda got use to having you around."

"I really don't know for sure," Weston told him. "I'll probably stay awhile and get reacquainted with my family. I can't wait to see the look on my sisters' face when she sees me returning with my father. We should be there just in time for her wedding."

Weston propped his feet on the polished wooden desk and leaned back on the chair as he exhaled the smoke from his cheroot. The months since Brana's death had been painful so he had decided to sail home with his father. Any distraction would be welcome, he decided, as he agreed to accompany his father home to San Francisco to attend his sister's wedding even though all he could really think of now was his loss.

"I still can't believe he was the one that found Santelle," Rawlings reminded him." At least one good thing came out of that terrible ordeal. "You and your father were reunited. Sorry Wes, I didn't mean to remind you of what happened."

Assuring him that it did not matter, Weston hurried out and mounted his horse only to find his way blocked by a Phaeton, Beth toyed with the reins, a straw bonnet tied under her substantial chin. Her young maid sat next to her, holding a parasol, chatting boisterously. Weston snarled at Beth as she got out of the carriage.

"Good day, Weston," she said sweetly.

"It *was* a good day." Weston said sarcastically. But, as he had long since discovered, it was impossible to insult Beth.

"I'd like to thank you for not telling Rawlings the details of our last conversation," she said now, twirling her frilly parasol her maid had handed her. "I really don't know what came over me. I hope you realize I wasn't myself."

"Save your explanations, Beth," he told her. "We both know it was greed that came over you and nothing else. I'm sure you'll be glad to know that I'm leaving town."

"I have to admit I am glad, and frankly, I don't know why you waited so long," she said boldly. "You're an unscrupulous scoundrel and this town is lucky to be rid of you!"

Weston, leaning back on his saddle laughed.

"At least I'm willing to admit what I am," he said. "I'm sure you would never admit what you really are, Beth. You saw Rawlings as a meal ticket, nothing more. Your actions were clear enough. And frankly, Beth, even I was fooled by your charade, you were annoying, yes, but I never thought you would be unprincipled. Keep in mind, Rawlings is no fool, he'll catch on, sooner of later."

"How dare you!" she exclaimed and then forced a smile when she heard Rawlings approaching.

"You two are finally putting the past behind you."

Weston laughed rode off, unwilling to inform Rawlings of who Beth Jackson really was. Although, he left explicit instructions with his solicitor, should Beth start to meddle in the business, he was to be notified immediately, and would return, putting Beth in her place once and for all. He would spend his last hours in town with Lacy. Busy with his own plans, he had let her grieve, without intruding, understanding her pain and torment.

"I'll miss you, you rogue," Lacy told him tearfully. She and Weston had a bond like none other. They had both lost an innocent love and shared in their grief.

"I'll be back," Weston told her, knowing Beth the way he did, he was sure of it. "I just don't know when. It will do me good to get away for a while and spend some time with my family."

"Don't stay away too long," she said, sniffing. "The place won't be the same without you losing at cards,"

"You take care of yourself and make sure you watch after old Simmons," Weston said as he turned to leave.

"Wes, one thing, has always been puzzled me," she said clinging to his arm. "When did you and Brana first see each other? I know it wasn't on the ground floor of La Salone." Lacy arched her brow and looked at Weston.

"That's something you will never know." Weston said playfully and kissed her one last time.

Weston and his father grew even closer during their voyage to San Francisco. They shared a mutual love for the sea as their ancestors, who had built a rich empire in the import and export business, had before them. Weston realized that he and his father shared many things in common. Neither of them had ever about the wealth they had inherited, both of them content to make their own fortunes.

Weston and his father had booked passage on the same ship that had gone to search for the crew of Devil's Fire. Weston respected the captain and crew and paid handsomely for their passage home, and in the weeks during their voyage, he had even got used to the rows he had with the old doc.

"I didn't give you this sooner but I believe this belongs to you," the captain told Weston as he handed him the blue silk ribbon he thought he had lost.

"I found it the day you left. It was under the covers on my bunk. I'm assuming you left it there the day you cut your hand. Am I wrong?"

"It-it's a keepsake, "Weston told him. "Thank you for saving it,"

Holding the ribbon to his lips, Weston could still smell Brana's scent. He would never forget her. The ribbon brought back memories of her defiance and the color of her eyes flashing in anger, as well as the way she had yielded to his caresses.

"I love you, Brana," he managed to whisper. Sea mist sprayed on his face, covering the tears in his eyes. No one heard his confession of love as the waves of the sea crashed loudly on the vessel. He stood alone, remembering his beautiful temptress, when his father interrupted him.

"Son, you were right," his father said. "That old doc is the devil in disguise. He could beat me at cards blindfolded. He's just as sharp with cards as he is with his tongue."

And then, seeing that Weston's thoughts were far away, he put his hand on Weston's back to comfort him from the pain he knew would never heal. They both stood at the rail listening to the sounds of the sea they both had heard so many times before and looking into the icy blue depths of her soul.

Weston's father broke the silence, "We should be home in several days if the weather holds. Your sister is going to be so happy when we both arrive. She's probably fit to be tied because I haven't shown up. She made a promise that she wouldn't get married until I return. She's really grown up to be a beautiful woman, Weston. She's so sensible and proud, just like your mother. I'm sorry I missed out on all her growing years. But I'm not running anymore. I'm too old and tired. I'm going to be the father to her I should have been years ago."

"At least we'll be a family again, even if it's only for a little while," Weston said with an expressionless voice.

"Son, I was hoping you would change your mind and stay. You could run the family business. God knows I've left it for other people to manage far too long, but I think it's time we carry on the tradition."

"I'm sorry but right now I just don't feel like staying in one place for very long," Weston told him.

Weston's father held out hope, thinking that once Weston returned, he would have a change of heart. Lots of good memories were shared there, in a beautiful home over looking San Francisco bay, and prayed that maybe those would be the memories that would keep him home. Weston had remembered his childhood during the happy times, but he could never forget the image of his mother's dead body and the guilt that went along with it.

"Well, you don't have to make a decision now," his father told him. "You might just decide to change your mind." Weston's father was ready to walk away, but turned to his son and said, "It's been a long day; I think I'll turn in. Tomorrow we'll be in port and I have to send a message to your sister announcing our arrival."

"I'm going to stay up a little longer," Weston told him. "I'll see you in the morning."

Knowing that sleep would never come, pulling out the ribbon, he drew it between fingers, remembering the day he picked it up when it had fallen from her silky hair. And the he remembered the sharp sting of her slap and chuckled. He remembered the look of surprise on her face when he first kissed her. She was a passionate little flower that had bloomed under his touch. He put the silk ribbon back in his cloak pocket he headed for his cabin.

"Home," he said as he sat on the bunk and rubbed his hand under his chin.

CHAPTER 51

The horses raced on the green meadow, and the brilliant sun was beating down on the bay. A women's laughter sent a flock of birds scattering away in different directions, they squawked loudly at their displeasure. Although, enjoying his ride with his betroth, Bonnie, Cameron Prescott could not ease the frown of concern on his face.

"Darling, would you like to continue, or have you had enough for today?" Bonnie asked him with concern in her voice. Her deep green velvet riding habit shone as brightly as her eyes, the rich gold of her hair shone brightly through a green velvet ribbon that kept it in place. A few strands of gold managed to escape and frame her delicate face. Her cheeks had reddened from the playful rays of the sun, and the tip of her nose began to freckle.

"Are you tired my dear?" Cameron asked. He knew he had found a rare treasure indeed in Bonnie Yates. Her beauty was beyond that of a goddess, and her slender form had curves of perfection. Her smile lit her whole face, showing her feelings of love for all those she cared for.

"No," Bonnie said. "It's you who looks exhausted, Cam. I heard you pacing in your room all night. I am worried about you."

The war had left Cameron a bitter man. He had thought all was lost to him -- his family, his home, and all his friends who had died on the battlefields for a cause that had been lost. Bonnie had redeemed him, given him the gift of happiness but now, having found Brana, the past had come back to haunt him.

"I guess I'm just worried about Brana," he told Bonnie now. "She should have recovered by now. But she's still pale and she's not eating well. Perhaps I should have a doctor look at her."

Bonnie's heart went out to him. And the same time, she couldn't possibly tell Cameron the truth about Brana's condition until Brana was ready to tell him herself.

"Darling," she said now, " I know how much you love Brana and I know all you want to do is have her up and about feeling better, but she did tell you once before she didn't need to see a doctor. You know she can be quite stubborn, and I don't think she would appreciate it if you went against her wishes."

The weeks they had been home Brana remained in her chamber. She ate only a few morsels during the day and a few more at night, leaving her pale and weak.

"You're right, Bonnie," Cameron agreed. "I suppose I'm just being a little over-protective again. And I really don't feel like having another row with my dear sister. She's been through a terrible ordeal. We all have to be patient, I guess."

"I know that's difficult for you," Bonnie teased him. "Come along, Cam. Let's ride a bit further."

"I'm sorry, my pet, but I have to get back to business. I didn't intend to oversee you father's business this long, but now I have no choice but to make the major decisions in the shipping company. I hate to put business before pleasure but there are a few things at the office that I just can't put off until tomorrow."

Cameron smiled and Bonnie's heart melted as she saw that familiar twinkle in his eyes.

"Darling, why do you feel we have to wait until Father returns to take our wedding vows. I really wouldn't mind if we married tomorrow. I love you so much."

Bonnie edged her horse closer to Cameron's and took hold of his hand. She wanted to be his wife in every way and couldn't wait for the pleasure he would bring her. A few stolen kisses she knew were not enough now. She needed him to be her husband.

"I would love nothing more than to marry you tomorrow, my lovely," Cameron told her, "but the last time your father came for a brief visit, you promised him you would wait until he returned to take your wedding vows. It means a lot to him, and I owe him that much. If it weren't for his help in getting me started in the business, I don't know how I would have managed thus far. It's been torture for me not having you share my bed, but we just have to be a little more patient. I'm sure he'll be home soon."

Cameron bent over and gave her a long lingering kiss. Desire shot through him like fire. Controlling his emotions, he quickly pulled away, leaving is heart aching for more.

"I give him no more that one month," Bonnie told him. "If he does not show up you will be my husband with or without my father's presence."

Bonnie looked at him defiantly, and Cameron couldn't help himself from chuckling. He knew she was becoming more and more like Brana every day, probably because they chatted for hours on end. Heaven help him, but he liked the change in Bonnie. Some of Brana's defiance had definitely rubbed off on her.

"I have to agree, my pet," he said. "Now we'll ride to the house. I must get to the office, but before I do, I 'd like to check on Brana."

Brana watched through her chamber window as the two rode back to the house. The happiness they shared made her think of Weston, whom she loved with all her heart. Every waking hour she could see his face, smell his scent, and feel him making love to her. The mere reminder of his lovemaking made her shiver. Just the thought of carrying Weston's child brought a warm glow to her cheeks. The man she loved would always be a part of her.

When Cameron joined her, she threw her arms around him and hugged him tight.

"I'm glad to see you in good spirits this morning," he said. "You're looking better today, there's more color in your cheeks."

"I feel fine, and I'm in a wonderful mood. I'm in such a great mood, that I'll even take a stroll around the grounds and see what I've been missing for weeks."

Going to her armoire, Brana chose a skirt of dark pink silk, the apron attached was a lighter pink color, trimmed with white lace around the hem line. The apron accentuated a tiny waistline, however, the apron ties were long enough to go around her waist twice, leaving a smart bow tied in front which she held up on front of her for Cameron to see. The gown must have been Bonnie's idea, she thought.

"Well Brana, I'm happy to see you're feeling much better today," Bonnie said, coming into the room. "Cameron has been beside himself with worry about you, dear."

Both of them tried to avoid speaking of her pregnancy directly. For the time being, at least, Brana was willing to accept Bonnie's reasoning which was that Cameron had too much on his mind just now.

"As you can both see, I'm fine, and well on my way to a speedy recovery, so you don't have to worry any longer Cam," Brana said "I feel wonderful."

"That's a load off my mind Brana, but don't overdue it, "Cameron told her. " Assure me that once you feel the least bit fatigued you will rest."

"You have my word, brother dear. Lord knows it's been way too long since I've dressed for dinner. This is what I will be wearing tonight!"

"I'm delighted that take it my two favorite ladies will be joining me for dinner tonight. Until tonight, ladies."

Bonnie began helping Brana pull gowns of every color from her armoire, laying them on the bed. Bonnie wanted to approach the subject about the pregnancy, but didn't have the heart, since this was the first time she had seen Brana full of energy, happiness shinning in her eyes. "Oh Brana, you look lovely," Bonnie told Brana as she adjusted the ties around her waist. "I'm glad you stuck with the pink. Your hair is so shiny and black, I'm envious."

"Bonnie, I really wouldn't know what to do without you," Brana giggled. "What a creative idea you have invented with the length of this ties, just enough material for a nice size bow right in the front. Cam will never even have to know until I give birth."

"Now Brana, you have to tell him. I was hoping you'd take the chance I gave you earlier. You know how much I hate deceiving your brother. He's been really worried about you and he almost went against your wishes and if I hadn't argued him out of it, he would have called on a doctor this afternoon. But seriously, Brana, how do you think he's going to feel when he finds out the truth? He may never speak to me again!"

"I'm sorry for putting you in this uncomfortable situation, Bonnie, but I'm just not ready to tell him yet," Brana told her. "You and Cam are so happy. I just don't want anything to spoil it. I really hope you understand and don't hate me for it."

"Of course I wouldn't hate you," Bonnie said, hugging her tight. "Here now, let's not spoil your mood. Let's take our walk on the grounds and hope you work up an appetite. Cameron will be so pleased."

"I'm so glad you'll be my sister soon," Brana told her. "Have you heard when your father will be arriving? Cam told me you promised to wait until he arrived before marrying."

"I hope he arrives within a month's time because Cameron and I will be married if he doesn't," Bonnie told her. "I should have never promised him that knowing my father the way I do."

"I can't believe he would prefer traveling the seas instead of enjoying his wealth. It must have been very lonely for you when he was away. I can't believe he would do that to his only child."

"I'm not his only child," Bonnie replied. "I have an older brother."

CHAPTER 52

Derek Lancer had lived in the South, but not as one of the perfect gentlemen the South was known for. In fact, his poor family had endured more hardships than some of the slaves who depended on their masters for food and a place to live. At times he and his family had come close to starving, thanks to the fact that Derek's father had deserted them. And then fever had swept the valley and within days, at the age of fifteen, he had been orphaned.

When he read about the gold being found in the West, he signed on board a ship that was bound for San Francisco, as a cabin boy. Surviving off hard tack and stale bread, he endured his new home, with dreams of riches. As the sea tossed and heaved, he groaned, prayed with every violent turn that gold was well worth his suffering.

His journey at sea was not half as bad the privation he faced in a lawless town. Camps were crowded with drunks and migrants, and whores, flaunting their wares. Murder was common, as tempers flared for those who dreams were about to end. He never gave up, tried of being dirt poor; he worked day and night until he would find enough nuggets to maintain a crude shack for weeks at a time. Weeks went into months and months went into years, still searching for his precious gold but the nuggets only toyed with him, keeping him alive through the rush. He saw hopefuls come in groves, but left quietly in despair, in worst hardships then, when arriving. He met many people but kept few friends, one of whom, a ship's owner name Yates, whose family transported goods from every port in the world, had changed his life, often treating Derek more like a son than his own heir, Weston, a handsome, arrogant boy who Derek came to hate.

Derek almost gave up his search for his beloved gold when Yates convinced him to pull up stakes and try mining another spot, one know of be full of dangerous gases, hidden in the hills. Men had mined there before, but most seemed to die of strange afflictions before finding any evidence of the gold that was supposedly hidden there.

Derek took the advice and went with Yates to find his treasure. And when they did, everyone in the town could hear their shouts of joy. It was the biggest strike the town had ever seen.

Derek became one of the richest and most powerful men in the city. Still a young man, in his early twenties, he bought land, women, hotels and anything else that came his way. Life was good to him in San Francisco where times had changed, bringing law and order.

When Derek saw Weston in town, they were barely civil to each other. Weston's father told Derek that Weston felt jealous of his interest in him, Derek shrugged it off. And when, after his mother's death, Weston had gone back East, Derek had been glad to see him gone. Weston's father, however, distraught over his wife's suicide, was a different matter. It had been a sad day for Derek when he had made the decision to sail the seven seas, leaving Derek in charge of his San Francisco office.

The two friends never lost contact, however. Whenever Yates was in port they would dine together and when he was away, Derek always made it a point to visit Bonnie to make sure she was never in need of anything. Derek felt for his friend, particularly when he learned that his wife had killed herself and why. But he never passed judgment on Yates, supportive and compassionate he continued to invest money in his shipping empire.

The news of the war hit Derek hard. Reports of the firing on Fort Sumter spread like wild fire throughout the town. Derek sympathized with the South. His roots were there. It was the beloved homeland of his family, a family that would have fought gallantly for the cause. Being financially able, he aided the South with vessels and medical supplies until, realizing it was fighting men that they needed most, he enlisted and survived the many long hard battles between the states. But in the final stage of the war he would have lost his life if it had not been for Captain Cameron Prescott.

The South had been destroyed. Men were starving, and the supplies were gone. Fever took its toll among the injured that weren't strong enough to recover, some killed themselves with their own hands. Ending their lives was better than being pitied for their loss of sight, limbs, or pride.

Tired, weary, and weak from the loss of blood, Derek fit right in with the dead scattered bodies on the battlefields. Too scared to speak and too tired to move, he lay there waiting for his final fate. Through the darkness he heard shouts and felt his body being lifted and carried. When he awoke from his unconsciousness, pain shot through him and whiskey was poured down his throat. A surgeon stood over him, arguing with his captain. His leg had been spared, but a lifeless limp, would be his reminder. He owed Captain Prescott his life, being a diligent officer, he risked his life to make sure that no man was left alive on the battlefield; if not for him he would have been left in the hands of the enemy, which would have meant his certain death. Five years of hell was finally over, Derek and Cameron parted good friends, promising to put the war in the past and look forward to a future. Cameron left in a hurry to see his family, Derek left with a promise, that Cameron Prescott, would one day be repaid.

But only a few months later, Cameron appeared in San Francisco, still wearing the tattered uniform of the Confederate army. Too proud to accept charity, he soon went to work for Derek in the ship yards and proved himself worthy to both owners. He never spoke of the tragedy that clearly must have befallen his family, but Cameron was not the same person. He had become cold and hard, and most times ruthless.

Although he saved most of his earnings to pay the back taxes on his plantation in Georgia, Cameron allowed himself enough coin to be a regular at the waterfront drinking houses where he drank freely. A demon was torturing him inside, never letting him forget the pain and suffering of his past.

But when he met Bonnie Yates, all that changed. Her father liked the well-bred young man and welcomed him into his home and family. With his being away at sea and his only son defying him, he needed someone to help Derek to help run his business.

Cameron accepted the position with confidence, knowing he had proven himself to both his employers. But Bonnie was the only one he opened his heart to. And slowly let the demon of his past put to rest. She felt his pain and suffering when she heard the terrible stories of his childhood friends dying in his arms on the battlefield. Tears rolled down her face when he told her about his sister's begging him not to leave her.

His voice cracked with emotion when he repeated the last words she had ever said to him.

But now, far from the tragic scenes of battle, far from the memories of every thing he had lost, there was Bonnie. New hope for a golden future together, a hope she prayed nothing would dash.

CHAPTER 53

"Well Cameron," Derek said as he and sat on a leather chair with his hands holding onto a shiny wooden cane with solid gold adorning the tip of the handle. "I think everything seems to be in order. I know you're anxious to get back to your sister. It's just amazing how you two have found each other."

"Sometimes I just can't believe it's true. You get used to the fact that someone you love is dead and then you discover that they're alive. I still can't believe it." As he was looking at several papers stacked on his desk, Cameron looked up at Derek and smiled. His sister had been brought back from the dead, and every time he thought about it he shook his head to make sure it wasn't a dream.

"Is Brana feeling better?" Derek asked. "Some of those unworthy sea vessels should be at the bottom of the sea instead of risking the lives of innocent people. You risked your life and the lives of Bonnie and your sister. You could have waited for one of our ships to bring you back home."

"I didn't have a choice in the matter Derek," Cameron said defensively. "You see, I didn't tell you that Brana had been badly abused. She had been in the hands of a mad man and when she saw me she couldn't take the shock and I feared for her life."

Cameron's mood had turned stormy and a cloud covered his eyes.

"I'm sorry Derek," Cameron apologized, "but every time I think of how I found her I visualize myself killing who was responsible."

"Did you inform the authorities?" Derek asked as he shifted himself in the leather chair and put his lame leg forward. He folded his hands over the gold handle of his cane and looked at Cameron narrowly.

"Brana said she had killed him, but believe me, in my hands he would have died a slow and painful death," Cameron told him grimly. "I might not ever have recognized her if it hadn't been for the gold locket around her neck. Without Bonnie I don't know how I would have managed. Old memories and thoughts of my parents came flooding back. I'm just happy that Brana is feeling better and will even dine with Bonnie and me tonight. You know Derek, you've never met her, and since she's feeling better, why don't you join us. Bonnie was just telling me the other day that she has missed you. I think it will do Brana some good."

Derek wasn't a bad looking man. In fact, before the war, his features were perfect enough for him to be called "golden boy" by several ladies in town. His blond hair caught all the golden rays the sun had to offer. He was the youngest and most available bachelor in the entire town, and several women had tasted his lust. But since he had returned from the war with his limp, he hadn't seemed too interested in the women who threw themselves at his feet. He too had changed. The lighthearted boy who was generous with his riches was now a lonely young man.

"I don't know Cameron. The ladies might not want at guest tonight and Brana might not be in the mood for company." Derek replied nervously.

"Nonsense, and since when are you company. Brana was in a great mood and I'm sure she'll welcome a diversion."

Derek noticed Cameron's eyes sparkled with mischief and Derek knew he might be up to something. He was intrigued by what he had heard about Cameron's sister, having heard a good many stories about how they had fought like brothers when they were young and how she could ride a stallion better than any man.

"You win Cameron, but only if you don't think it'll be upsetting to your sister?" Derek said using his can to help himself rise.

"Not at all," Cameron told him, "and now that we have that settled, have you heard from Mr. Yates? Bonnie and I have put off our wedding so that he may attend, and according to my calculations he should have been back by now. Bonnie's worried even though she doesn't show it. If he's not able to come, he should have sent word by now."

"Don't worry, Cameron," Derek said. "I don't think he's got himself into something he can't handle. If the old man promised Bonnie he'd be back to see her married, believe me he will. He's probably on his way as we speak."

Derek started to move toward the door. Looking out of the window he could see most of the busy city. It was hardly the city he had known when he first docked here as a young boy, too green behind the ears to drink successfully with the other miners and too pitiful and bashful to bed the trollops who would have given themselves eagerly for a few specks of gold dust.

The mansion he had built offered a view of the city from on top of what was known as Rincon Hill. At night he would look out of his windows and overlook the lighted city before a heavy fog would roll in and cover the highest rooftops.

Cameron put his hand on Derek's shoulder, "I'll see you tonight," he said and then stood watching as Derek limped to the waiting carriage. His driver nodded to Cameron and opened the shiny carriage door. Derek managed to help himself in with no assistance and all Cameron saw was a wave of a hand and the carriage took off in a slow trotting pace pulled by a beautiful team of roans.

Back in his office, Cameron picked up the same pile of papers he had put down earlier. The business of importing and exporting to every port in the world was making him a wealthy man. Even though he didn't own the company outright, he owned some shares, and was paid quite handsomely. Once Bonnie became his bride, he would be a full partner with Derek and Yates, no doubts he would be able to afford to keep Bonnie happy.

He would never have imagined that his life would have taken such a drastic turn, that he would find himself part of an empire being built in the West. The South was part of his heritage and the land had belonged to generations of Prescott's before him. It wasn't easy to wipe away the memory of all your loved ones. As much as he wanted no ties with the South, the Prescott plantation still held part of his heart in the family cemetery, even though the mansion that had stood proud for so many years was now nothing but blackened rubble hidden. Nothing of value was left because the vultures had who destroyed his home had taken from silver to family portraits. Material things were gone and long forgotten but the memory of happiness and love that had filled his home would always be buried in his heart. Cameron would die before he let his family heritage be owned by Yankees. The thieving murderers had taken enough that belonged to him and deep in his heart he knew he would return to the place his mother had bore him.

As Cameron stared out the windows of his office, deep in thought, he didn't notice that a mob had gathered in the streets, pushing and shoving a Chinaman threatening to chop off a long braid of his hair which hung to the middle of his back. But his attention was attracted, when he saw the angry mob kicking a Chinaman to the ground. He was out of his office directly pushing his way through the crowd.

Suddenly a stick someone had thrown struck Cameron full force in the eye and he staggered back, blood trickle down the side of his cheek. Grabbing the man who had thrown it, he ripped the shirt off of his back. Lifting him into the air and threw him at the angry mob.

"Are you crazy?" Someone shouted. "This is the enemy." He pointed to a broken man curled up in a ball on the dirt road.

"You all look like a pack of wild dogs," Cameron shouted. "Stop this insanity before you live to regret it."

"What are you, a China lover?" Someone else shouted as the crowd grew quiet. "You defend this man when he takes our jobs from us."

Cameron went to help the Chinaman up. His eyes were swollen shut and there was a deep cut on his lip.

"Look mister whoever the hell you are, this isn't your fight," the man who seemed to be the leader of the mob shouted. "We can't let these Chinamen take our jobs. Our families are starving and the railroad won't do anything about it. I say we kill this one to teach them all a lesson."

"Your fight is with the railroad not with these people," Cameron told them, supporting the man he had rescued with one arm. "These people are innocent. The ignorance you have proven here today tells me that the railroad knows what its doing."

"You'd actually go against your own kind for the likes of them? You'd better watch your back, mister. In this town you never know when you might get a knife stuck in it."

"Can't you tell by his fancy words that he ain't one of us," another slurred, putting a bottle of whiskey up to his lips. "Got a southern accent to him. He don't belong here. I say let's finish them both off."

"Anybody else have something to say?" Cameron asked, as most the men backed off. The welt on his check was a dull throbbing pain. His temper was on edge and he felt at this point he could have surely murdered someone with his bare hands.

Cameron understood their complaints and felt the railroads to be at fault for the murderous rage these men felt. The Chinese were being shipped in by the thousands to work for the railroads as cheap labor.

Tempers flared, and at every turn, innocent men like this one were killed for being at the wrong place at the wrong time. Chinese men and women were found murdered in dark alleys with knife wounds in their backs or their throats slit from ear to ear. Cameron thought he had seen enough war, but now it had become a part of life.

Men were starting to walk away, muttering but the leader of the group held his ground and stared at Cameron, sneering. For the first time, Cameron noticed his scraggly appearance. His hair was cropped short and uneven and from the odor of his breath Cameron knew a whiskey bottle had been his companion for most of the morning. His sturdy build and calloused hands told Cameron that physical labor was all he knew. The rips in his shirt had been mended with fine stitches which Cameron assumed he had a wife to support and probably a child or two.

"You ain't seen the last of me, mister," he threatened. "You may tend to the Chinaman's wounds now, but next time his wounds won't heal."

Assisting the Chinaman to his office, Cameron pulled the dark green shades, for privacy. Motioning for him to sit in the chair Derek Lancer had left a few minutes before, and handing him a towel to wipe the blood dripping down his nose, Cameron noticed he was holding his swollen fingers in his other hand and that his nose was flattened with a large lump at the tip.

"I'd like to know the name of the person I just risked my life for," Cameron said. "Do you speak English?"

The Chinaman waited for a few seconds before he mumbled. "Berry little," he said, wincing.

"Do you have a leader?" Cameron asked "Someone that can represent your people, here in this city?"

The Chinaman shook his head, unable apparently, to look Cameron in the eye.

"I can see what your problem is," Cameron continued. "You need a leader who can stand up for your rights as human beings, so bullies like the one you encountered today can be dealt with. Go to your camp and tell your people to pick someone to represent you. Someone that can speak better English than you, understand?"

The stranger shook his head, as if the words Cameron spoke were just now starting to register.

"Good, now I have to go now," Cameron told him as he leaned over and helped him off the chair. "Remember everything I have told you this sort of bigotry will continue to happen to your women and children, if you don't stand your ground."

Cameron watched him disappear down the alley before he pulled the last dark green shade covering the windows.

Cameron noticed the mist in the night air as he closed the office door tightly shut. His Dakota mid-thigh frock coat did not keep the chill that was rising at a fast pace. Quickly getting into the awaiting carriage, he headed for home. Telegraph Hill seemed steeper than usual tonight but the view was magnificent as ever. The mist had not yet enveloped the bay, lanterns swinging from the vessels in the harbor looked like a swarm of fire flies dancing wildly in the air. Fingering the bruise on his cheek, Cameron reminded himself not to let Bonnie see him before he had taken care of the signs of the recent struggle.

Meanwhile, Bonnie, Brana and Aunt Elizabeth were waiting dinner for him, thankful that Derek was there to distract them, and refill their glasses with wine. They all knew of the tensions that had invaded the town and Derek was all too well aware that Cameron would never turn away from a confrontation.

As soon as Bonnie had made the proper introductions, Derek had found himself lost in the deep pools of violet that were Brana's eyes. She was, he thought, one of the most beautiful women he had ever seen with her black hair, flowing past her waist in the back. And her slender figure, elegantly arrayed in a stylish apron gown, the color pink, to offset the richness of her black hair and the violet sparkle of her eyes.

When introduced, he had gently taken her hand in his and kissed it softly. He felt intoxicated by her touch as well as her perfume.

Bringing himself back to the present, Derek pulled a silver watch of the breast pocket of his vest. It was late. Too late. He remembered the cluster of railroaders gathered in the street. They were angry men. Some would debate with good reason. He hoped that somehow Cameron had not become involved with them. Aunt Elizabeth frowned and was about to speak when they heard his voice in the direction of the Library.

The servant bowed his head to them and Cameron entered behind him.

"Well, it certainly is about time," Aunt Elizabeth scolded. "Nothing could be that important at the office, a fine meal is getting cold."

"Well, I think that it's wonderful that Cam is so dedicated to his work, I am very proud of him." Brana stated matter of factly.

"My apologies," Cameron said walking over to Aunt Elizabeth and kissed her softly on the check.

"I was getting worried," Bonnie said. "We expected you hours ago."

Derek looked at Cameron amusingly, noticing the striking resemblance of him and Brana, the beauty sitting next to him. Derek was caught by surprise as he realized how attracted he was to Brana. He had never felt for any other woman the way he was feeling now. Not even Tanli, the China doll whom he had won in a poker game, occasionally shared his bed, a delicate, fine featured woman for whose services he paid handsomely.

Tonight he felt different. Brana's presence made him feel like more of a man than ever before. He wanted to caress her, hold her in his arms and assure her she would always feel safe with him. Her southern accent reminded him of his family and his homeland.

"I'm famished," Derek said, noticing a small welt on Cameron's cheek. "Shall we?"

"Please, let's not detain ourselves from this wonderful meal any longer," Cameron said as his eyes locked with Derek's.

Cameron had let himself in the back way, through the stairs in the kitchen, not wanting anybody to notice he appearance. He reached his bed chambers without incident and began to wash up at the basin. Dabbing his injury with a cold cloth, he swore under his breath and donned a clean white shirt and carelessly ran his fingers through his wet hair. He knew the situation was far from over and thought of what he was going to tell Bonnie.

"Bonnie has told me of the riches in gold and silver mines in your city," Brana was saying. "I have yet to see the city itself, but from what I can make out from the view, it looks quite lively. There's always activity going on. I'm intrigued by all the different people and customs."

Brana was starting to feel a lot better as the meal wore on. Grateful, that she was able to keep her food down.

"Just read the *San Francisco Star*," Derek told her. "Don't let the beauty of this city fool you, it's as ruthless as they come. For all its beauty and wealth, it's also a haven for murderers and thieves, taking easily from those who have worked hard at earning a living."

"The situation with the railroad doesn't help any." Bonnie interjected.

"With all the riches this land has to offer, why couldn't it have been used to help the South?" Brana asked innocently.

"My dear, we have just a few Southern sympathizers," Derek explained. "A handful of men, but really not enough to make a difference."

"I don't know the parties involved," Bonnie told them, "but it is said that a large vessel carrying a fortune in gold and silver once sank in that bay. A delegation was set up to recover the sunken ship by building a dam. The plan was to use the spoils to help defray the cost of the war."

"Well what happened!" Brana exclaimed with excitement.

"Nothing," Bonnie concluded. "They laid the plans out before Lincoln, and rumor had it, he was quite amused."

Brana's eyes widened, "You mean to say that there is a ship laden with gold and silver down at the bottom of the bay!"

It was, Cam thought, good to hear Brana being distracted by Bonne's stories of the city that was now to become her home. If only he could keep the trouble that he was becoming involved with from her, all might still be well. She had gone through far too much back in Vicksburg to have troubles follow her here.

CHAPTER 54

Cameron was intoxicated by the smells of the dishes on the finely decorated dinner table and the sweet smell of the candles. Aunt Elizabeth's centerpiece was made up to perfection with wild azaleas, violets, fragrant rosemary and deep red roses, directly from the garden. And he was mesmerized as he looked at Bonnie. The candle light left gold highlights dancing throughout her golden brown hair. Her eyes were bright and earlier in the day the sun had dotted her cheeks and nose with freckles, beautiful, sun kissed perfection. Her gown was simple yet elegant, a soft bustle fashion skirt, the fullness bunched up to the back of the skirt, accentuated her hips. As usual, just one look excited him.

Bonnie left her chair and went to Cameron, taking his hands and kissing him gently on the cheek. Noticing the bruise on his cheek, she searched his eyes for answers, but only to be distracted by his warm embrace.

Filling a wine glass with Chardonnay, Cameron, addressed himself to the dish of sole sautéed in a creamy white sauce that was placed before him, even though he was not hungry. "I apologize for my rudeness," Cameron told them. "I lost track of time today. Please don't let me interrupt your conversation. It sounds most intriguing."

"Bonnie and I were just filling Brana in on the history of her new home," Derek told him distractedly, still caught up in the emotions Brana had evoked.

He was happy to see that Brana was laughing at the jokes that she and Derek were sharing. It occurred to him suddenly that they seemed to be in a world of their own.

"Darling, what on earth happened to you?" Bonnie whispered. "I didn't want to question you in front of Brana and Auntie, but what happened?"

Bonnie's eyes were searching his face as she folded his hands with hers.

"Don't worry darling," Cameron told her. "Just a little disagreement, nothing more."

"How can you say it was just a little disagreement?" Bonnie protested in a low voice. "The bruise on your cheek is getting darker and your knuckles need to be tended to."

"Brana seems to be enjoying herself, don't you think?" Cameron said. "And it is certainly obvious that Derek is."

"Don't try and change the subject, Cameron," Bonnie told him. "I know how dangerous the waterfront is right now. I just couldn't take it if something happened to you."

Bonnie's eyes were misty and she looked away just as Brana's voice caught her attention.

"I'd never heard about Bonnie's brother until the other day," she was telling Derek. "Do you know him well?"

"Well, dear Sister, that's a subject Derek, will be unwilling to talk about," Cameron interjected. "Let's just say there's no love lost between those two. Right Derek?"

"I can think of more pleasant things to talk about than some hot headed scoundrel." Derek replied.

"Really Derek," Bonnie protested, "so much time has gone by can't you forget about the past and your difference with Wes---"

"You're right, Bonnie," Derek interrupted. "Let's concentrate on the future. How about some fresh air? I could use a good cheroot."

"I would like one myself, Derek," Cameron agreed. "I have a box of imported ones that I haven't tried yet."

Before anyone could leave the room a servant rushed in and quickly apologized several times for his intrusion.

"What's going on?" Brana asked Derek.

Just then three men barged into the room. One of them was the Chinaman that Cameron had defended earlier in the day and the other two looked enough alike to be his brothers. Cameron and Derek were on their feet in an instant.

"What is the meaning of this intrusion?" Cameron shouted, looking as if he were ready to do battle. "Bonnie! Brana! Take Auntie and go to your chambers!"

"What in the world!" Aunt Elizabeth gasped.

"I will not, Cam!" Brana protested.

"Nor will I." Bonnie said, walking towards Brana and her aunt.

"It seems that your women are as brave as you are, Mr. Prescott," one of the intruders said scornfully. "But really, there is no cause for alarm. We intend no harm."

The man who appeared to be the leader was dressed in black silk. A long braid hung past his waist and the slant of his eyes made him appear even more sinister than his sudden appearance might have indicated.

"If I thought you were here to cause my family harm, you would have been a dead man by now," Cameron told him. "A good choice bringing him with you."

Cameron nodded to the Chinaman standing in the very back of the room. He recognized him as the man he had helped earlier on the docks.

"I don't like my home or my privacy invaded," Cameron continued. "Especially when I'm with my family. State your business briefly and then you will be escorted out."

"We do apologize for the rudeness of our intrusion. Please ladies and gentlemen forgive us," the Chinaman said. "However, we were in fear that we would be turned away and this matter is of the utmost importance. May I be so bold as to ask if there is a private place for us to speak?"

The Chinaman had a look of desperation on his face that Cameron could not ignore.

With Derek following, Cameron led the way to the library, "I'm sorry my dears," he told the ladies as he passed them. "This conversation is not for your ears."

"How could he!" Brana said as they went upstairs. "It must have been important for those men to barge in the way they did. I just wish I knew what was going on. How can you be so calm Bonnie?"

Bonnie sat at the edge of the bed determined to remain calm for Brana's sake. But inside she couldn't stop trembling. What could Cameron be involved in? She knew it had something to do with his condition when he had arrived home and, she had noticed that one of the chinamen's face was bruised and very swollen.

"What, darling? Did you say something?"

"What does all this have to do with Cam?" Brana demanded.

"Calm down, Brana." Bonnie told her. "You're not doing yourself or your baby any good by getting so upset. I'm sure Cameron will tell us what this is all about after his meeting. Now why don't we ring for some tea and talk about Derek. Isn't he wonderfully nice?"

"Why do we have to ring for tea? We can go downstairs and have it." Brana was already heading for the door.

"No Brana, I don't think that would be wise. Cameron will be very upset if we defy him a second time. I think it's better if we have it up here."

As Bonnie spoke, she pulled on an ornate rope that hung loosely behind her bedpost.

"Ok," Brana said reluctantly. "I guess we'll find out soon enough."

"Now that's a good dear," Bonnie said as Brana threw herself on the chaise, her skirts billowing about her. "You know, I really think it is time you tell Cameron about your condition. I don't think it's fair that you keep something like this a secret from him."

Bonnie pulled all the pins out of Brana's hair and let it fall over her shoulders. Taking the gold handled brush that her father had given her when she was a girl, she began to brush her hair.

"I do intend to tell him Bonnie, "Brana said, "but I feel the time is not right. We both know how Cam will react, and I just feel I'm not ready to handle him just yet. You can understand that, can't you?"

Brana looked about the room. She knew she should be happy in this elegant house with its flocked wallpaper and Oriental rugs, the flowers grown in its own conservatory everywhere.

As Bonnie sipped her tea, thoughts of Cameron kept slipping into her mind. She wondered if he was in any kind of danger. He had been through so much lately. Finding Brana had certainly reopened deep wounds and scars he had suffered during the war. He had been through so much and Bonnie dreaded the possibility that he was about to be in danger again.

CHAPTER 55

"I gather this has something to do with this afternoon?" Cameron remarked when they were settled around the fireplace, sipping brandy. He knew that it would do no good to talk to the man he had defended hours earlier as he could not speak his language or understand it.

"What *did* happen this afternoon Cameron?" Derek asked him. "I noticed that your face was a bit battered."

"Your friend here saved Yom Ling's life," the man who had introduced himself as Sing Ling, said. "If he would not have intervened, my brother, Yom Ling would have surely been killed. That is the reason for our visit tonight. He told me how you stood up for him against those savages from the waterfront. Yom Ling told me that you took a beating yourself for him. It gives us great honor even to be accepted into your home."

Cameron had decided to hear them out. The servant who had tried to bar the door to them hovered uncertainly in the corridor outside until Cameron motioned him away.

"We need a man like you," Sing Ling continued. "Our people are being killed at every turn. It was not the first time that man has assaulted one of our men. Only the other man was not as fortunate as Yom Ling was today. He was killed. We need a strong man with dignity and honor to represent us. We would be honored if you would accept. Our money is very little, but all we have is yours."

"See here now, what you ask is clearly impossible." Derek interjected. Unknowingly Derek pounded his cane on the ground.

The Chinaman could not read the emotions on Cameron's face, a hidden mask that perhaps not even his closest friend could penetrate. The Chinaman's eyes went from Cameron to Derek.

He spoke softly "Please sir, we need a strong man, not to fight our battles but to talk to your people in a tongue they can understand."

"You seem to be managing that part of it very well on your own," Derek said gruffly. "Why do you need Cameron?"

The curtains had been opened and through the French doors you could see the fog starting to roll in leaving a thick mist in its wake. Fog horns in the distance warned ships passing through the bay or docking for the night. Derek could see the lights down in the city, dim. Derek's attention was drawn to a cloud that was forming in the air. He looked in Cameron's direction and noticed that Cameron had a cheroot clenched between his teeth and a smile formed at the corners of his mouth. Derek poured himself a generous amount of liquor and shook his head. He knew his friend too well to know that he would not turn his back on these people.

"I have heard of the situation between your people and the railroad," Cameron said. "I had a taste of the hostility today. But I fail to see what I can do. You and your people are a community and I am just one man."

At that Yom Ling hurried forward and placed a brown leather pouch in his hands. Holding it up, Cameron heard the clink of coins.

"He wanted to do the honors in offering you all the money we have managed to collect. In order to persuade you to help us," Sing Ling said "It is all that we have and we want you to have it. It would please us greatly. And now, we have taken up much of your time. We leave you now. You can let us know tomorrow if you can help our cause."

Before Cameron could return the pouch each man had bowed deeply and left the room. When he heard the front door being closed behind them, Cameron went to one of the library windows and looked out into the foggy night. From far below he heard the familiar sound of a foghorn. Tomorrow morning he would return their money and tell them that he would help them. He hoped that by tomorrow Bonnie's father would have arrived. Now, if ever, he needed his advice.

"Pretty thick fog out," Derek said. "I guess I should be going myself. No need to see me out, I know by now where the door is."

"Aren't you going to try to talk me out of it, Derek?" Cameron said as Derek prepared to leave as well.

"It wouldn't help," his friend said with a shrug. "I will say this, however. You not only have to look out for yourself, but Bonnie and Brana as well. These men on the railroad can get pretty tough and with all that you, your sister, and Bonnie have been through you wouldn't want any more harm to come to Brana as well as Bonnie."

"Don't worry Lancer," Cameron said sharply. "I can take care of my family."

Derek knew he had hit a raw nerve when Cameron called him by his last name. But he also knew that he had had no choice but to warn him.

Once home, he went directly to bed, only to find Tanli sleeping there. Her ebony black hair, so like Brana's spread out on the pillow. He sat on the bed and wondered if Brana was still awake and would he be in her thoughts as well. Remembering her beauty, he became bewitched again and as Tanli stirred, he immediately joined her in bed.

His coverlet was neatly folded at the bottom of the bed and he easily slipped between the bed sheets. Her body was warm as she drew him close to her. She moved her leg on his and rubbed it gently. She moved higher and with her knee, touched his manhood and laughed as it grew with life. Moaning he turned to face her, kissing her inviting lips and rubbing her small breasts. Her nipples hardened at his attention and her tongue was warm with excitement as he parted her lips to play with his. His thumb and index finger played with her nipple making her hips rub against his. She moaned as she took his throbbing member in her hands, his tongue drew circles around her dark pink rosebuds and his other hand gently caressed the succulent mound between her thighs. He rubbed and teased, feeling her dampness between his fingers.

Derek whispered words of love in Tanli's ears, as he became lost in desire. Parting her legs, he buried his face in her hidden flesh, the heat from Tanli's body consumed him. Unable to control his passion, his thrust was deep, hard and fast paced, calling out her name as he entered paradise. Brana's eyes were the last thing he saw, before exhaustion consumed him.

CHAPTER 56

Brana awoke when sunlight poured through her window, leaving a ray of sunshine dancing in her bedchamber. Thinking of Weston, tears flowed down her cheeks. His face had hsunted her dreams. It seemed that every time she closed her eyes the pain in her heart was unbearable. She lay quietly listening to the birds nest in the pine tree, next to her chamber window.

When she heard carriage wheels on the gravel drive below her window, Brana knew that Cam was off to the city. She hoped that he had explained exactly what had happened last night to Bonnie and that she would come and tell her soon. The thought had no sooner come into her mind when Bonnie appeared along with a servant carrying a tea tray.

"I talked to Cam before he left for the city," Bonnie said, curling up in one of the wing chairs by the fireplace and helping herself to a croissant. "I'm afraid he was rather angry with me or should I say us for defying him last night. He blames you for my new found defiance but I'm sure it was to avoid the scene from last night."

The dark circles under Bonnie's eyes told Brana that she hadn't got much sleep last night either. Bonne's hair was just brushed out and pulled back by a simple ribbon and her dress was a simple cotton frock of yellow and pink roses. For one fleeting moment, Brana was reminded of someone, although she was not sure whom.

"Did Cam tell you anything?" Brana asked, taking a careful sip of piping hot tea.

"It's what he didn't say that worries me," Bonnie told her. "He did admit that he had gone to defense of a Chinese man whom he had seen being beaten by some railroad men yesterday, but I know it's more that that. I guess we'll have to wait and see, or question Derek next time he comes over for a visit."

"Are you feeling ill this morning?" Bonnie asked. "You look a bit pale. Is everything alright darling?"

"Will my heart ever stop hurting?" Brana said, beginning to cry.

"There, there, darling," Bonnie said as she held Brana close. "You must try and go on with your life for the sake of your baby. The love you felt for your captain will never leave you, I know but you will be blessed with his child and the pain will go away in time. You are still young, Brana. Time heals all wounds. Just think of the precious gift you carry and concentrate on the future with your lovely child. There now dry your eyes."

"I feel better, thanks, Bon," Brana said. "I know I'll have more nights like last night but, it's comforting to know I have a good friend to help me through it."

"I'm not even sure I could take the advice I just gave you," Bonnie admitted. "I just pray that Cam will be careful and come home to me every night. You must know what I'm going through particularly since I'm not even able to be his wife."

"Don't worry Bon, things will work out. Cam is careful and I know he loves you with all his heart. He wouldn't do anything to hurt you."

When Brana dried Bonnie's eyes with her own soaked handkerchief, they both started laughing.

"Look at us!" Bonnie exclaimed. "Here I was supposed to be comforting you and it turned out to be the other way around."

"Let's just say that we are here for each other Bon, doesn't the day look just beautiful? What about a ride on the grounds? That would certainly take our mind off things."

"I don't think it's a good idea Brana," Bonnie told her. "You shouldn't be riding in your condition. It isn't safe. We could take a stroll."

"Nonsense. I'm sure you have a gentle horse and I'm certainly not going to race it. I really do miss riding, Bonnie. I promise to be very careful. Now let me get my riding habit on and I'll meet you at the stables."

Bonnie agreed but with reluctance. Brana was so impetuous and she had heard tales of how she loved to race horses but still, if she was determined to go, it was best that she go with her.

CHAPTER 57

The black velvet riding habit was snug around Brana's mid section and now too short in the front, which enhanced her swollen belly. Thinking of Weston, she patted her stomach and smiled, happy to know he lives within her. She smoothed a few strands of loose hair from her face and took one look in the mirror before going off to greet Bonnie.

As she walked to the stables, Brana noticed the wet dew that still lingered to the green grass but it did not bother her one bit. The sun seemed to be warming, and Brana took in mouthfuls of the sea air. The stables were not far from the house and as she got closer she could smell horse flesh and hear them snort. Bonnie was waiting for her, talking a stable hand who was feeding the horses.

"You get to ride Slow Poke here," Bonnie told her. "I do admit, she is rather old, but she will be safe. But I really wish we would go for a walk instead."

"How much trouble could I get into riding Slow Poke?" Brana asked her. "She's as old as worn out shoe, and probably as blind as a bat. She'll do just fine. We'll just walk the horses near the stream, let them drink some water, and talk a little and walk them back. Nothing too strenuous, I promise."

As they were talking, Bonnie motioned the stable hand to saddle the horses. They walked out of the stable and waited as they shared a joke or two. With the stable hand behind them, they were on their way.

"Well, Bonnie, this horse is certainly living up to her name," Brana said. "I'm not used to such gentle horses. When I was a child I rode a beauty of a beast. It sometimes felt as if we were flying. I loved that horse. We used to share secrets and she was as much of a friend as Cam was. Of course, Cam bought me Beauty for my birthday and my parents just about disowned him."

Brana suddenly became quiet. This was the first time she had shared a memory of her parents with anyone. She thought of how it had been when she was a child. She remembered her mother's smile and her father's laughter. She missed them terribly. But at least she still had Cam.

"I know how much you miss your parents," Bonnie told her. "I miss mine terribly. I do see my father at least once or twice a year. But I do miss him. Things have never been the same since my mother's death, and when my brother left."

"You never told me how your mother died. Was it the fever?"

Brana and Bonnie walked their horses to the stream and paused to watch the birds fly down to steal a drink. All the dew had almost melted and the sun was growing brighter with every minute.

"No, I was very young at the time and my father never did tell me what happened, but gossip has it that she killed herself."

"Oh dear, I'm sorry Bon," and then, quickly changed the subject. "Look at that, on the far side of the hill. Who lives there?"

"Derek. He has a beautiful home and he has been a wonderful friend and neighbor. Funny how that's another city, but were neighbors. I know him better than I know my own brother."

"It sounds like he dislikes your brother. When was the last time you saw him?"

"Not since my mother's death," Bonnie told her. "He left soon after. I miss him terribly."

As they chattered under a tall pine tree, the wind seemed to whisper her name, Brana had forgotten how much she loved to ride and it was irresistible to her not to feel the wind blowing through her hair as it had in the old days. And so, despite what she had promised Bonnie, she nudged the old nag into a trot.

"Brana, you promised!" Bonnie called just as Slow Poke stopped dead in her tracks and Brana went flying.

Brana!" Bonnie screamed as she raced to where Brana lay. Sliding off of her horse, she fell to her knees next to Brana.

"Get help!" She called to the stable hand. "Hurry!"

"What is it man!" Cameron shouted when the stable hand, panicked stricken, bolted into his office.

"Sister! Accident with Slow Poke!"

"Derek, I'll get the doc, you have the carriage ready." Cameron said as he ran out of the office down an alleyway.

It seemed like an eternity before they reached the hill and Derek could see the pale color of Cameron's face. Silently he prayed for Brana to be fine. He knew that Cameron could not bear to lose her a second time. And it surprised him to realize that he did not want to lose her either.

"She's a strong, girl," Derek told him trying to hide the tremor in his voice.

"I just couldn't bear to lose her again," Cameron cried.

The carriage ride was quiet and as soon as it came to a halt, Cameron jumped out and ran into the house, taking the steps to Brana's chamber three at a time. Derek followed the doctor, his lame leg had been forgotten.

"Cameron, where's the doctor? Is he with you?" Bonnie frantically questioned as he entered Brana's chamber.

"He's on his way up now!" Cameron assured her. "Is Brana alive? Please, Bonnie, I must know, tell me?"

"Yes, I'm sure she'll be alright," Bonnie told him. "She just took a nasty fall."

Derek made his way to Brana's chamber and saw Cameron at Brana's bedside.

"She's alive, Derek," he said as he wiped her brow with his hand.

"Thank God," Derek whispered.

"Why don't you wait downstairs with your friend, Mr. Prescott while I examine the patient?" The doc told them. "If I need assistance, I'm sure Bonnie can help. If we need you we'll call."

Derek and Cameron nodded and quietly left the room. They headed straight to the library and poured drinks.

"Did you talk to her? Is she conscious?" Derek asked, gripping the handle on his cane.

"She's somewhat conscious," his friend told him. His face was pale and drawn "Apparently the horse she was riding ran right into a gopher hole and broke his leg. We just have to wait until the doctor is finished examining her to find out if she has any broken bones."

Cameron and Derek both lit up a cheroot and paced back and forth, waiting for word from the doctor. There seemed, strangely enough, to be nothing to talk about but both of them had only one thought in mind. Nothing must happen to the woman they both loved so much. Nothing.

"She's young and strong," the doctor told them when he came downstairs. "It was lucky that she wasn't riding fast. No broken bones, a few bruises, but she'll be just fine with some bed rest. Now, Mr. Prescott, I've have told your sister that I don't want her riding any more. Another spill like that could harm the baby."

Cameron shook his head as if he wasn't hearing correctly. "What baby?" he demanded.

"I see that your sister hadn't told you, she's with child," the doctor said, clearly puzzled. "Well, never mind. I'll check her on a regular basis. I'm sure this incident will not affect the normal delivery of the child. I'll show myself out."

As soon as he was gone, both men poured themselves another drink. Neither of them asked the obvious question. Brana pregnant! By whom?

"I wonder how long she knew," Cameron whispered. "I'm sure Bonnie knew."

As Bonnie entered the library, one look was all she needed to know that both men now knew the truth about Brana's condition.

"I'm sorry you had to find out this way, Cameron,' Bonnie said. "Brana wanted to tell you when she thought the time was right. I thought she should be the one to decide when you should know. She'd like to speak to you now."

Cameron turned his back to Bonnie as he lifted his glass and flung it against the wall. Amber liquid splattered everywhere, glass shattered into tiny little pieces as it hit the wall.

"You knew about her condition and you let her go riding?" Cameron said angrily. "Were you two going to wait till she gave birth to tell me?"

"It was Brana's decision to make, not mine. She didn't want you to worry about her."

"My god, woman, how could you think that I wouldn't be worrying about her anyway with all that has happened. I suppose she told you who the father is."

"Yes she did," Bonnie replied. "It's the sea captain who she fell hopelessly in love with."

Nobody saw Brana enter the room, her head pounded and her body ached but she needed to defend her best friend.

"Please Cam, let me explain," Brana cried.

"Brana!" Bonnie gasped. "You're not supposed to be out of bed."

Brana swayed and almost fainted, Cameron hurried to help her to the couch.

"I just wanted you to know that Bonnie is not to blame for my deceit, "she told him. "She begged me to tell you but I wanted to wait until I thought the time was right. If you have to be angry with someone, be angry with me."

She looked so pale and her hair, hanging loose around her face, made her look like a child. Cam's heart reached out to her. He couldn't bring himself to lash out at her.

"So I am to be an uncle," he said, sitting next to her and taking her hands in his. "Why didn't you tell me at the beginning? I would have understood."

"I couldn't bring myself to tell you," Brana sobbed. "You remembered me as the young girl you left before the war. But I'm a woman, Cam. I loved a man and now I'm going to have his child."

Forgetting his anger, Cam went to embrace his sister. But it was Derek who spoke next.

"I would be honored…"

CHAPTER 58

Brana was pacing back and forth, biting her lower lip when Bonnie came to join her.

"You are supposed to be in bed Brana," Bonnie scolded her as she fluffed the pillows. "Now get in."

"I just can't lie still right now while Cameron is downstairs planning my future," Brana protested. "Please tell me, Bonnie. What's happening down there? Surely he can't make me marry if I don't wish to!"

"I'm afraid I agree with his decision, darling. He is your brother and he loves you very much. He can't force you to marry but I really think it's for the best. Derek is a wonderful man and I know he will do his best to make you happy. You have to think about your baby now. The doctor said you are to rest."

Brana took off her wrapper and slipped under the bed sheets. She knew she didn't stand a chance against Cameron this time. And in a way she understood. The father of her child was dead. And they had never married, although they would have done had he lived. Because Weston had loved her. She was sure of it. And he would have hated to think of her banned from society, his child brought up a bastard. And that was what would happen if she didn't accept Derek's offer. But she didn't love him. She would never love another man as she had Weston.

"I'm sure that Derek would make someone very happy," she told Bonnie now, letting her friend pull the covers up around her. "But I don't love him. Would it be fair to him? He has been so kind to me. How can I do that to him?"

"Brana, you have to listen to me," Bonnie told her. "I know that you will never love again like you once did. But, you must think of your child. A child needs a father."

Before Bonnie could finish, a knock sounded at the chamber door and Cameron entered. He was still pale but his eyes were steely blue with determination.

"Bonnie," he said. "I would like to speak to Brana alone please."

When he and Brana were alone, Cameron stood in silence by the window, looking down at Derek's carriage. He had been amazed when Derek told him that he loved Brana, that he was willing to have her any way he could and that he would accept her child as his own. It was decided that wedding would take place on the following day and with Cam and Bonnie taking their vows as well.

He turned to look at Brana. How Brana reminded him of his mother. With her stormy eyes when angry, her voice, that carried the same tone. And her defiance reminded him of his ornery father. He knew his parents would be proud of the woman she had become.

"I know that in time you'll come to love Derek," he began. "He really cares a great deal for you, Brana. It's the only sensible thing to do. We have arranged for the wedding to take place tomorrow. With the blessing of Aunt Elizabeth, Bonnie and I will marry as well. I can't see why we should wait any longer."

"What if I don't want to wed?" Brana asked him. "Derek is a nice man, Cam, but I don't love him. I could never love him. My heart belongs to another and always will. Can't you understand that?"

"Brana, how long can you go on loving a dead man," Cameron protested. "Believe me, if this man were alive I would move heaven and earth to bring him to you. Damnation Brana, this isn't easy for me. Think about your child. Do you want it to be labeled a bastard? You know how cruel people can be."

"Yes," Brana told him in a low voice, "I know how cruel people can be. Oh Cam, how can I make you understand how much pain I'm in? My heart aches. I think of him with every breath I take, every dream I dream. How can I marry Derek feeling this way about another man?"

"I had a long talk with Derek," her brother told her. "He understands. He won't make any demands on you until you are ready, if that's what you are worried about. He's a good man, Brana. In time you will forget this sea captain and learn to love Derek."

"I will never forget him!" She cried. "I'll never learn to love Derek. I won't let myself."

"I'm sorry Brana, but this is what must be done, you shouldn't think of yourself right now, think of your child. It is my wish that you will become Derek's wife tomorrow and I hope that in time you'll see that it was the right decision." Cameron stated as he quietly walked out of her chamber.

Brana knew Cameron spoke the truth, she was being selfish, she knew, but she couldn't help herself. She thought of Lacy and how she would comfort her and tell her it would be ok.

"Oh Lacy!" She cried, "I miss you so. Please forgive me."

It was Derek who made the plans, even seeing the doctor to make certain that Brana was strong enough to go through with the ceremony. Bonnie's gown had been ready for weeks in anticipation of the great day, and he solved the problem of what Brana would wear by having his maid go through every cedar chest in town until she found a wedding dress, an elegant white tulle affair which, with a few minor alterations, would fit Brana perfectly.

Excited, he pictured Brana in her wedding gown. She would be his tomorrow and he vowed to make her forget the love that she felt for the dead man. He was very much alive and intended to shower her with love, affection, and gifts that a mere sea captain could never afford to give her. He felt a pang of jealousy for the dead man but, quickly remembered that if it hadn't been for him, Brana might never have been his.

Derek arrived at the office to find Cameron staring out the window.

"There's the same group gathered over here in the alley," Cameron told him. The man I had the confrontation with yesterday is apparently the leader. But he hasn't made a move to come in so I assume they want no trouble." He had scarcely finished speaking when a rock shattered the window, narrowly missing him. A note was fastened to it.

Derek handed him the paper which read, "Stay out of our business!" scrawled in a messy hand.

"Who do you suppose wrote this?" Cameron asked.

"The leader no doubt," Derek said. "Well, now we know that he is a coward. I just hope he comes to his senses before pulling another stunt like this."

Before they could continue their conversation, two Chinamen walked in carrying pieces of wood and began to board up the broken window. One carried a broom and swept up the glass off of the floor.

"Well now Derek, did you expect that to happen?" Cameron chuckled.

"It seems I underestimated your new friends," Derek said. "Looks to me like you have many eyes watching you. But what happens next time? Do you think these cowards would try this again, maybe set fire to the place?"

"They're cowards, alright," Cameron said. "If something does happen they know we would retaliate. Look at them. Not one of them seems to be sober. This was done by someone in a drunken stupor; I don't think we have anything to worry about." Cameron assured his friend.

As he spoke he thought of Bonnie and Brana. His heart felt heavy, knowing that Brana was truly unhappy. He could not bring himself to speak of it to Brana, to tell her that he knew what she was going through, that he had felt the same way when he realized that his family had been murdered. His heart had ached, and he had felt so lost and lonely that he had made a path of destruction everywhere he had gone, wanting nothing more than revenge. Now finally, with Bonnie's help he realized that he could not fight the entire world to ease his suffering. He could remember the look in Brana's eyes as she told him she did not want to wed. She was much like the child he remembered before the war, but he had to remember that she was no longer a child, and she had to do what was right for her unborn child.

He remembered Bonnie's face when he told her that they would also wed tomorrow. He had to kiss her tears of happiness away, and ease her mind over Brana's pain. He knew Derek would try and make Brana forget her sea captain, and yet he knew that there was nothing Derek could do that would heal her broken heart.

CHAPTER 59

The vessel that Cameron and Bonnie had been waiting for had finally docked. The crew scattered to the many taverns that lined the shore. The harbor was the center of a frenzy of activity with vessels coming and going with none to notice that Weston and his father had finally returned.

What Weston noticed first was the new buildings that crowded the waterfront. Brick buildings, some three stories high had replaced the shacks that he had seen the last time he had docked here. Now the waterfront looked like the market place of the world. Merchants were selling everything from fish to gold nuggets on makeshift tables.

"Well, son, how does it seem to be back in Fan Francisco?" his father asked him, slapping him on the back.

"I would hardly recognize the place," Weston commented, pushing past the whores who crowded around them. "But some things never change."

Weston's father reminisced as he heard the old doc mutter under his breath. A sound he had gotten used to.

"Well, what are you two waiting fer?" the doc barked. "This Old Doc is might thirsty."

Weston's attention was caught by the face of a cabin boy, his eyes full of excitement mixed in with a little fear. The lad reminded him of himself when he had taken his first long voyage. Somehow he had survived, he thought dryly, and knew he had survived many things that could have easily taken his life in an instant, and he knew he would survive the pain in his heart. But, he also knew that it would scar him for the remainder of his life.

The blue silk ribbon in his trouser pocket was frayed from having been drawn through his fingers so often. Now, staring at the pieces of driftwood floating about the dry docks, Weston remembered all to well the last piece of driftwood he had seen floating in the sea after Devil's Fire had been wrecked.

"Something I can help you with?" a skinny whore asked whose face was covered with rice powder.

Weston ignored her and headed to the saloon his father and Old Doc had just entered, finding them sitting at a battered table, playing cards with several other grizzled cronies. The smoke was thick and the music was loud but Weston could still hear the old wooden floor boards creak under his weight. Old men and young swapped mining stories and trollops flaunted their wares.

The old doc just won a hand and the loser was none to pleased. He stood up and pushed the table, drinks splattered and cards flew everywhere. Weston's hand was already under his cloak cocking his prized pistol.

Suddenly there was a hubbub and a man shouted, "I say you're a cheat, old man. Nobody cheats me out of nothing. We kill people here for less!" The music, laughter and chatter had subsided and everyone turned to look at a bearded man who rose from the gaming table, his face twisted angrily.

"Look here now, I won fair and square you brainless fool!" Weston heard the ship's doctor roar. "And nobody gets away with accusing me of cheatin' at cards. I've been playin' a fore your daddy spilled his rotten seed in your ma's whor'n belly."

Before the sore loser had a chance to draw his gun, Weston's pistol was cocked and aimed at him between the eyes.

"Not a very wise move," Weston said in a voice that was just as deadly as the look on his face.

"He didn't mean nothing," one of his cronies called out. "The man just lost his job on the railroad to those slant eyed bastards and took a beating from a foreign sympathizer just yesterday. Prescott's to pay for all of our troubles!"

"Shut up Duke!" The loser shouted angrily. "I'll deal with this."

"It seems to me that you owe the old doc here an apology," Weston said, smiling ominously. "Where *I* come from we kill a man for less."

He held his cocked pistol with a steady hand. The other man swallowed hard and wiped the dirty sweat from his brow.

"It seems I was mistaken, sir," he said, adding, "he's a better card player than I reckoned."

"I told you so," the doc snorted.

"One of these days, you're going to get that ugly face of yours blown off, Doc," Weston said as the piano player began to pound the keys again.

"Don't worry about me you young whippersnapper," the old man said slipping a pistol about the size of the palm of his hand back into his boot. He chuckled loudly and drained his glass of whiskey in one gulp.

"I think we better head to my office, son," Weston's father told him. "The man they said was responsible for their troubles is Bonnie's betrothed."

Weston quirked his brow in amusement and followed his father out of the saloon and down the road to a brick building the sign of which read Yates and Lancer import & export.

"Nobody's here, it's not like Derek or Prescott to close up so early." Weston's father said as he tried the door.

"Lancer still has an interest in your business?" Weston's dislike for Derek was apparent in his voice and the scowl on his face.

"Among other things, yes," his father said as he fetched a key out of his jacket pocket and unlocked the door. "We're still very good friends and business partners. Give him a chance, Wes. He's a good man. He's overseen Bonnie's welfare and the business since I've been away. I pray you two can work things out."

Once inside, both men looked around and Weston's father examined the broken window and the crumpled message that lay on the floor.

"'Stay out of our business!' What the hell does that mean?" Weston asked as he read the note aloud.

"Bonnie's betroth must have intervened between the railroaders and the cheap labor going on here. I must say, things haven't changed that much around here. Something tells me that you two are going to get along just fine. I think we should get a room at the inn, get cleaned up, shave, and have a good nights sleep before heading up to the house tomorrow morning. For all I know your sister may even be married as we speak."

It has been so long since he had seen Bonnie, Weston thought. And yet, with Brana gone, this could not be the homecoming had had dreamed of. How difficult it was to think of anyone except her. And yet he knew he must try for his family's sake.

"Yes, I'm very interested in meeting this Prescott fellow," he said. "I do believe we already have a few things in common."

. As father and son left the office, they were the object of some considerable attention.

"Now what business did those two have with Prescott, I wonder?" one of the men said. "They sure made a fool out of you Ritchie. If I wouldn't have spoke up you would be dead fer sure. We warned him and that partner of him off but I reckon there's more of them than we thought. P'haps we ought to lay off them for awhile."

"Just shut your trap!" Ritchie told him, snatching the whiskey bottle out of Duke's hands.

"What'd ya do that fer?" he complained. "I need another swallow. I weren't finished yet."

"Just shut yer trap. They'll all get what's coming. I happen to know where Prescott lives. We'll show them China lovers who runs this town."

The grey light of evening brought a cool chill to the air. As the sun fell deeper and deeper behind the horizon, the voices in the alley became louder and bolder.

"That house is just waitin' fer us to get our riches," one of the men declared.

"Well I don't know, Ritchie," another said. "Prescott and them strangers in that saloon seem to mean business. How do you know they won't be expectin' something to happen?"

"You chicken!" Ritchie chuckled. "There are more of us than them and that's all that matters. Let me tell you how sure I am. If Prescott has a woman, I'll let you have her first. Now tell me, ain't I a good sport, Duke? Ain't I a damn good sport."

CHAPTER 60

Brana awoke when Bonnie entered her bed chamber the next morning and opened the heavy drapes to let the sunshine pour in.

"The fog rolled in early last night, but luckily the sun is shining already and melting the dew on the grounds," Bonnie chattered. "It's a beautiful day Brana. The happiest day of my life. I just wish that my father and brother were here to share it with me."

Brana sat up abruptly, letting her hair tumble over her face. She sat silent, and limp.

"My dear," Bonnie said "You must put your past behind you. Today you will start a new life. Be happy for yourself and your baby."

"I could never put my past behind me, Bon," Brana told her. "But you're right. I must start thinking of my beautiful child. It's the only reason I let myself live. And I'm happy for you and Cam, Bonnie, I truly am. And I won't let my sullen mood put a damper on your wedding day."

"I've seen the beautiful dress that Derek found for you." Bonnie told her trying to cheer her up. "It's fit for a queen."

"The vows I will take today are mere words," Brana said sadly. "They will not mean anything to me. It wouldn't matter to me if I take these vows in a simple cotton frock or my riding attire."

A rap was heard at the door and a servant entered carrying a box. Others followed until the room was littered with them.

"Oh my," Bonnie exclaimed "It seems Derek thought of everything. Well, I must help Auntie with her dressing. She can be tiring at times. She never lets the servants do what they are supposed to. I'll send Jessie in to help you."

Brana slipped out of bed. Wrapping her arms around her body, she let the sun rays caress her gently. Taking the top of the largest box; she gasped as lace and brocade spilled over the top. Lifting the wedding gown out of the box, she held it up to her. The sleeves were of pure lace and puffy but tapered from the elbow to her wrists. The collar was high and tight and the brocade bodice was dotted with baby pearls.

Suddenly nausea swept over her. She clutched her wedding dress tightly, waiting for the bout to dissipate, praying for her parents to give her strength, to help her find the graciousness to deal with what Derek was about to do for her and her unborn child. Hearing footsteps in front of her door, she lay the gown down on the bed and smoothed out the creases.

"Brana." she heard Cameron call out, just before her body hit the ground. She felt him scoop her up and carry her to her bed.

"I shouldn't have pushed you into this, Damnation!" Cameron growled.

"No, Cam," she assured him. "I'll be fine. The doctor told me I would experience these little set backs. I don't want you blaming yourself!"

"No, Brana," her brother insisted. "I will not risk your life or the life of your child. You should stay in bed until the baby is born."

Brana was touched by his overwhelming concern for her baby, particulary since she could tell that he did not get much sleep last night. His eyes were bright but yet she could see faint lines of exhaustion. She smiled as she remembered how they used to be as a family when her mother and father were alive. Cam would tease her unmercifully and she would always retaliate with one of her mischievous ideas. But now there were hard lines around his mouth. The war had aged him, but he was still starkly handsome. His jet black hair showed a few sprinkles of gray which made him all the more distinguished looking. He would make a handsome bridegroom indeed.

"I'm fine now, Cam," she said. "I'm sure I can make it through the ceremony and I promise to rest right after. Really, Cam. I recognize that I must do this for my child. Jessie will help me dress. Did you see all the things Derek brought for me?"

"You have really become a strong young woman," Cameron's voice cracked with emotion. "Mother and father would have been proud." Unable to continue, he took Brana's hands and held them in his.

"They would be proud of you, too, Cam," she told him. "You lost everything and in spite of that you managed to become a successful and caring person. And now you are about to marry a wonderful woman who loves you deeply." For a few minutes, the two were silent, united in their memories of the past as well as their hopes and fears about the future that was to come.

CHAPTER 61

At the inn, Weston joined his father for breakfast. His beard was gone, leaving his skin looking soft and unmarred, his good looks more apparent. The young girl taking his order could not keep her eyes off of him as he ordered, the special, the hot breakfast plate.

"A good night's sleep did you good, son," his father told him as he sipped his coffee. "You look like a new man. I saw the ship's captain and the Old Doc this morning and promised to meet them out front after breakfast. They want to see the mines. Lord knows, it's been a long time since I've seen them myself."

"I thought you wanted to see Bonnie this morning?" Weston asked.

"I figure by the time we get done it will start to get dark and we can head up then, just in time to dine. What better way to surprise her than at the dinner table."

Doc and the ship's captain were already arguing when Weston and his father met them out front.

At the mining camps, men swapped war stories or told of backbreaking labor searching for gold camps. But most were drinking and fueling their hatred towards the slanted eye foreigners who took their jobs on the railroad, leaving them with an uncertain future. Many cursed the sea captains and damned them for taking a big part in their misery, blaming them for transporting the foreigners into their town. It was easy to see why San Francisco was known for its thirst for murder. No decent wages, the railroad paid the Chinamen for their labor and gold was scarce now. The rush was over and those like Yates and Lancer owned almost all the producing mines. Hatred fueled, and the Chinamen were an easy target.

The brightness of day dimmed with every passing hour as they returned to town, and Weston grew inpatient, wanting to see Bonnie and meet Prescott, who may have a few things to add to the day's conversation.

Salty mist was escaping from the turbulent sea, reminding those who cared a storm may be brewing and shelter was needed of the night.

Weston and his father left Doc and the ship's captain at a gaming house and they took a hansom cab out of the city. As they neared their destination, Weston remembered his mother and the terrible way that she had died. He could tell that his father was also reminded of the terrible memories that had kept them apart for so many years.

The beautiful house was lavishly decorated for the grand event and the frenzy within the last twenty fours hours was certainly worth the final result. Oriental rugs had been beaten just hours before the guests had arrived, and the floors were still damp from being polished minutes before. Flowers from the conservatory filled every room, casting a variety of floral scents throughout the house. Candleflame danced from the Candelabras that were placed in every room and noisy chatter drifted throughout the cold night, in anticipation of the dual nuptials.

Derek and Cameron stood beside the preacher, both of them handsome in black tail coats, white bow ties, black vests and black trousers, with a white, heavily starched shirt. Almost identical if it wasn't for Derek's fod watch, hanging from his pocket. Bonnie's Aunt Elizabeth sat at the pianoforte and on cue she began to play the familiar wedding march. Bonnie looked radiant as she floated down the stairs, with Brana, stunningly beautiful, behind her. Suddenly, three men, holding pistols, stormed into the hall where the company was gathered.

"See here, what's the meaning of this?" The minister demanded while Bonnie and Brana huddled together, their wedding gowns billowing around them.

"Stay out of this, Preacher," Ritchie demanded. "We have nothing against you. It's Prescott and his meddling friends we aim to teach a lesson to."

People gasped, and Aunt Elizabeth fanned herself, trying to ward off the vapors.

Cameron moved quickly from across the room, but stopped dead in his tracks as Ritchie grabbed Bonnie by the arm and held a gun to her head. Brana couldn't move, memories of Jeb flashing through her mind. She could see his face and remembered his laughter as it echoed throughout the room.

"No, this can't be happening again," she cried.

"Well now, me and my boys are mighty hurt that we weren't invited here," Ritchie said, laughing as he rubbed the tip of the gun's barrel on Bonnie's breast, "right boys?"

Cameron didn't speak until he assessed their perilous situation. He looked at Derek, motioned him with his eyes to do the same.

"Well, you're sure right, Ritchie," Duke said "Lots of riches here. Women too, don't ferget your promise. It looks like the uppity Mr. Prescott has no manners at all, not askin' if we want something to eat. What happened cat got yer tongue?"

Cameron saw that Bonnie's eyes were bright with fear, yet she held her chin high and continued to struggle. She had, Cam thought, never looked more beautiful to him. And she was his, his to love, his to protect.

"Your fight is with me," he told Ritchie, his voice cracking the air like a whip. "Let the woman go."

"Stay right where you are, Lancer," Ritchie sneered. "Looks to me like both of you were just about to take your marriage nuptials. Well now, appears my men get to taste your women first."

Ritchie turned to Bonnie and kissed her hard on the lips, while pointing his loaded gun to her side. His free hand touched her body, feeling every hidden curve, as she tightens under his bold caresses. He could hear Cameron breathing heavily, and could almost feel the hatred pouring out of his gaut body. She winced as he grabbed her breast and squeezed tightly.

Brana covered her ears and wept. She would never let Bonnie go through what she had with Jeb. Thoughts of Weston came to mind and she decided to sacrifice herself and their baby to be with him once again. Brana looked and Derek and noticed for the first time how dashingly handsome he looked in his wedding attire, she would never forget his kindness.

Cameron had seen the mischievous twinkle in Brana's eyes, one he had seen so many times before. Brana lunged for the gun Ritchie held and covered Bonnie's body with her own.

"No Brana!" Cameron cried and lunged forward at the same time Derek did. The sound of the gun fire echoed throughout the house, along with a piercing scream.

Neither Weston nor his father waited for the carriage to come to a halt upon hearing a gun shot. Up the curving stairs that led to the portico, together they reached the door at the same time. But it was Weston who led the way into the gracious hallway, Weston who saw his sister clutching another woman to her. And then he heard father's voice and the sound of flesh against flesh, as a man he recognized as Derek Lancer struck out at a group of men who, given the way they were dressed, were common laborers.

Weston joined in the brawl, punched a man who had kicked Derek in his ribs. Attacked from behind, he managed to flip the assailant and knock him out cold with one punch to the jaw.

Wiping away the blood that was trickling from the side of his mouth, Weston helped his father to his feet and watched him stagger past the two men who lay unconscious, toward his sister who came running down the stairs to throw herself into his arms.

"Father!"

As for Brana, she could not believe her eyes, clinging to the banister, she slowly rose to her feet. A shot rang out and suddenly she was in Weston's arms. And Derek. Derek was sprawled at the foot of the stairs, covered in blood while beyond him Cameron faced the bearded intruder, with both pistols in hand. Once more a shot rang out and then another. It was the bearded railroader who toppled to the floor.

Weston paled as he saw Brana fall limp in his arms. He could not believe it was the same woman who had haunted his dreams for so long.

"Brana!" He cried as he lifted her up into his arms and slowly carried her down the stairs.

"Get some water!" Weston shouted to servants hovering about.

Cameron leaned over Derek's body and gently closed his best friend's eyes, fighting for control. Derek. The golden boy. His dear friend, gone forever like so many he had known before.

Meanwhile Weston had placed Brana on a chaise that stood beside the grand piano.

"Cam." Brana murmured.

"I'm here, Brana," Cameron replied, looking directly into Weston's face. Their eyes locked for several seconds. And then, pouring a snifter of brandy, Cam took it to his sister's side, pressed it to her lips.

Revived, Brana's eyes fastened on Weston. "Oh my darling, you're alive." She sobbed.

"Shush," he murmured, falling on his knees beside her. "It's been a shock for both of us."

"You don't understand," Brana protested. "Jeb told me that he killed you. I wanted to die too. I love you Weston."

"Jeb told me he had killed you," Weston told her, holding both her hand in his. "When he told me that, a part of me died too."

"How did you ever find me?" Brana cried as he pressed her against him.

"I'm sure Bonnie can explain all that," Cameron said. "Right now Weston and I need to talk."

"It seems that I got here just in time," Weston told Cameron when they had joined the minister and Bonnie's father in the library. "What did you do? Convince my sister to marry Lancer, so you could marry Brana? I'll tell you one thing Cam or Cameron or whatever you call yourself. If you even think about taking Brana away from me you are as good as dead!"

"It seems that you are a little confused," Cameron told him, keeping his voice even with an effort. "It's you that should be good as dead. You took advantage of Brana's innocence and for that alone I should kill you. As for toying with your sister's affections, we'll be married as soon as Brana recovers. And so will you. You will marry my sister!"

"Your sister!" Weston shouted, "Why the hell would I give a damn about your sister and what gives you the right to tell me who to marry? Why the hell would I want to marry your sister? Surely you don't know who you're toying with."

"I was under the impression that you loved Brana," Cameron told him. "Heaven knows she almost killed herself grieving over losing you."

Finally Weston understood. He started back as though Cameron had struck him.

"You mean Brana? You're Cam? Cam in the locket? You mean you're her brother?" It didn't take Cameron long to tell Weston about the events that had lead up to Derek's death. Seated by the fireplace, the reverend White and Weston's father nursed their brandies and listened while Cameron explained about the child and Derek's willingness to give him a name. "And in a sense," he concluded, "Derek gave his life for both of you, although he never knew it."

"Well it seems you two have settled your differences," Bonnie said hurrying into the room, "Weston, I've missed you so much," She hugged him tight. "Brana's waiting for you in her chamber. We just can't believe the turn of events. You and Brana. Me and Cam. I would like to

think mother may have had a hand in all this."

CHAPTER 62

Several weeks had passed since the burial of their dear friend. Cameron and Weston had quickly become friends as they had helped the women they loved deal with the trauma of the untimely death of Derek Lancer. The city mourned the loss of its golden boy and rejoiced in the death of Ritchie, who had threatened to bring terror to the populous.

As the sun shone brightly leaving an orange glow on the green sea, Cameron and Weston closed up the office and headed for home. Both could not stop thinking about the women who would soon become their brides.

As the carriage past Derek's house, Weston thought about the man who had saved his life and deeply regretted the hatred he had felt for him for so many years. He realized that, all along it had been jealousy that had kept them from forming a friendship.

Cameron was also thinking of Derek and the ultimate sacrifice he paid for friendship.

Cameron could see Bonnie and Brana waiting for them in front of the house as the carriage came to a halt. Both women stood anxiously waiting to greet their men.

"How are the wedding plans coming along, my darling?" Cameron asked as he poked his head out the carriage window.

"Just fine, the preacher's waiting, to discuss our plans," Bonnie said hurriedly. "Now let Weston talk to Brana. She's finally recovered from the shock."

"You know Bonnie, your brother is just right for Brana. I'm sure he'll tame her wild spirit."

Bonnie only smiled. Because she, at least, knew that the Brana she loved would never change.

CHAPTER 63

The brides looked radiant as they walked down the stairs on the arms of Weston's father, who smiled first at one and then at the other, knowing that these matches were made in heaven.

"Isn't she beautiful," Cameron whispered to Weston looking at Bonnie.

"The most beautiful woman I've ever seen," Weston replied his eyes fixed on Brana as she descended the stairs with his father, his heart ached with love.

CHAPTER 64

The house on the hill was quiet except for the laughter of the man and wife who occupied it. Weston had vowed to Brana that their house would be filled with love, laughter, and happiness and so it was.

"What are you feeding this babe?" Weston asked his new bride.

"I can feel him moving, Brana." Weston said in an awed voice as they lay together, holding one another tight under the quilted bed covers.

"He, darling," she said laughing. "The Baby is as wild and spirited as its father and mother, I fear. But that doesn't mean it is a boy. But if it is, I'd like to name him Derek."

Weston agreed. As he was just discovering, he could deny his new bride nothing.

"Did you get the letter off to Lacy?" she asked, kissing him gently.

"Yes I did and I wouldn't be surprised if she took the next ship out to see you for herself," Weston said. "And perhaps my father, too."

"I certainly hope so, I miss her terribly," Brana then quickly added "Simmons and Cook too!"

"I also sent a letter to Rawlings. I'm sure he'll be surprised at the turn of events."

"Is his betrothed as bad as you said she was? Or were you simply that wicked?"

"I am that wicked," he said kissing her lips. "But she is as detestable as I said she was."

"Why do you suppose Rawlings puts up with a woman like her?"

"Well, my sweet, I believe that those are the perils of passion!"

Brana giggled and the night was filled with whispers of love.

THE END

www.ingramcontent.com/pod-product-compliance
Lightning Source LLC
Chambersburg PA
CBHW031419240626
47154CB00001B/117